Dog Grant Me
a golden retriever mystery

Neil S. Plakcy

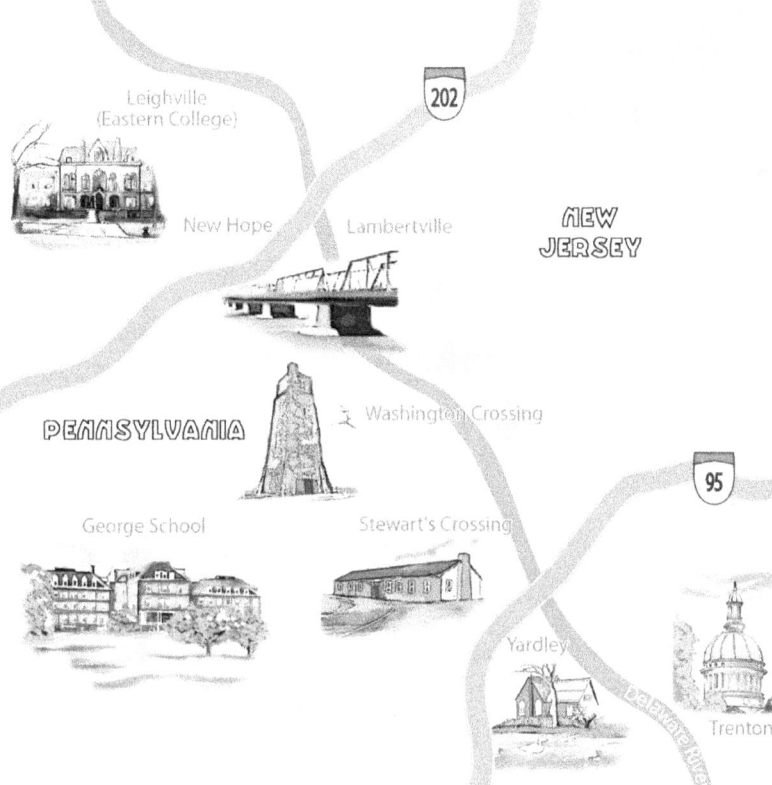

Copyright 2025 Neil S. Plakcy

This cozy mystery is a work of fiction. Names, characters, places, and incidents either are products of the author's imagination or are used fictitiously. Any resemblance to actual events or locales or persons, living or dead, is entirely coincidental. All rights reserved, including the right of reproduction in whole or in part in any form.

NO AI TRAINING: Without in any way limiting the author's [and publisher's] exclusive rights under copyright, any use of this publication to "train" generative artificial intelligence (AI) technologies to generate text is expressly prohibited. The author reserves all rights to license uses of this work for generative AI training and development of machine learning language models.

Reviews

Mr. Plakcy did a terrific job in this cozy mystery. He has a smooth writing style that kept the story flowing evenly. The dialogue and descriptions were right on target.

Book Blogger Red Adept

Steve and Rochester become quite a team and Neil Plakcy is the kind of writer that I want to tell me this story. It's a fun read which will keep you turning pages very quickly.

Amazon top 100 reviewer Amos Lassen

In Dog We Trust is a very well-crafted mystery that kept me guessing up until Steve figured out where things were going.

E-book addict reviews

Neil Plakcy's golden retriever mysteries are supposed to be about former computer hacker Steve Levitan, but it is his golden retriever Rochester who is the real amateur sleuth in this delightful academic mystery. This is no talking dog book, though. Rochester doesn't need anything more than his wagging tail and doggy smile to win over readers and help solve crimes. I absolutely fell in love with this brilliant dog who digs up clues and points the silly humans towards the evidence.

– Christine Kling, author of *Circle of Bones*.

Chapter 1
A Volatile Mix

"Are you sure we have enough garlic?" my wife Lili asked, weighing another bulb in her palm. The fluorescent lights of the IGA grocery store cast harsh shadows across the produce section, making the bulbs appear stark against the cold, white lighting. "My mother always said mojo sauce needs plenty."

The sharp, pungent aroma of garlic mingled with the earthy scents of the other vegetables as Lili carefully examined each one. A blast of cold air swept through the store as the front doors opened, and I pulled my scarf tighter against the chill. Around us, other shoppers bundled in heavy winter coats and hats hurried through the aisles, faces reddened from the biting wind outside.

I consulted the list on my phone. "Yesenia specifically requested three heads. We already have four in the cart."

Lili dropped a fifth bulb into our cart anyway. Her auburn curls were tamed behind her head, and she wore the same determined expression I'd seen when she was setting up a difficult photograph. "Better too much than too little. I want to make my mother's mojo chicken before Yesenia arrives tomorrow."

Yesenia Ubeda Goldstein was an old friend of Lili's from her days as a student, and then faculty wife, at New York University.

Yesenia was a Cuban American cook and food anthropologist who specialized in documenting the ways in which Jewish cooks had adjusted their recipes as they were spread through the diaspora of the Caribbean and Central America. She was joining us to co-teach a short-term class at Friar Lake, the conference center I ran for Eastern College.

"Testing out the recipe?" I asked.

"More like testing myself." She moved on to the citrus display. "Yesenia is a renowned expert on Caribbean cuisine. I don't want to embarrass myself when we're co-teaching this course."

I caught our reflection in the produce misters - me in my dark green parka that complemented my Mediterranean complexion, Lili in a tailored blazer and silk scarf under her wool trenchcoat. We made an interesting pair - the college administrator and the photography professor, brought together by love, a golden retriever, and a shared Ashkenazi Jewish heritage. We were now embarking on our latest academic adventure together, this time a culinary one.

"From everything you've told me about Yesenia, she'll be thrilled you're making your mother's recipe," I said. "That's exactly the kind of cultural preservation she studies - how Jewish families adapted their cooking in Cuba."

"And that's why I like Yesenia's approach to cooking. Because it's rooted in the foods of the home country, but adjusted to what's available where the cook is living. I'm so excited that she's coming to Friar Lake. I'm glad she's taking a break from all that travel through the Cuban countryside researching authentic recipes."

Lili selected several oranges and lemons. "I just hope the students appreciate what we're trying to do with this intersession course. Food isn't just recipes - it's history, culture, identity."

It was the evening of our last day of Christmas vacation, Monday January 4, 2016, and we'd be back at work at Eastern College the next day. "Speaking of students, did you get the final count?" I grabbed a bag of onions as we passed.

"Twenty-one total. A mix of Eastern students and special

students from outside. Some heard about it through Yesenia's online following." She consulted her own list. "We still need oregano, cumin, black pepper…"

I steered the cart toward the spice aisle, thinking about all the preparations still needed at Friar Lake before the students arrived. As director, I wanted everything to be perfect for Eastern's first January intersession program.

Though we had passed New Year's, the store was still playing Christmas music, and all the candy, pumpkin pie filling and boxes of stuffing that hadn't sold were stacked on tables by the registers, looking sadly neglected.

"Did you see Yesenia's latest Facebook post?" Lili asked as she compared two bottles of olive oil. "She's bringing all kinds of traditional root vegetables from a Caribbean market in Brooklyn - boniatos, malanga, yuca. She's really going all out."

"As long as she doesn't bring controversy with her," I said. "President Babson is counting on these intersession courses to succeed."

Lili gave me a look. "Just because she occasionally visits Cuba for her research doesn't make her controversial. She's a scholar documenting food traditions."

I held up my hands in surrender. "You're right. I'm sure it will be fine." But I couldn't quite shake my worry that combining academic politics, Cuban politics, and cooking might prove to be a volatile mix.

Chapter 2
Too Much Garlic

We drove home, where my golden retriever Rochester barked his head off as we walked in, not happy at being left all alone in the house. Then he nosed his way around us as we carried the groceries to the kitchen, sniffing to see if there was anything he could eat immediately.

Golden retrievers have no sense of time. We could be out for ten minutes or ten hours, and he felt the same sense of bereavement, worrying that we might never return. And forget telling him that I'd fix his dinner in half an hour. He wanted it now!

We unpacked everything, leaving out the items Lili would need to prepare her mother's mojo chicken for our dinner, including a package of skin-on, bone-in chicken thighs. In honor of the late Benita Weinstock, Lili donned an old apron printed with a cartoonish map of Cuba. On her feet were the fuzzy slippers I'd given her for Hanukkah, in the same color as Rochester's fur.

He'd given up on expecting anything from me, and was sniffing around Lili's feet hoping she'd drop something to the floor.

"Wherever we lived, my mother made chicken for Shabbos dinner," Lili said as she worked. "And always with the mojo sauce that my father loved. If she couldn't find sour oranges, she'd mix regular oranges with lemons. And if we lived somewhere she couldn't get fresh oranges, she'd buy a carton of orange juice and one of those little plastic limes that had juice inside."

"A true immigrant cook," I said. "Make do with what you have. My grandmothers and my great-aunts were the same way. They used canned pie filling for strudel when fruits were out of season."

Lili combined garlic cloves, shallot, kosher salt, zest, cumin, oregano, black pepper, juices, and olive oil in the blender and set it on high. Rochester didn't like the noise, so he moved out of the kitchen.

Yesenia's work was particularly intriguing to Lili and me because of Lili's background as the daughter of Ashkenazi Jews born in Cuba. Lili's mother's recipes often combined ingredients found on the island with Old World recipes. Jews usually stuffed baked pastries called knishes with potato, but in Havana Benita had substituted yuca, a similar starch common in Caribbean cooking.

Yesenia was one of the first scholars in this field, and she had extracted the recipes in her doctoral dissertation and created a cookbook which was popular among first-generation Cuban Americans. She was a visiting professor at Columbia and regularly traveled to conferences around the world, and her work had already begun to influence a new generation of scholars.

Lili poured the marinade over the chicken, and while we waited for all that garlicky goodness to soak in, I took Rochester for his evening walk. He was eager to befriend a yappy Yorkie whose barks turned into growls, and I had to pull him away. "Not everyone wants to play nice," I said.

We returned home, and I looked over some college e-mails while we waited for the chicken to finish marinating. President Babson had sent several mass mailings to everyone involved in the intersession, reminding them of how important this programming was to the future of the college.

"Like we need any more pressure," I grumbled. Eventually Lili grabbed the tray of chicken which had been coming to room temperature and slid it into the heated oven, and as I prepared a salad the kitchen was filled with a delicious aroma. Lili flipped the chicken over in the oven and as I sat back at the table, Rochester kept nosing my leg. I finally gave him a peanut-butter cookie. He crunched it down, leaving crumbs on the floor, and I had to point at them to get him to lick them all up.

Finally Lili pulled the pan of chicken thighs out of the oven. She sliced off a tiny piece coated in the oily mojo sauce and held it out to me. The chicken slid off the fork and flopped onto the floor and Rochester quickly gobbled it. Even at ninety pounds, he moved quickly.

"¡*Ay, Dios mío!*" Lili said. "Your dog!"

Then just as quickly, Rochester spit the chicken out on the floor.

"Rochester! This is my mother's special recipe. Your *abuela!*"

She leaned down and picked the piece up and tossed it in the trash. Then she dipped a spoon into the mojo sauce and tasted it.

"I see what's wrong," she said. "Too much garlic."

"Good thing he didn't eat it, then," I said. "In large amounts garlic can be poisonous to dogs." I reached down and chucked Rochester under his chin. "You're a smart boy. You know what's not right to eat."

"My mother used yogurt to mellow the taste of the garlic when she cooked for her brother Tio Moises," Lili said. "There should be some in the refrigerator. Can you get it for me?"

I stepped over the big golden retriever sprawled on the kitchen floor. "Dogs. They're everywhere you want to be," I intoned, in a version of the credit card slogan. I got the container of yogurt and handed it to Lili. She began delicately adding it, drop by drop, into the reserved marinade until she had the flavor the way she wanted it, then drizzled it over the heated chicken.

Yesenia had been in touch with Lili in the late fall, because she was intrigued by the work of a monk named Brother Gervase, who had spent time in the islands at the turn of the 19th century and compiled a book of native recipes intended to improve health. She found references to the book in other volumes but hadn't been able to track down a copy, and she'd learned that Brother Gervase spent his last years at the Abbey of Our Lady of the Waters in a rural area of Bucks County, Pennsylvania.

Lili had responded that Eastern College had purchased the abbey and repurposed it as a conference center, and invited Yesenia for a visit. They were still negotiating dates when Eastern announced its first-ever January intersession.

"Why don't we invite Yesenia to lecture during the intersession?" Lili had asked me at the time. That simple request led to the development of a four-week course Yesenia and Lili could co-teach, involving residence and cooking at Friar Lake.

It was timely because Yesenia was in talks with a producer at the Food Network about a potential show to combine food anthropology with cooking demonstrations. The network wanted to see how she performed on camera with a mix of academics and entertainment. She was bringing a videographer with her to document her ability, and to develop content for use on social media. "I hope this intersession works out," I said. "Babson has a lot invested in it."

The previous year, Eastern's president had hired an image consultant to help market the college. Its slogan, "A Very Good Small College," had worked for a long time, but we were facing increasing competition from other good private colleges, as well as cheaper state universities that offered a broader range of majors and opportunities.

One of the consultant's ideas was to postpone the start of the winter term for a month and create an intersession, where the college could offer short classes for a deep dive into special topics.

It served two purposes. First, we could allow our career-focused students to dig into enrichment classes without threatening the accumulation of major-related credits. Second, he hoped we would draw in students from other colleges as well as non-traditional students who wanted a quick academic experience.

Along with their tuition revenue, of course.

The faculty had come up with twenty courses to offer, from "The African-American Roots of Today's Music" to "Short Stories by

Women" to the course Lili had created to teach with Yesenia, "Exploring the Food Traditions of Latin America and the Caribbean."

It was outside her usual domain as chair of the Department of Fine Arts, but very connected to her personal history and a chance for her to spend time with Yesenia.

They were both Jubans, raised by Eastern European Jews in Cuba until Castro took power and they moved on. They had met years before, when Lili was a professional photojournalist, and they'd kept in touch as Yesenia finished her PhD in food anthropology, the study of the way that food and ingredients had social and cultural significance to different populations.

As we planned the course, I heard about how soon after they met, Yesenia and Lili had gone to Union City, New Jersey, also called Havana on the Hudson. They spent a day eating garlic-marinated pork, yellow corn porridge, and Cuban pressed sandwiches, accompanied by fruit-flavored milkshakes called batidos and flaky pastries called *pasteles de guayaba*.

"Ay, Dios mío, by the time we got to the end of Bergenline Avenue we were waddling," Lili said, when she described it to me. "Yesenia kept saying, 'oh, we have to try this,' and 'just a taste of that.'"

The next year, after Lili's first divorce, Yesenia had taken her on a food tour of Astoria, Queens, to cheer her up. The neighborhood was home to people from over 80 countries, and it sounded like they'd eaten their way from the Dominican Republic to Greece to Bangladesh. "You should have heard Yesenia quizzing this woman who only spoke Urdu about ingredients," Lili said. "Lots of hand gestures and laughter."

Lili and Yesenia worked together to come up with a syllabus that incorporated reading and hands-on cooking, and the curriculum committee approved it. Then Lili had to sell it to students, through a mouth-watering description of a mix of lecture, research, and cooking and tasting. The plan was for Yesenia to lecture about food origins and traditions, and Lili to help her prepare meals for the students based on the course materials. I was looking forward to some excellent eating.

Though most of the teaching would take place in college classrooms, and most students would stay in the dorms, we had two long-weekend programs planned for Friar Lake.

Lili and Yesenia would use the kitchen there to create a welcome dinner, and students would get to prepare dishes with recipes Yesenia provided. Over the four weeks of the term, they'd write an academic paper and discover a recipe that they would cook at the culmination of the course.

"How are the preparations coming at Friar Lake?" Lili asked, as she placed the chicken on a platter. It was roasted to a crackly brown, and glowed with golden beauty as the juices dripped down the sides. The mojo sauce went into a gravy boat that Lili's mother had used.

"We're scrambling," I said. The intersession was to start on Thursday, three days later. We planned to have them arrive on campus that morning, and be bussed out to Friar Lake. Monday the 11th we'd bus them back to start the on-campus portion.

"In what way?" Lili asked. She sat across from me and began slicing up the chicken.

"All the bedrooms and bathrooms need to be cleaned and checked," I said. "We're taking delivery of a new convection oven for the kitchen, and repairing a couple of loose windows there. Then a general run-through of every building and every room. The people from the psychologists' conference in the beginning of December reorganized the whole chapel and we haven't put things back properly yet."

I took my plate of chicken, accompanied by rice and black beans, and inhaled the fragrance, setting my taste buds tingling. I ladled a few drops of mojo sauce on one piece of chicken, then slid it into my mouth.

"Wow," I said. "The garlic is mellow and lets the sour orange shine. And the chicken is so tender."

"You're not just saying that, are you?" she asked.

I shook my head. "No, honestly, it's delicious." I cut a tiny piece of the chicken without the mojo sauce and fed it to Rochester, who gobbled it up eagerly. "See, even the dog approves."

My phone buzzed with another email from President Babson. 'Just heard from a faculty member concerned about Dr. Ubeda's political activities,' he wrote. 'Please keep a handle on any reflection on Eastern.'

I looked across at Lili in the kitchen. The intersession hadn't even started yet, and already it was threatening to spin out of control.

Chapter 3
Juban Journey

"Want to have lunch this afternoon?" I asked at breakfast on Tuesday morning. "I'm coming over to campus to make sure Yesenia's room is ready before she gets in." While Lili and I ate oatmeal and chocolate-chip mini-muffins, Rochester chowed down noisily on a bowl of pellets dusted with chicken powder.

"How are she and her camera person getting here?" Lili asked.

"She has a car, so they're going to drive down from the city," I said. "I'm glad I won't get roped into chauffeuring them back and forth from campus."

"Why don't I come to Friar Lake with you this morning? I'd like to look around the kitchen before she arrives and see if there's any equipment I need to bring from home. And I thought I'd scout out the library and see if I can find any information on that Brother Gervase Yesenia is interested in. And then we can have lunch."

"Yeah, she sent me three emails yesterday about him," I said. "I told her that I've never looked through the abbey records and I don't have time to do it right now."

"She emailed me about him, too," Lili said. "Along with a list of ingredients I should have on hand. She wanted this special Cuban-style mustard only sold at Sam's Club and I told her we don't have a membership and I'm not spending $50 to get access to one ingredient. And she wanted to know if I had a supplier for caimito."

"What's that?"

"Star apple in English. But it's only in season from February to April. You can buy it frozen online, but the couple of places that carry it are out of stock."

"She'll have to suffer, then," I said.

"Which she won't do quietly. I told her she could substitute mamey sapote for caimito but she said the texture is different."

"Is she going to be a diva?" I asked. "Like those rock stars who don't want any brown M&Ms in their dressing rooms?"

"Always possible," she said. "But so far she hasn't asked for M&Ms in any color."

"That'll be in the next email."

I gave Rochester a quick walk, and then the three of us piled into my SUV for the drive up along the Delaware. Rocks sat at irregular intervals in the river as the frigid water rushed past them. Across from us, the Jersey shore was brown with only occasional pops of green in the stands of fir and Scotch pine. I kept the heat in the car on high, and Rochester poked his snout between the seats to take advantage of it.

The sun came out from behind clouds as I turned inland, shining on the fieldstone farmhouses and red clapboard barns. The road up to the converted abbey property was steep and twisty, but when we pulled into the parking lot we were rewarded with a vista of farmlands and the river in the distance. Bowman's Tower, a historic site a few miles away, had a similar outlook and it was easily visible through the barren trees.

Friar Lake's location had its pluses and minuses. Its hilltop isolation was great for reflective activities, and the slopes provided a habitat for deer, raccoons, porcupines, and wild turkeys. But if it snowed heavily, we had to shut down and wait for the college's snow removal service to come out. Since they had a whole campus to cover in Leighville, that took a couple of days. I'd learned to keep an eye on the weather forecasts in winter.

As I got out of the car, buttoning the top of my coat and tightening my scarf around my neck, I said, "Let me know how long you want to stay here, and I can run you back to the campus."

"I'll stay until lunch," she said. "Matilda can hold down the fort at the office, and I can browse through the library and answer emails after I finish in the kitchen."

Matilda Santos was a constant presence in the Fine Arts office. Her petite frame and perfectly pressed clothes suggested a quiet presence, but those who knew her understood she was one of the college's information hubs. She'd emigrated from the Philippines thirty years ago and had worked at Eastern ever since, cultivating an intricate network of administrative assistants, custodians, and cafeteria workers who seemed to know everything happening on campus before anyone else did. Her desk was positioned to see everyone who came into the office, and she had an uncanny ability to predict which faculty members would be late turning in their grades or which students were struggling in their courses.

As I opened the rear door so Rochester could hop down, Lili stepped out of the car, adjusting her long dark gray wool coat and the black hat that came down over her ears. She pulled her scarf tighter and set out for the library, a small stone building with a pitched roof that sat adjacent to the Gothic-style chapel.

Particularly in the winter, Friar Lake resembled a small village in Eastern Europe. The cluster of stone buildings huddled together, the leafless oaks and maples providing little protection from cold winds. At times like this it was easy to imagine the monks in their woolen robes hurrying to prayer, their wood-soled shoes heavy against the cobblestone paths.

When Eastern College bought the property from the monastic order, it had already been closed for a year or more. I was hired to supervise the renovation, with the plan that I'd manage the property afterward. We had done a lot of work to repair roofs and insulate stone walls. Once the property was secure, we'd moved on to converting the buildings to ways they could be used.

The gatehouse became my office, the infirmary was converted to classrooms, and the dormitories were updated to modern standards, with en-suite bathrooms and wi-fi connections. We hosted meetings and parties in the chapel, and modernized the refectory as a kitchen and communal dining hall. We kept those names for the buildings, though.

Because the property had been abandoned for a while, thieves had used it as a hiding place, and we still occasionally found unexpected items as we worked in the buildings. A breviary stuck behind a statue in the chapel, a sheaf of food bills in a refectory closet. They were a constant reminder that we were living with history.

With a couple of brief breaks for Rochester to sniff and pee, my dog and I walked over to my office. I turned up the heat and started my computer. Rochester settled in a patch of sun by the window for his morning nap, his head on a small rug and his legs stretched out.

Though I'd checked my email occasionally while the college was closed for the holidays, I still had many messages to go through. Yesenia had sent an email while waiting for her rental car, copying Lili. Because she had access to a good Caribbean grocery in Brooklyn, where she lived, she was bringing three different kinds of yams: white boniatos, pink malanga, and the bark-covered edible roots called yuca.

But she wanted to make sure that either Lili or I had picked up chicken (preferably organic), pork shoulder (preferably with lots of fat attached), a dozen cans of a particular brand of black beans, several boxes of long-grain white rice, and a host of other ingredients that she expected we could find at our local stores.

I knew Lili would manage that, so I dove into the rest of my emails. Most of them were from outside the college, though there were a few from faculty and administrators, including a welcome back message about the faculty meeting the next day.

Fortunately, as an administrator, I wasn't required to attend faculty meetings, although I did when something that mattered to me was on the agenda. Since one of the items was "intersession policies and practices" I thought I'd better show up.

Joey Capodilupo came in as I was finishing with email, bringing a gust of cold air with him. He was in his early thirties, ten years younger than I was, and he still had the strapping build he'd developed as a college baseball player and then maintained through years of carpentry and other building trades.

Rochester jumped up to greet him, putting his front paws around Joey's waist. I thought I'd cured him of that trick long ago, but Joey didn't mind. He rubbed the back of Rochester's neck and then let him slide back to the floor.

Joey oversaw Friar Lake's physical plant, and his handyman skills were useful in everything from unstopping toilets to fixing loose cobblestones. "While we were away, there was some rain damage in the classroom at the end of the infirmary," he said, as he pulled off his gloves and his wool watch cap.

"Bad?" I asked.

"Not really. It looks like a couple of the roof tiles have come untacked, probably from that bad windstorm we had in December, and they lifted, letting water get in underneath them. I'll climb up and tack them down again, and I can replace the damp part of the ceiling and the drywall myself. Some spackle and a coat of paint and it'll all be fine."

"Let me know if you need help. I can hold the ladder, at least."

"It's a low roof and I can lean the ladder against the building. Just wanted to let you know."

Working on a two-hundred-year-old property had its downsides, and constant repair was one of them. We insulated all the buildings when we renovated, replacing all the windows with double-plated glass and bringing in energy-efficient appliances. But stuff was always breaking, and I was glad I had Joey there to manage the repairs.

Rochester came over to me and rested his head on my knee, and I scratched behind his ears as Joey and I talked. He also coordinated with Eastern's groundskeepers to have the grass cut, the leaves swept up, and the snow removed, and a dozen other small tasks, leaving me to concentrate on budgets, programming, and fielding requests from faculty for class visits and special lecturers.

"You can help with something," he said. "The new convection oven is arriving today. You can deal with the delivery, if you don't mind."

I agreed, and Joey put his coat back on and went back to the infirmary. The delivery truck arrived about fifteen minutes later, and Rochester and I directed them around behind the refectory. My golden was always eager to meet new people and sniff new smells, and he danced around them as they carried the oven.

While they took out the old oven and plugged in the new one, I sat on the floor with Rochester to look through the manual, stroking his golden fur as I read.

I was surprised that the oven had its own internet connection. "Why would you want your oven online?" I asked Rochester, but he had no answer for me. The oven had a preset internet address and password, and there was nothing in the manual about how to shut it off or change the password. Once the oven was plugged in, it was connected to a satellite network run by the manufacturer.

I tipped the delivery men and they left. Rochester was eager to follow them back to their truck, but I held onto his collar until I could shut the door behind them. "You have it too good to leave here, puppy," I said. "You have a whole hilltop to explore here with a fringe of woods, and you know I spoil you rotten."

I pulled out my phone and went to the company website to figure out how to turn the network connection off. I had been reading about "the internet of things," where eventually one day all our appliances would be online. You'd be able to log in and turn on your oven from work. Your refrigerator could notify you that your milk was about to expire, and add it to the shopping list on your phone.

We wouldn't need any of that at Friar Lake. Unfortunately, the company's website didn't have anything about how to disable the oven's internet connection, so I had to call customer service. While I sat there on the floor listening to Latin-accented hold music, I petted Rochester and when he rolled over, scratched his belly. He yawned with pleasure, showing a mouth full of white teeth.

Finally an agent came on the line. "May I have the home phone number associated with the account?" she asked.

"It's not a residence. It's a college. Do you want my direct line, or the main number?"

"What's the number associated with the account?"

I had no idea. Purchasing was handled centrally, and I'd sent in a purchase order months ago. "I don't need anything specific for my account," I said. "I just want to know how to turn off the internet connection on the oven."

"You need technical support," she said, and put me back on hold.

More Latin music, more belly-rubbing. Fortunately the act of petting a dog helps reduce stress and generate endorphins in humans.

The tech support rep wanted the same information, but I repeated my request. "Why do you want to turn off the internet connection?" he asked. "You may want to turn the oven on while you're at work."

"I am at work," I said. "We only use the kitchen here a few times a month. I don't want the oven to come on randomly because it gets some internet prompt by a hacker."

The rep laughed. "Oh, you don't have to worry about that."

"Oh, I do," I said. "I have a background in computer security. An open port on a machine where I can't control the connectivity or the password is like waving a flag saying, 'Criminals, come on in.'"

"Sir, there's no reason why a criminal would want to turn on your oven."

"Have you ever heard of a distributed denial of service attack?" I asked. "That's where a hacker gets hold of the access to a bunch of machines, and uses their internet connections to disrupt a server with a flood of requests."

"You can't use an oven for that."

"You don't need an oven. Just a whole lot of unsecured ports. Can I speak to a supervisor, please?"

More Latin music, more belly rubs, and then a dial tone. "Probably their protocol for what they consider crank callers," I said to Rochester. "I'll deal with this another day."

I stood up and stretched. I was excited when President Babson announced the intersession, because it was an opportunity for Friar Lake to participate even more in the academic life of the college. There had been some movement in the past to close us down as a cost-saving measure, but we were Babson's pet project and he'd been able to deflect those problems in the past. But who knew how long he could keep that up? Integrating Friar Lake more closely into academics would make it harder for any rogue faculty members to insist on closure.

I was back at the office when Lili came in at noon, carrying an old book in her hands. "Look what I found in the library." She handed it to me, then pulled off her gloves.

Rochester came over to sniff her calf-high leather boots as she pulled off her coat, hat and scarf.

The leather-bound book had no title so I opened it. The handwritten title page proclaimed it to be "An account of Brother Gervase's travels in the Isles of the Caribbees." I scanned through a few pages.

"This must be the book Yesenia was looking for. Odd that it should show up here," I said.

"I checked the list of all the monks who ever lived here," Lili said. "Brother Gervase took his vows at Belmont Abbey in England. He had an interest in healing, and he joined a ship of priests going to Jamaica to take care of them on the long voyage. Then he stuck around, traveling from island to island learning about traditional methods of healing."

"Okay," I said.

"He left Cuba during the Spanish-American War in 1898, and when he retired he ended up here. The book has an appendix of

Caribbean fruits and vegetables and how they can be used for medicinal purposes."

"That is interesting," I said. "I'm sure Yesenia will want to see it."

"I agree. But I'm not giving it to her until I've had a chance to read it myself."

"Better read fast. She's only going to be here for four weeks."

"I can manage that. Ready for lunch?"

"Sure. I checked online and the Cafette is open, and with only faculty and staff on campus it won't be too busy."

The Cafette was a sandwich shop in an old carriage house behind Fields Hall. During the warm weather, we could take Rochester there and sit outside, but because it was too cold I left him in my office with a peanut-butter cookie. He stared at us mournfully as we left, but I was sure he would slump down against the wall and sleep until I returned.

I parked in the faculty lot at the college, which was only half-full. Faculty wouldn't return in force until classes started on Thursday. With so many cars missing, I saw the damage the winter weather had done to the paving, a series of dips and cracks. The stately maple trees that lined the lot were leafless and the mansard roof of Fields Hall showed through the bare branches.

We walked along an asphalt path lined with low bushes to the Cafette. It was a homey-looking place, with weathered wooden picnic tables and benches. During the term, it was busy with faculty, administrators, and students who weren't on the meal plan. That day, though, the light clatter of plates and conversation echoed against the high ceiling.

After we ordered our sandwiches, with tea for Lili and hot chocolate for me, we snared one of the few single tables, off in the corner next to the remains of a brick chimney. "Did you get the grocery list from Yesenia?" I asked.

"I did. We have some of the spices she wants at our house already, and the rest I can get at the IGA market."

"You've never told me how you met Yesenia," I said.

Fire crackled behind us, setting off golden sparks. "NYU sponsored a panel on the Jews of the Caribbean, years ago," Lili said. "A couple of years after I graduated. One of Adriano's friends was organizing it, and because she knew about my background she asked me to participate."

Adriano was Lili's first husband, her professor at NYU when she was an undergraduate. While they were married, she'd hobnobbed with many faculty members.

She picked up her tea and sipped it. "Yesenia was one of the other panelists, and we got to chatting. We discovered that we had a lot in common, and after the presentation she took me to her favorite Cuban-Chinese restaurant on the Upper West Side. I remember the menu was split, Chinese dishes on one side, Cuban dishes on the other. We made up stories about how the ghosts in the kitchen kept mixing up the recipes, so you'd have wontons stuffed with oxtail or the lechon asado would come with a side of pork-fried rice."

She laughed. "I think there was a lot of rum consumed that night. That seems to be common denominator of every time we got together. Cuba libres, mojitos, daiquiris. And toward the end of the evening lots of shots of specialty rums including ones from Guatemala and Barbados. Whenever she can, she manages to smuggle back some authentic Havana Club rum—the one they make in Cuba is so much better than the one the Bacardis make here."

"Have you worked out with her how you'll balance the lecturing and the cooking?"

"She was in Cuba over Christmas with limited internet access, so we decided we'd figure things out when she gets here."

"You said she travels there often. Is that possible?"

"It's not a prison," she said. "You can get a visitor's visa if you're part of a cultural exchange. She still has family there, so she comes up with opportunities to give presentations and talk with cooks as part of her research."

"Has she gotten pushback from the Cuban-American community?"

A group of rowdy students came into the Cafette, laughing and pushing at each other. "Some," Lili admitted. "There are a lot of hard-liners who believe that any engagement with the Castro brothers is bad. Fidel is retired, but Raul is still holding his thumb over everything."

She nibbled her sandwich. "I'm of the opposite opinion. The more we show people on the island what the rest of the world is like, the more they'll push for change."

"Do you think her being here will cause problems? I don't want to see a line of protestors at the entrance to Friar Lake."

"Yesenia can be controversial," she said. "The police had to be called at a program at the New School when people in the audience started yelling and throwing things."

"At her?"

"Well, she was one of the speakers. And she certainly stirred things up online afterwards. Sometimes I think her desire to be famous interferes with her common sense. Especially when it comes to Cuba."

"You might have mentioned this when we began talking about this program a few months ago," I said.

She reached over and took my hand. "Don't worry, I'll keep an eye on her. One Latina to another."

Chapter 4
Past and Presents

When we finished eating, Lili went to her office and I walked over to Fields Hall on a cobblestone path filled in with green moss.

The grand stone building had been the home of the family that endowed the college in the mid-1800s, and now housed the college's administrative offices. When it was renovated a dozen years ago, four rooms behind the top-floor dormer windows were installed with en-suite bathrooms for special guests of the college. We'd secured one of those guest rooms for Yesenia and one for her videographer, though both would stay at Friar Lake on the weekends.

I had good memories of my time working at Fields Hall, even though one of my mentors as an undergraduate had been killed during a party there. I walked in through the front door, and noticed changes had been made since the last time I'd visited.

New offices had been built in the lobby, reducing the once-grand entry to a small marble-floored space. The circular staircase that led to the upper floors had been replaced by a modern elevator. A woman I didn't know sat at a reception desk with a phone, a computer, and a stack of Eastern viewbooks, the promotional materials made up for potential students.

"I'm Steve Levitan from Friar Lake," I said to the woman, whose name badge read Anita. "Just checking on the two rooms I have reserved for our guest, Yesenia Ubeda."

"Yes, I have keys ready for her," Anita said. "Would you like them? Maintenance finished cleaning the rooms this morning, and they usually leave the doors open."

"You can hold the keys for her," I said. "I'll just take a look."

Her phone rang, and I rode the elevator to the fourth floor. Yesenia had been assigned the front room, facing the campus, and the door was ajar. The room next door had been reserved for her videography assistant.

I pushed the door to her room open and looked in. The double bed had been made, the wooden floor swept, and the rag rug beside the bed had been vacuumed. I put a box of candy Lili had given me on the bedside table.

As I was ready to leave, Yesenia herself appeared in the doorway. I held out my hand to her. "I'm Steve, Lili's husband," I said. "Welcome to Eastern College."

As she shook my hand, her long, elegantly manicured nails grazed my palm lightly. "I didn't expect to get a personal welcome," she said. She had a light Spanish accent, and with her black leggings, her white blouse, and her bright-red lipstick, she was the epitome of a classy Latina. The way Lili looked when she wanted to dress up—though Lili would never wear that shade of lipstick.

"Just a coincidence. I wanted to make sure everything was ready for you."

"That's very kind." A young Asian woman with very tan skin and a nose ring stood behind her, with two rollaboard suitcases. "This is Deepti. She's going to be videotaping my lectures."

I shook hands with Deepti. "Welcome. If you need any help with the Wi-Fi let me know."

"I have some boxes in the car, along with Deepti's equipment," Yesenia said. "Do you think you could help us with everything?"

"It might be easier to take it all directly to Friar Lake," I said.

"Why don't I walk you over to Lili's office and the two of you can talk, and then she can direct you out to the conference center. I can unload everything there."

"If it's all right, I'll stay here," Deepti said. She had a pleasant voice, with the hint of a British accent. "I have some online work to do. And I can set up my equipment tomorrow."

As Deepti went next door, Yesenia pulled her suitcase into the room and looked out the window. "So pretty," she said. The land sloped down to a broad lawn, and beneath it Main Street in Leighville. "Nice to get out of the city in the winter."

"We're lucky," I said. "Leighville is a pleasant college town, and Lili and I live just downriver."

Yesenia and I took the elevator downstairs. "Did you have any trouble on the road?" I asked.

"*Dios mío*, I don't know how the cab drivers manage. It took me ten minutes just to get on the Verrazano Narrows Bridge from the Belt Parkway. And the smell of the gas along the Jersey Turnpike! But once we got off the highway the country started to remind me of Cuba."

"Lili said you were there over the holidays," I said, as we walked out into the cold.

"When Lili and I were growing up, there was no such thing as Christmas. Fidel made sure of that. But after the pope visited in 1998, the goyim could celebrate again."

It was funny that Yesenia, who appeared so Latina, would use a Yiddish word to refer to non-Jews. But that was the way Lili spoke as well, mixing all three languages.

"You probably already know about Noche Buena, the night before Christmas," Yesenia said, as she stepped carefully over the cobblestones in her high heels. "It's traditional to roast a whole pig in an underground oven called a caja china, a Chinese box. But in the city, people don't have access to those so they cook with whatever they have."

She stopped for a moment. "That's one of the reasons why I think my work is so important. To document those old traditions so that when Cuba is free and prosperous again, people can return to them."

As we approached Granger Hall, the Fine Arts building where Lili's office was located, she said. "Is that where Liliana works? It looks like a giant pill!"

I nodded. "It does. Mr. Granger was a pharmaceutical magnate and he was very involved in the design of the building. Fortunately the glass walls bring a lot of light to the studios and classrooms."

She looked around. "But the other buildings are so old-looking, all stone and slate. *Esta sobresale como un pulgar dolorido.*"

"You're right, it sticks out like a sore thumb," I said.

She turned to me. "*¿Tú hablas español?*"

"*Un poquito*," I said. "I've been with Lili long enough to pick up many words and expressions. And we had a lot of her family here in October for our wedding, so I was forced to communicate."

We walked into the airy lobby, which was chilly. The big windows hadn't been insulated properly, something Lili complained about regularly. We climbed a staircase to the second floor and walked into the chair's office. Student artwork hung on the walls, a rotating selection Lili curated from prize-winners and other pieces she liked.

I introduced Yesenia to Matilda, and Lili must have heard us through her open door because she came right out, and she and Yesenia exchanged hugs and *besos*, or kisses to the cheek.

"Yesenia has some stuff in her car that needs to come out to Friar Lake," I said. "Why don't you bring her out there later, and then we can all go out to dinner?"

"Sounds like a plan," Lili said. "Come in for a minute, Steve, and we can look over the student profiles together."

She held her hand out to Yesenia and led her into her office, and I pulled two chairs up beside Lili's desk. "I asked each prospective student to write me a note explaining why they were interested in food, the culture of the Caribbean, or both," Lili said.

She opened a folder of printed sheets. "For many of them, *esa una conexión familiar.* Like this boy here, Bobby Cruz, who was born in Havana and raised in Miami. He says he misses his mother's cooking and all the flavors he grew up around, as well as *el sentido de comunidad.*"

I noticed that with Yesenia, as with her family, Lili included a lot more Spanish words and phrases in her speech. My great-aunt had told me once that she loved speaking Yiddish with anyone who could understand her. It was the way she connected to her childhood.

Lili showed us Bobby's form, and Yesenia and I leaned in to read it. She wore a perfume that reminded me of gardenia flowers.

Bobby wrote that his family had been split by the diaspora, with his mother estranged from her brother over politics. His uncle lived in New York, and Bobby was hoping that if he learned more about *cocina Cubana,* he could make a connection to his uncle.

"My brother and his family live in Miami, and my mother did until she passed," Lili said to Yesenia. "So I know a little about *esa comunidad.*"

"*Yo también,*" Yesenia said. "I've lectured several times at Florida International University, which has a big hospitality management program. And of course I've spent a lot of time at the restaurants along Calle Ocho. I'm fascinated by the fusion cuisine down there—Peruvian Japanese, for example. And don't get me started on *fritas!*"

"Lili makes a delicious one," I said. "Half beef and half pork topped with the crispiest French fries."

We went back to the student letters. There were twenty-one students in all, roughly split between college students and outsiders who were interested in the topic. A few had heard about the class from Yesenia's online community, including her Facebook group.

"Ah, her, I know," Yesenia said when we came to Maria Cabrera. "She's *una verdadera* fan, a member of my online community. She gets *muy defensivo* when anyone criticizes me for engagement with the Castros. I've met her a couple of times at events in New York. *Es muy brava.*"

"She's brave?" I asked.

"More like she's strong-willed," Lili said.

"Yes, that's Maria," Yesenia said. "Not afraid to stand up in a crowd and wave a Cuban flag, or argue with anyone who disagrees with her."

"I hope you won't have any arguments about food," I said. I recalled what Lili had said about a protest at the New School in New York. I didn't want Eastern College or Friar Lake to make those kind of headlines.

We looked through the rest of the list, and then Lili and Yesenia got into a conversation about mutual acquaintances. I excused myself and drove back to Friar Lake to see how Joey was coming with the repairs to the infirmary. If he couldn't get it all done by Thursday, we'd have to bring in outside contractors, and that was going to knock a hole in my budget.

Chapter 5
What Was Hidden

First I had to stop at the office and mollify Rochester, who was upset at having been left alone so long. But I'd brought him a few scraps of roast beef from my sandwich, and that made him happy. He sat on his haunches and gobbled them quickly. "Watch my fingers!" I said once. "I don't want you to get a taste for human flesh!"

I didn't take off my coat— I knew he'd want to go out, and I had to walk over to the infirmary and see Joey. When Friar Lake was quiet, I didn't bother with a leash for the dog. He was well-behaved enough to come when called, and though he liked to chase squirrels, he hadn't yet caught one.

He romped around as we walked. Golden retrievers have a two-layer coat, so pockets of air between the layers kept him warm even on frigid days. I couldn't say the same for myself. A gust of wind hit my face and my cheeks got cold, and I hurried him along.

It was a relief to pull open the solid oak door and walk into the warmth of the classroom building which had once housed the sick and infirm, as well as the monk who treated them with herbs and potions.

We walked to the far end to find Joey. "Just in time to help me," he said. "I've got to take this whole sheet of drywall down and I could use a hand."

Rochester hurried over to the damaged wall and began sniffing there. Then he looked up at me and barked.

"I know, the wall is damaged," I said to him. "Don't worry, it's coming down right away."

It was warm in the room, so I shucked my coat, hat and gloves and walked over to where Joey stood. He grabbed one end of the sheet and I took hold of the other, and we pulled.

Because of the moisture that had seeped in, the drywall was loose and pliable, and came off easily, tearing only at the places where it had been nailed to the metal studs.

With the drywall down, we saw through to the stone wall, and the area in between. A wooden box lay on the ground. "Where did that come from?" I asked as Rochester raised a paw and scratched at the box.

Joey shrugged. "The monks had already sealed up these exterior walls, so we didn't touch them during the renovation."

"Then this must have been left behind by the monks." I squatted down to take a closer look at the box, my dog right beside me, crowding my space.

The mahogany box was well-made, about twelve inches long and six inches high, with a lid that folded down. The lock on the lid was old and rusted by the humidity inside the walls, and the flap lifted easily even without a key.

The rich aroma of tobacco rose into the air as I opened the box. Inside, resting on a soft piece of blue cloth, were eleven cigars with Spanish markings on the bands.

"These might be Cuban," I said. "Over a hundred years old." I told him about the book Lili had found in the library. "I wonder if that monk brought these back from Cuba and hid them here so his brothers couldn't find them."

Joey nodded. "There are eleven left, probably twelve to start with. He might have died before he had the chance to smoke them all."

He smiled. "My dad would have been delighted to find these on his watch. A great cigar can age for decades so long as the temperature and humidity are stable. This humidor looks like it kept them well."

Joe Capodilupo Senior had been the facilities manager for Eastern College, and he'd hired his son to manage the renovation of Friar Lake. Joe Senior had since retired, but Joey had leveraged himself into his position by virtue of his skills and his knowledge of the facility.

"He still smokes cigars?" I asked.

"When my mom isn't around," Joey said. "We gave up warning him about the consequences a long time ago. He says he's seventy years old and he only has a few pleasures left."

"He's a character," I said. "Let's get this box out so you can finish fixing the wall."

I nudged Rochester aside and grabbed the box by the handles on the side, then stood. The dog was still very interested in what was in the box and he stayed by my side.

"You need help hanging the new drywall?" I asked.

"I can manage. If I need anything I'll give you a holler."

I put my stuff back on and walked back to my office carrying the box. Rochester stayed right by my side despite all the smells around us.

"Why are you so obsessed with this box?" I asked him, as he got tangled in my legs while I was trying to take off my coat. "You don't smoke cigars. And you can't eat tobacco."

I put the humidor on a high shelf in the office, and Rochester, looking disgruntled, lay down on the floor beneath it.

I had a lot more to do before the intersession began on Thursday, so I was busy all afternoon until Rochester sat up on his hind legs and barked. I looked out the window and saw a sedan pull up in the parking lot, and Yesenia and Lili got out.

"Yes, that's Mama Lili," I said, scratching behind Rochester's ears. "We'll show her the cigars and see what she thinks."

The two of them were laughing and talking as they crossed the parking lot. "You guys look like you're getting along," I said.

"So much to talk about!" Yesenia said. "The course, Cuba, *la vida!*"

I was glad to see Lili looking so happy. She'd been worried about the course, because it was her idea and because she was stepping out of her comfort zone in the fine arts to help teach it. I hadn't helped by getting upset about controversy. Yesenia appeared to be clearing up Lili's fears.

Rochester sniffed Yesenia experimentally, and she smiled down at him. Then he went back to nosing around Lili's boots, and settled on the floor in front of them as they sat.

They bubbled over with ideas they'd been talking about. Resources they could use in teaching, recipe ideas their mothers had shared with them, and of course the old book that Lili had found.

"On that note." I stood and retrieved the humidor. "Look what Joey uncovered while he was repairing a wall in the infirmary."

"Cigars!" Yesenia said as she opened the box. She inhaled. "They're marvelous. How old do you think they are?"

"They might have belonged to Brother Gervase," I said.

"That makes sense," Lili said.

"Too bad he didn't get to smoke more of them," I said. "There were probably twelve."

"Maybe more," Yesenia said. "This only looks like the top layer." Very carefully, she lifted the cigars out and placed them on my desk, then lifted out the soft cloth.

Beneath them were a stack of papers. Yesenia peered at the top one, without touching it. "*Dios mío,*" she said. "This is an official document from 1898."

"Rochester was very interested in that box," I said. "He must have known there was something in there besides the cigars."

Yesenia looked at me, and then Lili, who shrugged. Yesenia began lifting the papers out, one by one.

"What do you think they are?" Lili asked.

"At first glance, like *acuerdos oficiales* between the US and Spain and Cuba," Yesenia said. "*¡Esperar! Eso es interesante.*"

We both looked over at her. "It's my name," she said. "Ubeda. I'm translating here, but it grants a plot of land in the Vedado neighborhood to Joaquin Ubeda Hernandez in recognition of his service to Cuba."

She put the page down. "I did some genealogical research a few years ago, and discovered that my great-grandfather was Joaquin Ubeda Hernandez, and that he lived in Vedado. My grandfather and my father were both born there. The story I heard from my abuelo was that their home was confiscated by Carlos Prío Socarrás in 1943 because he liked the area. He commissioned an architect to design the seat for the Supreme Court and the Attorney General."

Her voice was quavering and Lili looked concerned.

"In 1965, Fidel Castro ordered the seat of government to be relocated there, including the presidential office."

I had no idea where this was going. What did some old papers have to do with the present?

Yesenia put the paper down. "*Mi abuelo* was an only child, and so was *mi padre*, and so am I. I am the last living descendant of Joaquin Ubeda Hernandez." Her voice became more surprised. "If these documents are correct, I am the legal owner of the ground the Cuban Presidential Palace sits on."

Chapter 6
Controversy

"That can't really be true, can it?" I asked. "It's been a long time. And didn't Castro confiscate a lot of personal property over the years?"

"You're thinking of Title III of the 1996 Helms Burton Act, the law that allows the original owners of Cuban properties confiscated by the Castros to sue foreign companies using those properties," Lili said. "I don't know if that includes property taken before the Castros took power, or claims against the state."

"I'm sure the Cuban government would never turn over ownership of the Presidential Palace to a *gusano*," Yesenia said. "But I might be able to use this document to leverage the government to grant me access to their archives. There must be so much rich material I could use there in my research. Having that research could make my name as an academic. Get me a tenured professorship somewhere."

"What's a *gusano*?" I asked. "Is that Spanish for exile?"

Lili shook her head. "It means worm. Castro used it to describe people who fled the country after the revolution." She turned to Yesenia. "You need to slow down, *mija*."

That word I knew, because Lili used it among all her female relatives and close friends. It was an abbreviation of *"mi hija,"* or my daughter.

As she spoke with Yesenia, Lili's whole demeanor shifted - her gestures became more expansive, her voice taking on a melodic Spanish lilt that contrasted with her usual measured English. She leaned forward in her chair, occasionally touching Yesenia's arm for emphasis in that characteristically Latin way.

"You have a good relationship with the Cuban government already, don't you?" she continued. "What if you push forward a lawsuit and they shut off all your access? No more visits to the islands, no more dinners at *paladares* and *casas particulares.*"

She turned to me apologetically. "Sorry if we're losing you with so much Spanish. Those are restaurants people set up in their homes to feed tourists. Yesenia has gotten a lot of recipes from them."

"And a lot of cultural history, too." She sighed. "You're right, I need to think this through. I want to expand my food connections, not cut them off."

Rochester must have heard the word "food" because he barked twice. "We should head to dinner," I said. "Lili, you have any restaurant ideas where we can take Rochester? I'd hate to dump him at home after he missed out on lunch with us."

She frowned. "Every place I can think of has outside dining, and it's too cold for that."

"Why don't we cook together, Liliana?" Yesenia said. "I can make a quick picadillo if you have the ingredients."

"I'm a Cuban cook," Lili said. "I always have ground beef, tomato sauce, onions and rice in the house."

She looked at me. "You don't mind, do you? We'd have to drive Yesenia back to Leighville after dinner."

"Don't worry about me," Yesenia said. "I have a rental car and a GPS. I can get myself back easily."

"Then it's settled," I said. "Lili, why don't you ride with Yesenia and show her the way, and I'll take Rochester."

"Good plan," she said. "Yesenia and I can stop at the IGA in town and pick up anything else we need."

They left in Yesenia's car, and I closed the office. Rochester and I followed a few minutes later. I stopped on the way to buy a bottle of good red wine, and by the time Rochester and I got home Lili and Yesenia were in the kitchen. I took Rochester for his evening walk and he tugged eagerly forward, pausing to sniff and send his own pee-mail to neighboring dogs.

I was chilled by the night air by the time we returned to the house and the smell of ground beef simmering on the stove.

It was great to see Lili working with Yesenia in the kitchen. She had learned so much about cooking from her mother, and sometimes there was a tinge of sadness as she prepared a recipe Benita Weinstock had perfected. That evening, though, there was joy. We played Celia Cruz on the stereo, we drank the red wine, and the kitchen was filled with rhythm and laughter.

"It's a pleasure to get out of Brooklyn for a while," Yesenia said as we ate. "Not just *porque la ciudad es tan sombría en invierno*, with all the barren trees and the dirty piles of snow." She paused and took a deep breath. "I've been getting some threatening emails."

"Really?" Lili asked. "¿A cerca de? You're a food anthropologist. Why would someone threaten you?"

"Because of my perceived close ties with the Castros," she said. "When I was in Havana once, I was asked to cook at a benefit for the Cuban National Center for Sex Education."

"Run by Raul Castro's daughter Mariela," Lili added for me. "Did you do it?"

She nodded. "I wasn't the only one. There were five of us, and I didn't think it was a big deal. The Center is one of the most progressive organizations on the island. I posted a lot of photos on social media, and a special recipe I created for a rainbow flan, with stripes of blueberry, lime, caramel, and guava."

She looked at Lili's face and laughed. "I know, it sounds awful. But I muted the flavors so that the caramel stood out and the other flavors were very mild. It was a big hit at the event." She frowned. "Not so much on social media, though. People accused me of all kinds of things. There was even a protest before one of my talks at the New School."

That must have been the event Lili had mentioned, and it reignited my fear that we'd bring controversy to Eastern as the college was experimenting with intersession programming. One big problem could bring the whole concept to a crashing halt.

"Do you think anyone will protest here?" I asked Yesenia.

"All the way out here in the country?" she asked. "Liliana, are there even other Cubans here?"

"We're everywhere, *mija*," she said. "There's a Caribbean students' club at Eastern, and a couple of the members who are here during the intersession will be in our class. That boy, Bobby Cruz, the one from Miami? He'll be there. But I doubt anyone will make a fuss."

I looked at Lili. She caught my eye and shrugged.

The picadillo was delicious, and I thought I tasted something different. "You don't usually use potatoes, do you?" I asked Lili.

She shook her head. "Yesenia suggested them. What do you think?"

I was torn. Compliment our guest, which Lili might take the wrong way. Or tell the truth, which was that I liked Lili's better. I opted for the truth, cloaked in my own nostalgia.

"My mother used to buy stuffed cabbage at a Hungarian grocery in Trenton," I said. "When I eat Lili's picadillo, because of the ground beef and the rice and the raisins, it reminds me of that dish."

Fortunately, Yesenia wasn't upset. She pulled a pen and pad from her purse. "That's a great connection, Steve. Between the food the Jews ate in the old country, and what they ate in America and the Caribbean. I want to remember to mention that."

I was relieved, and Lili looked pleased. For dessert, we had mango sorbet they had found at our local grocery, though it didn't have strong enough mango taste to please either of them.

By the end of the meal, we'd all had plenty of red wine to drink, and Lili brought out a bottle of rhum Agricole from Martinique, and served us all shots. Then a Celia Cruz song came up on Lili's playlist, and Yesenia jumped up and struck a pose with her back to us. She raised her left hand and moved it sinuously through the air while swaying her hips.

She picked up the hem of her long skirt and began lifting it up and down to the rhythm of the music. Then she extended her right arm and right leg in exaggerated movements. "*Baila conmigo, Liliana,*" she said. "You must know the habanera."

I nudged my wife. "Go on."

She stood up and began to mimic Yesenia's movements, bowing to her and twirling in time with her. They laughed and clapped their hands and eventually collapsed onto the sofa laughing.

"I haven't danced that way in years," Lili said. "Not even at our wedding." She poked Yesenia in the side. "You're going to be a bad influence on me."

Yesenia opened her mouth in mock horror. "Me? Never!"

Yesenia assured us that even after all the wine and the rum, she was quite capable of driving. "I once drove an ancient pickup truck from Matanzas to Havana, in the middle of the night, when I had a lot more to drink than this." She blew us both air kisses. "*Adios, mi amigos,*" she said, and then she swept out the door.

Rochester watched her leave with something like awe.

Lili and I looked at each other and laughed, and then I helped her clean up. Rochester hovered around for a few minutes, hoping we'd drop something on the floor. Then he gave up and clambered up onto the sofa, where he could watch us through the kitchen door.

"I'm worried that someone will cause trouble at your course," I said. "Are there other Cubans coming? Any of the special students besides that one we talked about at your office?"

A special student was one who was not pursuing a degree at Eastern. They included senior citizens taking classes for enrichment and those visiting from other institutions. We often got kids from the community college taking a class or two, and those who wanted a semester away from their home institution for whatever reason.

"She encouraged her social media followers who have the time to sign up for the class. I checked the roster yesterday, and there are two members of her Facebook group coming. They both have Cuban backgrounds. One of them is the woman we talked about, Maria Cabrera. The other is Raquel Jaceldo. From what I've read, she's a retiree who sticks up for Yesenia against any criticism. I think she'll be very interesting. She was a line cook at a Cuban Chinese restaurant when she was younger. Eventually she retired after a few decades in food service administration for the New York City public schools."

"You mentioned a Cuban Chinese restaurant you and Yesenia went to. Is that really a thing?"

"The sugar plantations brought in Chinese men to work in the late 1800s," she said. "They often married Cuban women and they created a blended cuisine. When those people left Cuba, many of them moved to New York and opened restaurants, primarily in Latin areas, not in Chinatown. Most of the people who own those places identify more as Spanish than Chinese."

She put her hands together. "I had some time this afternoon so I did some research on Maria Cabrera, who goes by Maria de los Angeles Cabrera on Facebook. She still has several family members in Cuba, so she's been very outspoken on social media. She wants a normalization of relations so she can reconnect with her family there. She was in school to become a science teacher when she and her family had to leave the island, and she couldn't continue her education here because they were too poor and she didn't have the English skills. She and her husband lived on the Upper West Side, near Columbia, where he was a janitor. She worked in factories and then raised her children, so she's basically a home cook."

"Is she the one Yesenia said was very strong-willed?"

"Yes. She's widowed now and she devotes a lot of time to writing to politicians about Cuba."

"Great. But if she likes Yesenia, then she shouldn't be a problem, right?"

"I agree."

"Well, Bucks County is not exactly a hotbed of Cuban dissent," I said. "And it's not that easy to get here from the city. I hope Yesenia's problems won't follow her out here."

"*Fun zayn moyl, in Gots oyer,*" Lili said. Because her grandparents were all from Eastern Europe, she had grown up with some of the same Yiddish sayings as I had, and we both used them. So I knew that she was saying "From your mouth to God's ear."

We had a very multicultural relationship. Our joint Ashkenazi Jewish heritage brought us together, and I was always eager to learn more about the Cuban and Spanish culture she had absorbed from her Havana-born parents. And while I'd spent most of my life in Stewart's Crossing, aside from brief detours in New York and California, Lili's family had moved around through her childhood as her father got better and better jobs. Then she'd eaten her way around the world while she worked as a photojournalist.

We finished cleaning up the kitchen and sat in the living room to read, with Rochester sprawled on the tile floor across from us. I was just getting into my book when Lili's cell rang. I expected it to be another of her many cousins, and prepared to go upstairs so she could talk in Spanish to her heart's content.

But instead she said, "It's Yesenia. I hope she didn't get lost." Rochester rose from the floor and walked over to her, nestling against her leg.

"Hola, *mija*," she said. Then, "No! You have to call the police. We know a detective in Leighville."

I looked over at her. Had Yesenia gotten into an accident? It hadn't snowed for a while, but sometimes water built up on the country roads and led to ice slicks and treacherous black ice.

"Well, if you think so," Lili finally said. "Call me if anything else happens."

She ended the call and turned to me, then put her hand on

Rochester's head. "When Yesenia got back to her room she found a threatening note slipped under her door. Telling her to give up teaching the intersession course and get out of town, or there will be trouble."

Chapter 7
Family Recipes

I was not happy to hear about the threat Yesenia had received. Because she was Lili's friend, and I was insulted that someone in our culturally diverse community had threatened her. And because I didn't want anything bad to happen at Friar Lake while she was there.

"What do you think?" I asked Lili, as Rochester pushed against her leg. "Is this a follow up to the threats she got in New York?"

"I have no idea. There were protests in person, yes, but all the negative comments came online." She reached down to pet the dog beside her.

"People are a lot more willing to say mean things behind the protection of a screen," I said. "It's like they type without thinking. I follow one of my favorite authors, and she posted something about the difference between "in to" and "into," and how a book she read had numerous errors in usage. And people came out of the woodwork to criticize her. One woman dissected her post, and another said the next time she read the author's book she was going to look for errors and report them to the publisher."

"I told her not to worry. But do you think she should?"

"She ought to talk to the police. At least to campus security. If she won't, then I'll call Dan Lazerow tomorrow." Lazerow was the head of that department, and I'd met him in the past when we served on the same committee.

"I'll talk to her in the morning," Lili said. "I don't want to make a big fuss if it's only a one-off."

"If you think so." I stood and stretched. "Time for Rochester's bedtime walk." He either knew the word walk, had an internal timer set, or recognized what it meant when I started putting on my coat and hat, because he left Lili's side and started dancing around me in circles.

Then he barked when I didn't move fast enough. "I'm working on it, puppy," I said. "I don't have a built-in fur coat like you do."

We walked out into the quiet night, and he tugged me forward. When I was a kid, I hated taking the garbage cans out late at night. We lived in a safe neighborhood, yet I was always frightened of attackers screaming down the street in cars with guns blazing.

I guess my parents shouldn't have let me read all those crime stories in the Sunday *New York Post*, where the centerfold was always dedicated to some heinous crime. Often they involved violence against kids or teenagers. One year I relocated my bed from under the window to across the room because of a story about a guy who slashed through screens to knife sleeping victims.

River Bend was quiet, though. Only a distant motorcycle and the sound of someone's TV being played too loud. Even so, I hurried Rochester through his walk, back to the security of our own home.

Wednesday morning Lili was scanning through her phone after breakfast and suddenly said, "Tell me she didn't do that."

I was at the sink washing dishes and turned to her. "Who do what?"

"Yesenia. She posted on Facebook about the threat she got last night, and how defiant she is. It's like throwing *gasolina* on a fire."

"She does have a certain personality," I said.

"Don't even get me started on the Latina temper," she said. "Or you'll see what it's really like."

I held up my soapy hands. "Nothing more from me." Rochester was staying out of the argument, too, slumped against the wall staring at us.

"Oh, I should tell you - Matilda already heard about the message that was slipped under Yesenia's door," Lili said. "She texted me first thing this morning."

"What else did she hear?" I asked.

"She says President Babson was already getting calls from some faculty worried about security during the intersession. You know how news travels through the secretaries' network faster than official channels."

Lili grabbed her phone and navigated to Yesenia's Facebook group. "Listen to this," she read. "'I am here at Eastern College in rural Pennsylvania preparing to teach a one-month course on the food traditions of the Caribbean. Innocent topic, right? Last night a threat was slipped under my door telling me I am a disgrace to the Cuban people. Really? A disgrace because I teach and write about food? Get a life.'" She looked up at me.

"She has a point," I said. "Why would anyone complain about food? Unless it doesn't taste good." Rochester barked once.

"Be serious."

"Did she mention the actual threat? That she should stop the course and get out of town or else there will be trouble?"

"Not in so many words. She went off on a tangent, one I know she's used before. She thinks the real undercurrent here is that she's been called a pawn of the Castros because they let her come to the island and travel freely. And because she refuses to denounce their regime."

"Regime is an interesting word." I finished with the dishes and turned around, leaning on the counter. Rochester rose and came over to lean against me. "You often hear it used with the word authoritarian, don't you? You never hear people talk about the Obama regime."

"That depends on who you talk to," Lili said and she smiled. "You're right. The Castros have been ruling Cuba with an iron hand for decades, and exiles and others have a right to protest anyone who is complicit with them. But it's not like Yesenia is posting social media updates from the Presidio Modelo, the prison where they send dissidents."

I knew better than to argue with Lili when she was passionate about something. Instead I focused on the delivery of the threat. "How do you think that paper got slipped under her door?" I asked, as I stroked behind Rochester's ears. "Someone had to know that she was coming here and where she was staying, and then get access to Fields Hall."

"She's been posting about this program online for a while," Lili said. "She took a picture of Fields Hall before she walked in, and then while she was waiting for me to finish up in the office she posted it with something about her room on the top floor and the view of the big lawn."

"So anyone who knew the campus would know where her room is," I said.

"Or anyone with an Internet connection," Lili said. "You just have to Google Fields Hall and you'll see pictures and the Wikipedia entry on the building and the Fields family. Then yesterday while we were at the IGA market she posted an update about coming to our house for dinner. Anyone who read it would know she wasn't in her room."

"Back when I worked at Fields Hall, they didn't lock the front door until eleven o'clock at night," I said, as Rochester slumped to the floor in front of me. "Anyone could have slipped in, especially after five when the receptionist goes off duty."

"I don't like this," Lili said, as she put her phone down on the table. "I'm going to have words with Yesenia. I'm co-teaching this class and I don't want trouble."

I couldn't disagree with that. I didn't want trouble either.

We both left for work soon after, with Lili headed to her office on campus and Rochester and me going to Friar Lake. As soon as we reached the parking lot and I opened the passenger door, he jumped out and took off after a porcupine, who waddled quickly into the tree cover.

"Come on, dog," I said, and slapped the side of my leg. "You don't want to mess with a porcupine." He bounded over to me and we checked in with Joey in the infirmary classroom, where he was stirring white paint in a bucket.

He'd already put up the replacement drywall and spackled the joints, and he was dressed for painting, in white overalls splattered with a rainbow of colors. "Just waiting for everything to dry before I start painting," he said as we walked in. "What happened with that box?"

Rochester sprawled on the floor as I told Joey about the papers Yesenia had found underneath the cigars. "She took those away with her last night, so I didn't get a good look at them," I said. "But she found her great-grandfather's name there and some kind of land grant."

"You think we could smoke some of those cigars?" he asked.

"I'm not a cigar guy. Are you?"

He put the paint can aside and stood up. "Only with my dad, and a glass of Irish whiskey," he said. "Preferably Bushmill's Black Label."

"I'll see if I can liberate a couple for you," I said. "Technically they're college property but I can't imagine what else we'd do with them. Maybe you and your dad will invite Babson over for a smoke."

He laughed. "My dad would like that. He and Babson always got along. I probably wouldn't even be here if it wasn't for their relationship."

"You're great at what you do," I protested. "Nobody could have complained."

"Back when we started, I was just a carpenter," he said. "After I graduated from Penn State I was still in the closet because I wanted to play pro baseball. I tried out for a bunch of teams. My arm was good enough for college but not for the majors."

He stretched his right arm and rotated it. He'd been a star pitcher on the Penn State team. "When I gave up on that dream, I went on a downward spiral. Started working as a carpenter, but I hated myself and my life so much I was getting drunk or stoned every night and I kept losing jobs."

"What turned you around?"

Rochester rose and moved over to Joey, leaning against his leg, and Joey reached down to ruffle the golden's hair.

"My dad, of course. I was living in a trailer in Levittown and he came over one Saturday morning. I had puked the night before and hadn't cleaned it up before I passed out. He took a look around and just shook his head."

I knew how much Joey valued his father's opinion, so that must have been hard. "He grabbed a rag and started cleaning up. I told him to leave it but he wouldn't."

Joe Senior was a formidable man. Six feet tall, broad-shouldered, and tough as nails when he had to be. He had worked his way up at Eastern from carpentry to the director of facilities, and that was partly because John William Babson believed in him.

Babson had believed in me, too. Perhaps because I was an Eastern graduate and I was lost, like Joey was back then. After my divorce and my return from prison, I struggled to build a freelance writing business because it was hard for an ex-con to get a job. I started teaching at Eastern as an adjunct in the English department, and Babson recognized my data management skills and slotted me into a job with the Alumni Relations office.

From there, he'd asked me to take over Friar Lake. He'd done the same thing with Joey, though I didn't realize it at the time.

"What happened after your dad cleaned up your trailer?" I asked.

"First, I got my sorry ass up and helped him. Scoured the kitchen, put aside a batch of linens for the laundromat. Even washed the windows."

"That must have been intense."

"It was." Joey sat down and Rochester followed, leaning his head into Joey's lap. I sat on the floor as well. I couldn't be jealous that my dog was paying attention to someone else. Rochester had empathy and he could tell when anyone was struggling.

Joey looked down at the floor. "My dad told me he didn't care who I slept with as long as that person cared about me as much as he and my mom did. I started to cry and I asked him how he knew. He put his hand on my shoulder and said, 'You're my boy. I saw how handsome you are, what a great personality you have, and yet you didn't date girls. At first your mom and I were impressed at how dedicated you were to baseball. But eventually we figured it out.'"

"That's so kind," I said. "Your dad has a crusty exterior but a good heart."

"That's true." He straightened up. "I moved back in with them and I stopped drinking. Started to date—well, really, hook up at first. Then Babson was over at our house one night talking to my dad about this abbey that he wanted Eastern to buy, and he wanted Dad's opinion."

I'd never talked about this with Joey before, and it was fascinating to see how Friar Lake had come to be.

"He and my dad made plans to see the property, and my dad had me come along, and one thing led to another."

"I'm glad it did."

"Me, too. Working with you, seeing how you manage things, helped me connect with the part of my dad inside me. And of course, without you I wouldn't have met Mark."

Mark Figueroa was one of the first people I met when I returned to Stewart's Crossing. He ran an antique store in the center of town, and we'd originally bonded over a shared love of mystery fiction.

"You know why I fixed you two up?" I asked.

He shook his head. "You never said."

"It's embarrassing to say now. But you were both gay, and both tall." Joey was a robust six-four, and Mark was a gangly six-five. I figured that was enough to put them together, and fortunately they clicked.

They had eventually moved in together, gotten a dog, then

recently bought a house in River Bend that renters had wrecked, and Joey was renovating it.

"Marriages have been made on less than that," he said.

"What about you guys? Thinking about marriage?" Joey and Mark had both participated in my wedding to Lili, handling Rochester, though handling was a generous word for it.

"We're thinking about it," Joey said. "Mark has been paying way too much for crappy health insurance, and if we get married I can put him on my policy here. But we both agree that's not enough for marriage."

"You're committed to each other," I said. "You own a house together. You have a dog. What more do you want?"

"I don't know," he said. "We'll see." He stood up. "I should get started painting."

As I carried the box to my office, I couldn't shake the feeling that finding this box of Cuban cigars now, just before our program started, was more than coincidence. And given what Lili had told me about her friend's flair for drama, I wondered if there might be more fire than smoke in Yesenia's presence.

Chapter 8
Academic Warning

Rochester and I went back to my office, with a brief detour so he could chase a squirrel. At least the squirrel didn't have spines.

"Give the little rodent a break," I said, when I called him back to me. "He's looking for a nut. Probably has a family to feed."

That reminded me of Yesenia and the food course, and when we got inside I checked her Facebook page. Many of her followers had chimed in with support, and both Maria and Raquel said they'd see her when class started on Thursday. They both promised to stand by her if anyone tried to disrupt the class.

As I ate my sandwich and gave Rochester a dental chew, I remembered that I wanted to warn campus security that there might be a problem. Since I wanted to attend the faculty meeting while I was up there, I left Rochester with Joey out at the infirmary building.

The security office was in a relatively new building on the edge of campus, where town met gown. To one side was a row of old Victorian houses, all of them converted to student housing. On the other was an open area where the lacrosse and soccer teams practiced, and beyond that the solid wall of the gym.

I'd served on the Honor and Discipline Committee with Dan

Lazerow, the head of campus security, so I knew him well enough to drop into his office for a brief visit. He was a Philly cop who had risen through the ranks and then made a career shift to move out to the country and work for Eastern.

I told the work-study student at the front desk that I wanted to speak with Dan, and she buzzed his office, and he came out to meet me a few minutes later. "Hey, Steve," he said. "What brings you here?"

"I wanted to give you a heads up on something," I said.

"You'd better come back, then," he said. He was a few inches shorter than I was, and in his dark blue business suit, he looked more like a mid-level corporate executive than a cop. Managing people and budgets probably represented the bulk of his work.

"We've got an intersession program scheduled that will take place in a classroom at Granger Hall, with introduction and conclusion out at Friar Lake," I said. I explained what we were doing, and he nodded.

"We might have a situation with our guest speaker," I continued, and I told him about Yesenia Ubeda Goldstein and the threat that had come into her room the night before.

"In Fields Hall?" he asked.

I nodded. "Is the front door still unlocked until eleven?"

"Let me check." He turned to his computer and typed. "Yes. Electronic door lock that kicks in from eleven to seven. During that time you need card key access, but otherwise anyone can go in or out."

"No cameras?"

"This isn't a prison, Steve," he said. "It's a very good small college in nowhere Pennsylvania."

"So there's no way to track who slipped that threat under Yesenia's door?"

"You say she posted where she was teaching and where she was staying on social media?"

"Yup."

"Then you've got all her followers on Facebook who knew, and whoever else stopped by her page. When does your program start?"

"Students arrive at Friar Lake tomorrow afternoon. They're all staying there through the weekend. Eastern students who have dormitory assignments or other living situations move back to campus on Sunday night. Special students can stay in the rooms at Friar Lake all month. Then everyone reconvenes at Friar Lake for the last weekend of the course."

"How are you moving the special students around? And is someone staying with them at Friar Lake?"

"They're all responsible for their own transportation," I said. "As you know, it's hard to get to Leighville unless you have access to a car. On the off chance a special student arrives on their own, we'll match them up with someone with a car. And Joey Capodilupo and I are taking turns staying out there during the week. He'll have his partner Mark and their dog Brody with him, and I'll have Lili and Rochester with me."

Dan steepled his fingers. "I can't say I'm happy that we've got a controversial speaker coming to campus, but we'll do our best to make Ms. Goldstein feel safe."

"It's actually Dr. Ubeda," I said. "PhD, and she uses the Spanish tradition of tacking her mother's maiden name on to the end of her name."

"Dr. Ubeda, then. It would be nice if you could convince her to stop making controversial posts on social media, at least as long as she's here."

"I will do my best," I said. "But like Lili, she's Latin and she's Jewish, and I know that's a potent combination."

He laughed. "My wife is Jewish and doesn't have a drop of Latin blood, and I have trouble keeping her from talking trash with her sisters, so I know what you mean."

I stood and shook hands with Dan. "I'll tell you what," he said. "I can send one of my guards out to Friar Lake on Thursday afternoon if you like."

"That would be great. I'll make sure the guard gets some good Cuban food."

"Make it sound that good and I might come out myself."

"You'd be welcome," I said. "If you're free, it would be a good chance to meet Yesenia and hear the description of the course. And get fed, too."

He said he'd let me know, and I left the security office and walked up to Pennsylvania Hall, the biggest building on campus. It housed the physics, chemistry and mathematics departments and its classrooms were the largest. A few faculty members were huddled in the cold outside, smoking cigarettes, but I wanted to get inside, and Lili had promised to save me a seat.

I slid into a padded seat beside her and kissed her cheek, still cold from the outdoors. "You speak to Yesenia today?" I asked.

"We had some words," she said. I wanted to ask what kind of words, but I could tell from her face they hadn't been happy ones. Then President Babson came onto the dais and the audience quieted.

He welcomed everyone back from winter break, and acknowledged that many of those in the audience didn't need to be there as the spring term wouldn't start until February. "But I am very grateful you've joined us, and particularly so for those of you who have agreed to teach in the intersession."

There was a general rumbling of affirmation. The crowd was much smaller than a usual faculty meeting, probably because those who weren't teaching in the intersession didn't bother to show up. And those who were teaching were getting an extra stipend for doing so, the equivalent of one extra class. That had been enough to convince many faculty to put together a short-term syllabus.

There were also those who welcomed the chance to do a deep dive into their area of specialty. Lucas Roosevelt, chair of the English department, was the first one to take a chance on me, having remembered me as one of his students long ago. He was teaching a class on the short story. Naomi Schechter, who had left Eastern after failing to get tenure, had returned to teach a course on non-fiction writing. And my friend Ewan Stone was doing a seminar on the roots of moral philosophy and ethics.

Jim Shelton of the history department was the president of the Faculty Senate, and he stepped up to provide his own welcome back from break.

A lanky guy with unruly gray curls, he went through several upcoming issues, including negotiations with the administration for a salary increase. Finally, he said, "There has been a lot of discussion in the past few months about the idea of an intersession, and its effect on the faculty and the student body. The Faculty Senate considers the upcoming intersession an experiment, and we will be collecting data about student success and faculty satisfaction. I hope you will all participate in a survey in early February."

Then he opened the floor to questions, asking folks to line up behind the microphones placed on each aisle. That was it? I'd expected a much deeper look at the mechanics, politics, and finances of the intersession, but I understood that Babson probably wanted to save debate until he had some real proof that his experiment had worked.

Or failed, of course.

People began lining up at the microphone. Barry McDermott was a professor of Eastern European history, a sallow-faced man with a long Rasputin-like beard. "The compensation plan for faculty teaching during this session which has been imposed on us by the administration favors those who agree with President Babson's totalitarian control of all things Eastern. It is completely unfair that one four-week class should be paid the equal of one class in the full term. How does the Faculty Senate plan to address this?"

There was some rumbling in the audience. Jim Shelton said, "As I have indicated, this is an experiment. In many cases, faculty teaching in the intersession have created entirely new courses with a narrow focus. This is very different from the kind of broad survey classes many of us teach. So to encourage this creativity and extra work, the Faculty Senate negotiated this pay schedule with administration.

And as I further said, we will examine every aspect of the program in our follow-up study."

McDermott didn't look pleased, but he sat down. A few other faculty members followed. Some made statements about upcoming special programs, including a Valentine's Day flower sale organized by the honors society. For a dollar a stem, you could have flowers delivered to your favorite professor or member of the college's support staff.

Others raised questions about a cap on travel reimbursements or the requirement to watch a new series of videos on sexual harassment in the classroom and the need to respect students' personal pronouns. Eleanor Fitzgerald, who ran the composition program, insisted that she would not use the plural pronoun "they" to refer to an individual student, regardless of that student's gender identity.

Jim responded, "One of our faculty members has complained about this policy. They have made their position clear."

It took a moment for the audience to recognize the joke, and Fitzgerald, a stately Black woman who was called Ella behind her back, looked like she smelled something bad as she turned away from the microphone.

The last at the mike was Elena Salazar, a professor of Latin American history. "Don't tell me that old witch is going to speak up," Lili said.

"You know her?"

"We've clashed a couple of times. Her idea of Latin American history ended in the 1940s."

Lili pulled out her phone and started typing.

Salazar, who was barely five feet tall, had to pull the microphone down to her level. "I'm concerned that Eastern is sponsoring a known supporter of the Castro regime," she said. "At a course being co-taught by a photography professor who has no understanding of the subtleties of Latin American politics."

Lili jumped up and stepped over me to head to the microphone. She moved with the confident stride of someone used to commanding attention, her leather boots clicking purposefully against the floor. Her tailored charcoal blazer and wide-leg trousers projected academic authority while still allowing glimpses of the artistic flair she was known for in her geometric silver earrings and colorful silk scarf.

"Thank you for your concern," Shelton said to Salazar. "All the proposed courses were vetted by the curriculum committee. In the future you may want to volunteer for that committee if you would like your voice heard at the appropriate time."

Salazar looked like she wasn't happy with that response, but when she turned and saw Lili behind her, she hurried back to her seat.

"For those who don't know me, I am Dr. Liliana Weinstock," Lili began. "It's true I am a professor of photography, but I am also an American of Cuban descent who has spent my life eating and cooking Cuban food and studying it, which provides me with subject expertise, as well as the courses in pedagogy I took while earning my PhD." She smiled. "I know some of the faculty members whose degrees were granted much earlier might not be aware that today's PhDs have that kind of education behind them."

Ewan Stone, one of Eastern's younger professors, applauded that.

"My co-teacher is Dr. Yesenia Ubeda Goldstein, who has a similar cultural background as well as a PhD in Food Anthropology from Columbia University. She is a renowned writer and teacher on the food of Latin America and the Caribbean basin. I'd be happy to share the syllabus for the course with Professor Salazar to prove there is no political motivation."

She smiled. "However my esteemed colleague only teaches one course, and the textbook she uses was published in 1964, and her last publication was over twenty years ago, so she might not be aware of the growing interest in food anthropology and how it relates to culture."

Tanya Lieberman began applauding, joined quickly by Gracious Chigwe, Naomi Shechter and me, and then by many other faculty members in the audience. Elena Salazar was clearly less well-liked than my intelligent and well-spoken wife.

Shelton said, "That concludes our question-and-answer period. I encourage any of you who are interested to review both the credentials and course work of both Dr. Salazar and Dr. Weinstock, and raise any concerns you have to me or President Babson."

Lili returned to us, and everyone congratulated her on her measured response to Salazar. She got some nasty looks from the History department, including McDermott and Salazar, as they walked past us.

But as we gathered our things to leave, I overheard Salazar muttering to McDermott. "Just wait until they see who's registered for this course," she said. "'Then we'll see how well Dr. Weinstock handles controversy."

Chapter 9
Digital Footprints

When we left Pennsylvania Hall, the breeze had turned bitter, and I pulled my scarf tighter. The confrontation with Elena Salazar had left me uneasy. If senior faculty were already expressing doubts about Yesenia's qualifications, what other problems might arise during the intersession? I needed to get back to Friar Lake and make sure everything was ready for tomorrow's start - the last thing we needed was logistical issues on top of academic politics.

"What is Yesenia up to this evening?" I asked Lili.

"Probably more trouble," Lili said. She pulled a pair of leather gloves out of her coat pocket and slipped them on. "She's going to do some rehearsals with Deepti in front of the camera and they'll get dinner in town. I asked her to hold off on social media posts, but she insisted that it's important to her brand to post regular content."

"Do you think we'll have better control of her in person?" I asked. "Starting tomorrow?"

Lili shook her head. "She'll do what she wants." She pulled her phone out of another pocket. "I should see if she's put anything else up."

She read as we walked back toward Granger Hall, her leather-clad finger moving through the posts. "Nothing new from her, but her last post has generated a lot of comments, and she's responded to some of them." She looked up and saw that we'd almost reached her office.

"Why don't you come up and we'll read through them together," she said.

We climbed the circular staircase to the second floor, said hello to Matilda, and walked into Lili's office. "I have to order some of those Valentine's flowers for Matilda," she said as she sat down at her computer.

She hit a key to wake it up, logged in, and answered the email from the Honors Society about the floral delivery. Then she opened a browser to view Facebook and tilted the monitor so we could both read.

The new comments were all in response to Yesenia's post about the threat slipped under her door. Many of them agreed that it was silly to think she was an apologist for the Castro regime. One summed it up nicely. "You're a cook, and you're honoring the food traditions of the Cuban people. That has nothing to with politics."

Others, however, disagreed. A poster named Juan Alfarero wrote, "Visiting Havana when there are still travel restrictions. Cooking for government officials, and then bragging about your connections. That's all about politics."

His response triggered a lot more. Some people gave him a thumbs up, while others a thumbs down. Raquel Jaceldo wrote, "If you are so opposed to the Castros, what are you doing about it besides complaining on social media? Get active!"

"What do you think that means?" I asked. "She's coming to the course tomorrow. Is she going to bring protests here?"

"I don't know," she said. "Yesenia is not taking this threat seriously. She's using it to generate comments online, probably to show the Food Network people that she has an engaged audience."

I pushed my chair back. "I'd better get back to Friar Lake. I'm sure Rochester is keeping Joey from getting any work done."

"Your dog is probably lying on the floor sleeping," Lili said. "But go. I'll see you at home."

The cold wind whipped around me as I trudged back to my car, and I turned the heat on full blast and kept my gloves on for the first few miles. When I arrived at my office, I texted Joey. "Where are you? Is Rochester behaving?"

He responded with two words. "Infirmary. Snoring."

I laughed. I believe in letting sleeping dogs lie, so I went through my college emails and handled the ones I had to, then pulled on my sweater and my coat and walked over to the infirmary. I snuck up on the side and looked in the window. Sure enough, Rochester was sprawled on his side, his legs stretched out. He looked like the perfect golden angel.

I tapped on the window and he woke up immediately. He lifted his head and looked around, then let it fall back to the floor. "Lazy dog," I said.

I walked inside the building and down the hall, and as I opened the door Rochester popped up and came rushing toward me, barking. "I know, I abandoned you," I said, ruffling his fur. "Bad daddy."

I unzipped my parka even though the air was still chilly. We did our best not to overheat the buildings in winter, because the electric costs came directly out of my budget.

Joey had finished all the painting and I couldn't tell where the old drywall stopped and the new began. "I extended the electric line down and added an outlet," he said. "People need so many places to charge their stuff these days."

"Good idea. You need a hand cleaning up?"

"You could carry the paint bucket back to my office. I'll get the rest of this stuff."

I grabbed the handle and Rochester led the way out of the building. He romped around, eventually following us to the one-time machine shop for the abbey, where Joey had his office. Half of it was devoted to the storage of equipment, including an open space where he could tinker with anything that needed repair. I spotted a snow blower in parts.

We locked up the property soon after, and I drove home, Rochester sitting on his haunches beside me, staring out the front window. Eventually he settled down, curling himself into a ball to fit on the seat and resting his head on my leg. I petted him as I drove.

When we got home, Lili was making a big salad for us with grilled chicken strips, olives and artichoke hearts. I fed Rochester bits of chicken as Lili and I talked.

"I have the class roster, and I did a quick cross-check against the list of Yesenia's followers," she said. "Five of them will be with us. You think you could do a little snooping? Make sure none of them are going to be trouble?"

"You know I'd be delighted," I said. Back when I was married to my first wife and living in Silicon Valley, I was a technical writer for a web company and assisted the security team in researching and writing about hacking tools. I began playing around with them so that I could understand them and write about them more accurately. Then Mary suffered her second miscarriage, and to prevent her from going on a retail therapy spree I hacked into the three major credit bureaus and put a flag on her account.

In retrospect, I should have talked to her instead. My hack led to a year as a guest of the California penal system, a divorce, and my return to Stewart's Crossing. But I still kept a laptop with those tools, which I used to help my police detective friend Rick Stemper with his investigations – almost always legally.

I had stopped storing my hacker laptop in the attic. It was too much trouble to retrieve, and I wasn't hiding it from Lili anymore. Now it sat on a shelf in her office, so at least she could see if it was missing and know I was up to mischief.

Rochester was behind me on the stairs as I walked up to the office, and then again as I went down. When I sat at the dining room table he sprawled behind my chair.

There are all kinds of names for people who use the internet for illicit purposes, starting with script kiddies. Those were unskilled people who used scripts or programs developed by others, primarily for malicious purposes.

A security hacker explored methods for breaching defenses and exploiting weakness in a computer network. White hat hackers did the same thing, aiming to expose and repair those breaches. Black hat hackers were criminals who exploited online weaknesses for profit.

I considered myself a researcher. I used the tools created by good and bad actors to find the information necessary to protect people, help Rick and in general right wrongs. I could protect my identity and navigate my way through the dark web looking for the tools and information I needed.

Sometimes, I admit, I used pirated versions of legitimate software, the kind that would charge you to see if your daughter's boyfriend had a criminal record, or how many traffic violations your neighbor had. Some of the programs I used had been posted for free in exchange for reviews or notification of problems.

I fed the names of all the students into the criminal records tracker and set it to work. Some might consider that a breach of personal privacy, but if anyone in the class was a violent offender, or had a record of arrests at protests, we needed to know.

Behind me, Rochester snored gently as I opened another program which culled results from social media. You could do a lot of that searching yourself, but you'd need an ID and password for each site, and the process of entering keywords and searching for results would take a long time. Since there were over a dozen social media sites out there, with hundreds of thousands of users, that would take me days. This program automated that process.

Once again, I threw in all twenty names, though I added some qualifying words like Castro and Cuba, and *gusano*, that derogatory term for Cuban exiles.

Lili looked over my shoulder as I was inputting the data. "Add the word *exilio*," she said. "In case some of the results you get are in Spanish. That's a popular word."

I did. Then I took Rochester for a long walk around the neighborhood. I hated the way it got dark so early in the evening. I usually had to drive home from work in the twilight. Some neighbors had their exterior lights on timers, so they were on every night, while others were only lit when someone remembered. And others were too cheap to light up their driveways.

It was easy to stumble in the dark, and hard to know what Rochester was up to. I thought about the year before, when we'd spent part of the Christmas holidays in South Florida, visiting Lili's mother and then staying on for her funeral. Going somewhere warm seemed like a good idea then, and I was pleased we were planning to head to El Salvador over spring break to attend the wedding of one of Lili's cousins.

Rochester wouldn't be able to accompany us, but he'd stay with Joey and Mark and Brody and have a fine time without us. Of course he would make me feel guilty for a few days after our return.

By the time we got back, both programs had generated results, and Lili sat next to me at the table to look them over. After drinking copious amounts of water and then trying to dry his mouth on my leg, Rochester sprawled beside my chair, keeping me in place.

I was pleased to see that none of the students had any substantial police records. One had gotten drunk in public, and two had speeding violations. That was it.

We turned to the social media results. Fourteen were Eastern college students, and I couldn't find much information on any of them on the Internet. Lili knew two who had taken her photography class, but the other twelve were mysteries to us. Neither of us were willing to abuse our privileges with the student database system without evidence of wrongdoing.

The final five were special students, like Maria de los Angeles Cabrera and Raquel Jaceldo. Maria was active in a lot of Facebook groups relating to Cuba and Cuban culture, including "Friends from Cuba," "*Cuba: Algo Mas que una isla*" and "*Seguidores de la libertad de Cuba.*"

I pointed to that last one. "What does that mean?"

"Followers of Cuban Freedom," she said. We clicked through, and all Maria's posts were in Spanish, so Lili had to translate. "She's pretty fervent, just as Yesenia said. But she's not promoting anything illegal or dangerous."

We moved on to Raquel Jaceldo. The only Cuban group she belonged to was Yesenia's, but she was just as fervent in her support as Maria was. Her hobbies were cooking and salsa dancing, and she had a lot of photos posted on her page of her engaging in both.

"I hope I'm that active when I'm retired," Lili said.

My program had picked up one more link for Raquel, on Twitter. It looked like she followed a lot of people with Hispanic surnames, and as we skimmed through their posts we found one thing in common. They were all journalists who covered Cuba. Two were fervently anti-Castro.

She didn't engage much beyond the occasional heart on a post, but that list worried me. "What do you think?" I asked Lili.

"I know Rodrigo Valdés and Carmen Elena Fuentes," she said. "Both of them are very respected writers. So it's possible she's following them for news and trying to see what both sides are saying."

Enid Garelick was studying at the Institute of Culinary Education in New York. She had been born in Jamaica to a British businessman father and a Jamaican homemaker mother, and lived there until she was twelve and her family moved to New York. She loved to recreate the recipes she learned from her Jewish and Jamaican grandmothers. And like Raquel, the only Cuban group she belonged to was Yesenia's, though she rarely posted there.

Zenobia Willis was a food blogger who belonged to more than a dozen food-related groups on Facebook. Like Yesenia, she aspired to have her own TV show, and she had tried out for several reality programs, including *The Next Food Network Star*. She made YouTube videos, and we watched three of them in sequence because they were so enjoyable.

Rochester sat up on his haunches and stared at the screen, almost as if he knew Zenobia was preparing something delicious.

She paired wrap dresses in African prints with Art Deco inspired dangling earrings, and addressed her ingredients with catch phrases like "Bless your heart" and "Aren't you a doll!" Her goal was to take traditional Southern dishes like fried chicken, gumbo, and sweet potato pie and update the recipes to retain the taste without as many calories or carbs.

When we got to Max Abraham, Lili pointed to his name. "Don't we know him?"

I leaned in close. "I'm not sure, but I think we've been to the café he and his husband run in Potter's Harbor. Maybe with Naomi Schechter and Jeff Berman? They both live there."

Max was also a follower of Yesenia's group, though he had never posted there.

We pulled up images of the café from its website. "I'm sure we've been there," Lili said. "I specifically remember a pain aux raisins that was delicious."

Max's personal tagline was "From Broadway to the Bakery," and he listed all the productions he'd performed in before relocating to Bucks County. Somewhere in the middle of all that singing and dancing he'd also studied pastry arts at the École Ducasse in Paris. In a photo in front of the pastry case, we saw that he was in his mid-forties, bearded and bearish.

The last two students were difficult to find any information on. Neither belonged to Yesenia's group. Lili pointed to the next to last name on the list. "That guy, Ken Gould," she said. "He's a computer guy, and he said on his application that he'd be working remotely when class wasn't in session. He emailed me last week to make sure we had good Wi-Fi at Friar Lake."

"Did he use a business email address?"

She shook her head. "No, a domain I never heard of. Safemail.com. I figured he was like you, maybe a little paranoid about computer security."

"You say the sweetest things," I said.

She elbowed me. "That's all I know about him. And on John Potter's application, all he said was that he was a single guy and loved to eat Cuban food, and was hoping to learn how to cook some simple dishes."

It wasn't that unusual that we couldn't find anything about Potter or Gould online. Lots of people disdained social media and preserved their online privacy.

All the students were due to arrive at Friar Lake the next afternoon. We'd be able to make personal impressions of them and see how they interacted as a group.

Yesenia was coming over early to begin roasting the chickens for our welcome dinner and to test out the computer equipment.

Everything was falling into place. The only thing that worried me was the threat slipped under Yesenia's door. Why would someone threaten her? And would there be more during the intersession?

Chapter 10
Arrivals

Lili and I had already packed up for our stay at Friar Lake, including Rochester's food and bowls. I added the hacker laptop to the luggage on Thursday morning in case I needed to do any further research while I was there. Rochester and I arrived at Friar Lake promptly at nine. When I took off my parka, I tugged at the sleeves of my sport coat, a concession to my position that still felt strange after years of casual Silicon Valley dress codes. But I wanted to look good for our arriving guests.

I spent the morning on last-minute preparations. I tested the computer and internet connection in the classroom we were using, and Rochester sniffed the perimeter of the room for any intruders. I made sure all the bedrooms and the kitchen were clean, and he kept circling around me like he was herding me. Then we walked the property with Joey in a last-minute check. Rochester successfully scared away three different squirrels.

"You're a lot more worried about this than you have been about any other program we've had at Friar Lake," Joey said as we walked inside the chapel. It was chilly in there with the heat on low, but the sun cast beautiful colored spots on the stone floor through the stained-glass windows.

Rochester immediately began sniffing the stone altar. "This intersession program has a much higher profile than any of the other events," I said. "If we fail, we might take the whole idea of an intersession down with us. And that could be a disaster for Friar Lake's future."

"I'm sure it will be great," he said. "We've gone over everything. The property is going to shine, and I'm sure Lili and her friend will deliver an interesting course."

"I certainly hope so."

After Rochester was satisfied that all was well in the chapel, he and I ended up back in my office. Dan Lazerow had accepted my invitation on behalf of himself and his wife, though he hoped there wouldn't be any trouble. "I'd like to get the lay of the land," he wrote. "Maybe you and I can walk around and look for vulnerabilities."

I didn't want to think about ways someone could disrupt us before we'd even started, but I sent him a considered answer. Any outsider could drive up the hill to the property, though in case of trouble we could pull a chain across the driveway at street level and a security guard could be stationed there to vet entry.

The parking lot was well-lit, as were the pathways between buildings. Any building not in use was locked, and only Joey and I had the keys. The only trouble we'd had in the past was a graffiti incident by local teens, and they'd quickly been arrested.

I tried to concentrate on work, but I kept looking out the window, wondering when the first students would arrive, and what kind of trouble they might bring with them. Though I was just an employee, I had a proprietary feel for Friar Lake, having overseen its transformation. President Babson had entrusted me with responsibility, and I wanted to justify his belief.

As I was finishing lunch, Rochester jumped up and started to bark. I looked outside and saw a sedan pull up in front of the gatehouse. Two women got out, one from each of the back seats, and the driver came around to the hatch to retrieve their luggage.

They looked like the New York women whose photos we'd seen

on Facebook, Maria de los Angeles Cabrera and Raquel Jaceldo. Rochester and I went out to greet them.

"Aren't you a handsome boy?" Raquel said as she reached down to pet him. He liked her better than the other woman.

"I guess we're a bit early," she said. "We took the bus from Port Authority to New Hope and we recognized each other. Maria knew about this new ride share company called Uber and she got us a ride more quickly than we expected."

"You know, we've spent years hearing how we shouldn't get into cars with strange men, and now this app tells us to do just that," the other woman said. "I'm Maria Cabrera and this is Raquel Jaceldo."

I shook hands with both women. "Should we call you Maria de los Angeles?" I asked.

She laughed. "No, that's just to keep me separate from my cousins. There are four of us on Facebook—Maria Jose, Maria Luisa, Maria Christina, and me. I'm the keeper of family traditions, so most of my posts are about food and holidays and family, with an undercurrent of longing for a lost island home."

She was short and chubby, with a gray ponytail secured by a wooden clip painted with folk art flowers. She wore a long quilted coat in deep purple over a loose cotton dress, her feet snug in fur-lined boots decorated with embroidered flowers that matched her coat's buttons. She looked every bit the doting abuela, but there was nothing soft about her dark eyes or the way she leaned forward intensely when speaking.

Raquel, the one with the restaurant experience, was tall and angular, with a bearing that spoke of decades commanding busy kitchens. Her silver-streaked black hair was pulled back severely from her face in a tight bun, the kind of no-nonsense style favored by professional cooks.

Despite her retirement, she carried herself with a chef's upright posture, shoulders squared beneath a practical navy wool coat with deep pockets that reminded me of a chef's apron. Her black snow boots were sturdy and serviceable rather than decorative, and she'd paired them with wool slacks - someone used to being on her feet for long hours.

When she spoke, her hands moved in precise, controlled gestures, like she was still directing line cooks during a dinner rush. There was an efficiency to her movements that contrasted sharply with Maria's more excitable manner, and her voice carried the calm authority of someone used to being obeyed in high-pressure situations.

"Welcome to Friar Lake. Let me show you to your room." Since space was limited in the dormitory, as part of registration we'd asked if people would mind sharing, and Maria and Raquel had volunteered. Rochester and I led the two women to the monastery building which had once housed the monks' cells. We'd converted those into six double rooms and two singles. Lili and I would be sharing a double room in that building with them.

"It's colder out here in the country," Raquel said as she and Maria trundled their suitcases behind them, with Rochester trotting along. "I guess in the city the buildings block a lot of the wind."

"Is this your first time out of New York?" I asked.

"Oh, no," Raquel said. "When I worked for the school system we traveled to conferences around the country. All cities, though."

"And I go out to New Jersey regularly," Maria added. "I have lots of family in Union City."

"Havana on the Hudson," Raquel said. "The biggest group of Cuban-Americans outside Miami."

I mentioned that Lili and I had been in Miami the year before, to see her family, and we talked about how nice it would be to bask in the sunshine during the winter. I opened the door to the dormitory and led them to their rooms, which were key-carded. "We're having mojitos in the refectory at five," I said. "You'll find a map of the property in your room."

"We'll be there," Maria said. "I never pass up a good Cuban cocktail!"

As my dog and I were returning to the gatehouse, Yesenia and Deepti arrived, and Rochester romped over to Yesenia's rental car. "I stopped at the grocery in Leighville and loaded up, *por en caso*," Yesenia said, as I reached her. She wore the same stylish long coat, but she'd painted her nails to match her bright-red lipstick.

Deepti wore a pink puffer coat and sleek leather gloves, and her black hair was pulled into a ponytail that stuck up from the top of her head and reminded me of Pebbles Flintstone.

The three of us alternated carrying bags from the IGA grocery, boxes Yesenia had brought from Brooklyn and all Deepti's camera equipment as Rochester wove his way between the three of us, as if he was herding us.

The monks had used the refectory as a combination kitchen and dining hall, and while we kept the purpose, we brought in all new appliances and a prep island. We selected round wooden tables and Windsor-style chairs. Most of the programs we sponsored that offered food were catered, either by the college's food service or an outside vendor, but we had a stock of silver and tableware on hand.

I laid out cards on one table where Lili and I would be hosting our special guests: President Babson and his wife; Lili's friend Gracious Chigwe and her husband Edward; Joey and Mark; and Dan Lazerow and his wife.

It was going to be a full house. But from the amount of food Yesenia had brought I was sure there was going to be enough.

Deepti began setting up her camera and tripod, along with a laptop computer and stand for recording. Yesenia preheated the oven and I watched as she prepped her chickens, washing and then setting them in bowls of salt water and spices to brine them.

Rochester and I walked back to the gatehouse, and as we did, another car pulled up, with Enid and Zenobia. The food blogger was a stately black woman in her forties with a coil of braided hair, wearing an African print jacket and black corduroy slacks. Her earrings were in the shape of bright-orange carrots.

Twenty-something Enid looked like many Eastern students, with multiple silver piercings in her ears, and her wavy brown hair appeared to want to curl into an Afro. "We don't study much

Caribbean cooking at my school, so I was delighted to find this course," she said. "I'm hoping to learn more about all the ingredients I grew up using."

Zenobia was delighted to meet Rochester, though Enid was shyer. But my sweet golden looked up at her with such a gentle expression that she touched the top of his head. "It's so soft," Enid said.

"Goldens are wonderful," Zenobia said. "If I didn't live in the city I'd have at least two."

"I've watched a couple of your YouTube videos," I said. "You'd have a hard time keeping a dog like Rochester away from whatever you're making."

Each of them had brought a bag of groceries. Zenobia hoped that Yesenia could provide ideas for how to use more Caribbean techniques with the traditional Southern recipes she focused on in her videos. And Enid had splashed out at a Jamaican grocery in Flatbush, Queens, to be sure she had all the products she wanted to ask about.

Rochester and I led the them to the dormitory, though of course the dog had to stop periodically to sniff and pee, then run to catch up to us. As we walked into the long hallway, Raquel and Maria came out of their room. "Yesenia texted that she's already in the kitchen, starting dinner," Raquel said. "She invited us to join her whenever we're ready."

"Sounds goods," Zenobia said. I left the four women to introduce themselves and walked outside, where I called Lili. "Can you come over here now? Yesenia is cooking, and students are already starting to arrive. And the bus from campus is coming in an hour."

We'd arranged to use one of the college buses to bring the residential students over. "I'll be there in twenty," she said.

The idea was that we'd get started at happy hour, and I planned to make a batch of welcoming mojitos to get everyone in the mood. I'd also have a pitcher of virgin drinks in case some students weren't old enough to drink, but I wasn't going to card anyone.

I went into my office with Rochester by my side. I checked for last minute messages, then shut down my computer. I needed to get back to the kitchen and start preparing the simple syrup for my mojitos. I called Joey to hang out and wait for the rest of the students, but as I walked out another car arrived.

John Potter introduced himself. He was forty-something, with a muscular build evident even under a sheepskin coat and had a large gym bag on his arm. I'd had a lot of exposure to Latinx students at Eastern, and I was surprised that he looked like many of them, with dark wavy hair and a deeply tanned complexion. He even spoke with a Spanish accent. But hey, Lili was a Latina and she was as white as they come, so I knew there was a broad range of people in the Latinx camp.

I shook his hand and introduced myself, though Rochester kept his distance. I sniffed the air and thought Mr. Potter had used a lot of cologne, and that's probably what put my dog off.

"Strange place for a program on Cuban cooking," Potter said, looking around.

"Well, my wife, Dr. Weinstock, is Cuban and she's a friend of Dr. Ubeda. They came up with the program together."

"Oh, I'm very familiar with Yesenia," he said. "Does your wife have the same political leanings?"

I was surprised that he used Yesenia's first name. Did they know each other? Yesenia hadn't mentioned anything when she and Lili went over the class roster.

"My wife tends to lean into her camera more than politics," I said. "She's a photojournalist and a professor at the college."

He nodded. "I'll have to look up her work."

There was something almost menacing about the way he said that, but I shook it off and directed him to the dormitory where he'd be staying. He walked off, dragging his rollaboard suitcase behind him.

I couldn't think much about Potter, though, because Rochester took off at a gallop around the back of the gatehouse, in search of something, and I checked my roster. The only special student who hadn't yet arrived was the computer guy, Ken Gould. I wondered if he'd stopped off at a coffee shop along the way for internet access.

I wondered for a moment why a computer guy had no online presence. You don't have to be on social media if you don't want to be—that's a personal choice. But many of the computer professionals I knew were on sites like LinkedIn, making professional contacts, sharing interesting articles or participating in online discussions.

Was it that he was a low-level worker and had nothing to brag about, no positions to mention that might draw the attention of a recruiter? But if so, how did he swing working remotely while taking the class? It was curious.

By the time Rochester returned, Lili arrived. "Everything's going smoothly so far," I said, as I kissed her cheek and Rochester romped around us. "I want to get to the kitchen. Joey will wait for the bus from campus. I hope Ken Gould didn't get lost along the way."

"He's a computer guy," Lili said. "I'm sure he has navigational tools."

Lili, Rochester, and I walked over to the kitchen, which already smelled wonderful. "Butter and chicken," Lilii said, inhaling as we walked in.

We had hired two students who worked for the campus catering operation to set up, serve, and clean up. They were setting the tables. They both had multiple earrings and tattoos, but that was normal of Eastern students. One was blonde, the other brunette, and as soon as I heard their names I forgot them.

Lili joined Yesenia and the four women at the stove and started doing what I'd learned was called *mise en place*, a fancy term for getting all your ingredients in place before you started cooking. Deepti had her cameras and lights in place, and she sat in a corner, typing on her phone.

Because he's always interested in things that smell good, Rochester was by Yesenia's side as she was searching for something in one of the grocery bags she had brought when she said, "*¡Ay Dios mío!*"

I was measuring out sugar for my simple syrup. I turned toward Yesenia, who had Rochester sitting on his hind legs by her side. "What's wrong?" I asked.

She held up a piece of ordinary white copier paper that had been tucked into one of the grocery bags. "Another threat!"

Chapter 11
First Impressions

I put down the sugar and crossed over to her, and Lili and I looked at the piece of paper as Rochester nestled against Yesenia's leg. "You've been warned," it read. "Prepare for the consequences."

"*¡Esto es ridículo!*" Yesenia said. "Who do these people think I am? That I will just walk away from a threat?"

"Did anyone touch these bags at the store?" I asked, hoping that maybe her stalker had been with her at the grocery, not here at Friar Lake.

She shook her head. "I bagged the groceries myself and put them into a wagon. Then I wheeled it out to the car and loaded the bags. A boy came and took the cart away, but by then all the bags were in the car."

"That means someone put the note in the bag after you got here," I said. "I don't like that."

"But what can we do?" Lili asked. "Cancel the program? Send everyone home when they've just arrived?"

"Dan Lazerow from campus security will be here for dinner with his wife. He's a sharp guy, a former cop," I explained to Yesenia. "You'll be protected."

"I will not knuckle down to anonymous threats," Yesenia said, and began stuffing her chickens with intensity. Lili went back to her station, and I looked over at Deepti, who had been videotaping Yesenia's response. I wondered how she planned to use that material.

With Rochester lying against the wall, able to keep an eye on all that was going on, I began making my syrup. I added equal amounts of water and sugar to a heated saucepan.

Who had the ability to place those threats, I wondered, as I stirred. The only person I knew for sure had access to both the room in Fields Hall and the grocery bags was Yesenia herself.

I stirred a bit too vigorously and a bit of sugar syrup spilled onto the stovetop and sizzled. As I wiped it up with a wet paper towel, I realized the implications of that idea.

Could Yesenia be behind these threats? I stirred the syrup. Why? Because she was overly dramatic by temperament, and loved to stir the pot? Lili had a female cousin like that in El Salvador. Even the smallest problem was magnified, often to place herself at the center of the controversy.

She was the only witness to the paper threats. She said she'd found the first note slipped under her door, but she could easily have brought it with her from New York. The same for the note in the grocery bags.

Maybe she was having Deepti record everything so that she could add drama to what would otherwise be a standard academic project? I'd watched enough reality programs to know that a little spice was great for television.

I looked over at Lili, but she was engaged in measuring out her ingredients. I kept stirring until the sugar dissolved, still thinking about Yesenia and her motives. It was curious that Yesenia had only requested that book from the library when she knew she was coming to Eastern.

And then there was that chest of cigars and paperwork that Joey uncovered behind the wall of the infirmary. Could Yesenia have snuck into Friar Lake and planted it there? Maybe she'd come by while the property was closed, poured water on the roof and unstuck the drywall to place the chest where we'd find it.

It sounded ridiculous to me, and yet the facts hung together. The only question was why? Were Lili and I, and everyone at Friar Lake, characters in a drama she was creating?

She might be Lili's friend, and a respected academic, but I had to recognize I couldn't trust her.

Once the sugar syrup was ready, I poured it into a couple of mason jars and sealed them. I looked over at Lili again, but she was still engrossed in her work. Well, I'd have plenty of time to talk about things with her after dinner. And I might even mention my theory to Dan Lazerow when he arrived.

My phone pinged with a text from Joey. "Ready for the student invasion yet?"

I sent him a thumbs up and set up my bar. By the time they all trooped in, I had glasses of alcoholic mojito ready to serve, each one garnished with a slice of lime and a mint leaf.

Rochester acted as a greeter, welcoming everyone as they arrived. It was interesting to see which students were eager to pet him and which ones stood back.

Claudia Monson was a theater student, and she wanted to understand how food and culture influenced the characters she played on stage. She also had some AP credits and the intersession credits would allow her to graduate early and get to New York to become an actress. She kept her distance from Rochester, probably so she wouldn't get dog hair on her black slacks.

Bradley Clark had written that his parents didn't want him sitting around the house in January, and the class looked like it would be the most fun of all those offered in the intersession. He wore a lacrosse team sweatshirt and had a typical frat-boy enthusiasm. I noticed that he immediately attached himself to Claudia and wondered if they'd get caught making out somewhere on campus eventually.

He teased Rochester with a magic trick, pulling a handkerchief out of the dog's ear, and Claudia pretended to be his magician's assistant, bowing and gesturing along with him.

Emily Wattenberg was a robust blonde from Iowa, majoring in sociology. On her application she had said that she was taking the class to gain exposure to a different culture. She got down on the floor and put her face up against Rochester's and let him lick her cheek.

Matthew Wong was so tall he reminded me of the athlete Yao Ming, with the same square face and mop of black hair. On his application, he'd said he was a pre-med student who wanted a break from his heavily science-oriented curriculum. And that he'd grown up in New York, where one of his favorite restaurants was Cuban-Chinese.

He talked to Bobby Cruz, the Cuban-American boy from Miami, and both looked eager to get to the dinner table. Bobby had the lanky build of a former high school soccer player who hadn't quite filled out yet. He looked very short compared to Matthew, though he was probably about five-nine.

His thick black hair fell across his forehead, and his face still carried some teenage softness around the jawline, making him look more like a high school senior than a college student. He moved with the loose-limbed energy of someone not entirely comfortable in his rapidly growing body, often shifting his weight from foot to foot when standing still.

Both he and Matthew dressed like typical college kids, in hoodies, jeans, and sneakers. But Bobby's were carefully chosen name brands that suggested he was trying to fit in while still impressing his classmates. Like many of Lili's relatives I'd met, his hands were in motion when he talked. When he smiled, a dimple appeared in his left cheek - the kind of detail that I was sure would make older women want to pinch his cheeks and feed him more pastries.

We were still missing Ken Gould and Max Abraham, as well as our invited guests, so Joey went back to the gatehouse to wait for them.

The students had already begun introducing themselves, though the college kids tended to stick together, as did the special students.

Claudia and Bradley took turns entertaining, with magic tricks and theater monologues.

Rochester jumped up as the front door to the refectory opened and a nerdy-looking guy with short hair and glasses walked in. He had the forgettable appearance of a middle manager at any tech company. His wire-rimmed glasses sat slightly crooked on his thin face, and his brown hair was cut in that characterless short style that suggests regular visits to a chain haircut shop.

He arrived wearing a practical but unremarkable black down parka from L.L. Bean, the kind you'd find in any suburban mall - warm enough for the Pennsylvania winter but chosen more for function than style. Under the coat, he wore khakis and a button-down shirt that seemed slightly rumpled, as if he'd packed them hastily in his suitcase, and he had the pale complexion of someone who spent most of his time indoors staring at computer screens.

"Hi, you must be Ken," I said, greeting him with a mojito. "I'm Steve Levitan. Any trouble finding us?"

He shook his head as he scanned the room. "No, I have a GPS gadget. I just got a late start because I had an emergency project to finish." He zeroed in on Yesenia. "Is that Dr. Ubeda by the stove?"

"It is. Are you a fan?"

"I'm not that interested in food, but my company does a lot of work in the Caribbean so I thought this would be a good way to learn something about the culture of the area."

"I hope it will be," I said. "What kind of work do you do?"

"Nothing very interesting. Shipping and transportation software."

He shut that question down quickly. I led him over to the group of special students and introduced him. Within a half hour, all our guests but one had arrived and had mojitos in hand, including Dan Lazerow and his wife. I took Dan aside, Rochester sticking close to me, and showed him the note that had been stuck into the grocery bag.

"Any idea how it got there?" he asked.

"I asked Yesenia, and she told me that no one else touched the bags while she was at the grocery. When she got here, she and I carried everything in from her car, and then she went back to her room and I returned to the office. The refectory was unlocked and anyone could have slipped in while we were gone."

"Did she see any cars following her?"

I shook my head. "Though there's a switchback on the driveway where you can park and get a view of the abbey buildings," I said. "I suppose it's possible someone could have followed her up here from Leighville and stopped at the switchback. They could have watched us carry the groceries to the refectory, then hustled up here while Joey and I were busy. Run to the refectory then back to the car. But that would take a lot of nerve and timing."

"How about anyone already on the property?" Dan asked.

"I can send you a list of the students who were already here," I said. "All of them are special students, because the regular college kids came over in a bus after Yesenia arrived. Once I showed the special students to their rooms, I didn't keep tabs on them."

"Do you know much about these outsiders?"

I didn't want Dan to know about my computer skills, so I shrugged. "Just what they put on their applications. A couple of them are followers of Yesenia's on Facebook."

Dan pulled out a pocket notebook like the ones my friend Rick used and made a couple of notes. "You said there was another threat, stuck under her door at Fields Hall Tuesday night."

"That's true."

"I think I'll send a guard out here tomorrow, just to keep an eye on things," Dan said.

"I had one more idea," I said. I looked around to make sure no one could overhear us. "What if Yesenia herself planted those notes?"

Dan cocked his head. "Why would she?"

I shrugged. "To generate interest in her program? A little controversy goes a long way on social media. Or maybe she really is an agent of the Cuban government, and she's trying to flush out anti-Castro agents?"

Even as I said that I realized it was ridiculous. "Sorry, I'm getting caught up in the drama myself."

"No, it's important to look at every angle. Who benefits, and who loses?"

"She could benefit from stirring up trouble, I suppose," I said. "But at the same time, the controversy could hurt her. She told Lili and me that she's taping her lectures so that she can boost her academic profile and maybe get a show on the Food Network."

That reminded me of the papers in the cigar box and I explained what we'd found. "She said one of the papers is a deed giving her inherited rights to some property in Havana," I said. "And that she might use that paperwork to gain leverage with the Cuban government and additional research resources. To help her get a tenured professorship."

"I don't have much experience dealing with foreign governments," Dan said. "But I can't imagine a single woman, even with the right paperwork, can get much leverage with Havana."

"She recognized she was going overboard after she said it. But I'm going to keep an eye on her while she's here. Even if I have to protect her from herself."

The door opened and Max Abraham burst in, and I imagined him making that kind of entry on a Broadway stage. "Sorry I'm late," he said, as he came up to me.

Despite the cold, sweat beaded on his forehead. He pulled off his heavy parka and gloves. "We got busy at the café as I was getting ready to leave and I had to stick around."

"No problem. We're about to get started, though, so why don't you take a seat at one of the student tables." He found an empty place and began introducing himself.

For the first time since I'd known him, President Babson had begun to look his age. Maybe it was all the stress of trying to improve Eastern's finances, or the introduction of the intersession, but he had more gray hair and some dark circles under his eyes. He wore his standard dark suit and a blue tie with Eastern's rising sun logo in the center.

John William Babson had been dean of students when I was at Eastern, which meant he had to be in his late fifties or early sixties, but he ordinarily had the vitality of a much younger man, with slicked-back hair and enthusiastic gestures. I'd had a lot of opportunity to see him in action over the time I'd worked at Eastern, and he always impressed me. Now he worried me.

Babson motioned me over to him and pointed toward Deepti and her equipment. "I'm concerned about the filming," he said. "We don't want the whole course broadcast for free online."

"She wants to create a demo reel to present to producers on the Food Network," I said. "And she's planning to share snippets on her social media. But I'll make sure she knows she can't share the entire course."

He went immediately into presidential mode as Lili introduced him and his wife to Yesenia. Gracious and Edward came in right behind the Babsons. She called herself a woman of traditional Botswana build, and she wore a colorful dress in a yellow and orange print. Her husband worked on Wall Street, and matched Babson in a navy suit. I was starting to feel underdressed.

Fortunately, Mark and Joey came in then, wearing khakis and polo shirts, and I felt better. Around us, the guests were already chatting and remarking on the delicious smell of roast chicken that pervaded the room. Rochester stayed close behind my chair. He wasn't going to let me out without getting some of that chicken.

I remembered the way Lili had prepared the dish Yesenia was making, and how she'd used too much garlic. I hoped the food would be delicious, and that this would be a great kick-off to our intersession course.

I looked around the room. The special students were clustered at one table, away from the regular college students, though I noticed

Enid kept looking over at the other tables, as if she'd rather be with people her own age.

Max Abraham led the conversation, along with Maria Cabrera. They were already talking about cooking and recipes. I wondered if we'd start seeing more Cuban pastries at Max's café.

It was interesting the way that Maria's voice shifted seamlessly between a warm maternal coo when sharing recipes and a sharp, staccato tone when discussion turned to politics or protecting Cuban traditions. I noticed that she had a habit of touching people's arms when making a point, her fingers gripping just a fraction too long and too tight to be completely comfortable, even through winter coats. Even when silent, her constant scanning of the room and slight forward tilt of her head suggested someone always on alert, watching and assessing every interaction around her.

The two tables of college kids were boisterous. Though many of them probably weren't legally allowed to drink alcohol, their enthusiasm was surely fueled by my mojitos.

Ken Gould and Zenobia Willis were having a side conversation, while the others at the table listened. John Potter kept rearranging his silverware, and I wondered if he was nervous or had some kind of OCD. He wore a short-sleeved shirt that showed off his impressive muscles, and a couple of tattoos disappeared under his sleeves. One looked like the bottom blue and white stripes of the Cuban flag, with the tail of the red triangle just visible.

I took a couple of deep breaths and glanced around the room. Elena Salazar's warning about controversy echoed in my head. Was she referring to one of the special students? If so, which one?

I knew she and Lili didn't get along. But should I reach out on my own to ask her? I didn't want to go behind Lili's back, and besides, Lili had pointed out that the elderly professor was out of touch with the current situation.

Between the threatening notes slipped under Yesenia's door and the political tension that Salazar warned about, I had a feeling this dinner was just the calm before the storm.

Chapter 12
Patria Y Vida

At a signal from Yesenia, Deepti turned on her lights and prepared to start filming. Lili stepped up to the prep island and welcomed everyone to Eastern, and introduced President Babson.

"I'm delighted you can join us to kick off what I'm sure will be an interesting and delicious program." He lifted his nose and sniffed. "I can already tell this meal is going to be a great one."

He talked for a minute about the intersession, and Eastern College, and then sat, to a low round of applause. I figured Deepti was recording that as a formality, and it would never make it to Yesenia's YouTube channel.

Lili introduced Yesenia, who stepped up to the prep island, where she already had laid out a platter of brown tubers and her knife kit. "I hope the students have all read the materials we sent out, so you'll know what to expect from the next four weeks," she said.

"Tonight, Dr. Weinstock and I are going to cook a traditional Cuban dinner for you, and we'll talk about the ingredients and the methods of cooking as we go. You can take notes if you like, but there are no exams for this course, just a final paper you'll write on an ingredient, a method of cooking, or the unique aspects of an island's cuisine."

"What do you mean by traditional?" John Potter asked. "There are indigenous people on each island in the Caribbean, and different histories of invasion and slavery."

I was surprised by the aggressive tone of the question. If he was angry before we even got started, did that mean we were in for a lot of argument?

Fortunately, Yesenia turned the question around. "That's exactly what we hope to get at during this course," she said. "How did the existing food on the islands, as well as the ingredients that explorers and conquerors and enslaved people brought with them, combine to make the dishes that people eat today."

I thought her use of "explorers and conquerors" was clever. Spaniards, Portuguese, British, Dutch, and Jews were among the many people that came to the islands, often with very different goals.

A couple of people pulled out notebooks and pens, including Maria and Raquel and some of the college students. "We're going to start with malanga, a root vegetable popular in the Caribbean."

She held up a brown, shaggy tuber that looked like a mutant potato. "It's similar to taro, which is its Eastern cousin, and it's a root vegetable commonly used in Caribbean and Latin American cuisine. The skin on malanga is brown and has a wiry, shaggy texture. Taro is also brown, but lighter in color and the skin is smoother, less bristly."

She unrolled her knife kit and chose one with a unique carved handle. She sliced the tuber in half, holding it up so students could see the white inside. "Malanga flesh is almost bright white. Taro's flesh can be white or cream colored with purple flecks. Liliana is going to be frying these into *frituras de malanga*, or malanga fritters, as an appetizer," she said.

Lili was already behind her, heating up a pan with oil.

Yesenia talked about the history and uses of the malanga as she quickly created thin slices with her very sharp knife. It was like watching a program on the Food Network in person. "These fritters are made with grated malanga and egg and flavored with parsley, garlic, salt and vinegar," Yesenia continued. "They're crispy on the outside, tender and mild on the inside. In Cuban cuisine, *frituras de malanga* are served as an appetizer or snack."

She handed the platter of slices to Lili, who carried them back to the stove, and they sizzled as they hit the pan of hot oil.

Yesenia continued to talk as she checked a pot of rice and black beans on the stove. "We'll be accompanying our roast chicken this evening with *Moros y Cristianos,* a traditional Cuban version of rice and beans." She looked out at the audience. "Who can translate that for anyone who doesn't speak Spanish?"

Raquel raised her hand. "Moors and Christians," she said. "It's also the name of a festival held in Spain to remember the conquest of parts of Iberia by the Moors and their subsequent defeat."

"Very good," Yesenia said. "Cubans cook the two together in one pot, while on other islands they may be prepared separately."

"Just cooking them together doesn't ignore the fact that the Christians subjugated the Moors just as they did with the native islanders," John Potter said.

Yesenia looked flustered for a moment, but then said, "Cooking them together today is going to represent the way that cultures merged in the islands, despite the history of what happened in Europe."

She kept up a steady patter as she and Lili cooked, talking about their techniques as well as the history of the ingredients. "One of the reasons I feel tied to Cuban culture is that when I was a child, my mother was ill for a year. During that time, my parents hired a country woman to take care of our household." She looked up at us. "Romelda had Taino heritage and was an expert in using herbs and roots to cure illness."

She looked over at Lili. "Today, Dr. Weinstock discovered a book in the abbey archives that references those country remedies. While I'm seasoning the beans, why don't you tell the class what you found."

"Certainly." Lili stepped up to the center island and held up the book she'd found in the abbey library. She opened the book to one of the places she had marked. "The best remedy against diseases of the lungs is calabash syrup prepared with watercress and rosemary," she read. Then she skipped ahead. "When the nose is weeping, take a whole lemon, beat it and put it on the boil. When it starts giving off steam, breathe in the vapor for five minutes."

She looked up. "That's not all. "The herb they call *milenrama*, which others call yarrow, is a medicinal wonder. It has been used to stop bleeding of wounds and cuts; as a poultice for burns and open sores; and used to cure fevers and colds. The leaves should be mashed with water and put on wounds."

Yesenia took over then. "Yarrow has many uses in cooking as well. Its peppery foliage and bitter leaves and flowers bring an aromatic flavor to salads. They can be added to soups and sauces, or simply boiled and simmered in butter as a side dish. I remember Romelda would cut the flowering tops and sprinkle them on salads."

She smiled. "Does anyone know who said, 'Our wine is bitter but it is ours?'"

"Jose Marti," John Potter said immediately, and he stood. "He is a Cuban national hero, and it offends me to hear his name from your lips, when you continue to consort with the Castro brothers."

Maria's entire demeanor shifted in an instant, like a mother cat bristling at a threat to her kitten. Her short, sturdy frame went rigid as she half-rose from her chair, planting both palms on the table. Though her voice remained steady, her shoulders tensed and she subtly angled her body to shield Yesenia from John's direction. Her movements were almost unconscious, born from the same protective instinct that had driven her to defend Yesenia online against critics.

She turned to face John. "¡Sentarse!" she said. "We are here to learn about cooking, not to talk politics."

Her usually warm, motherly eyes took on a harder edge as they darted between John and Yesenia, assessing. The fork in her hand, moments ago just a utensil for eating her chicken, was now gripped more like a weapon, though she probably wasn't even aware of the change. Even the way she leaned forward slightly telegraphed her readiness to intervene if the man's agitation escalated further.

He sat, reluctantly. I looked across the table at Dan Lazerow, who nodded. Then I noticed Ken Gould tapping away at his phone. Was he replying to a message that had come in? Sending one? It seemed odd to do so in the middle of a class session.

Yesenia stared at Potter for a long minute and it was like she recognized something in him, perhaps an opponent she could not allow to get the better of her. And that must have led her to turn to the documents in the cigar box. "I am not a *bruja,* or witch, but I believe that things happen for a reason. Today I discovered some old documents buried in a cigar humidor, perhaps by Brother Gervase, who also left us that book Dr. Weinstock found."

Lili spoke up then, bless her. "Yesenia, the chickens are ready to come out of the oven. Why don't we save discussion of the documents for later."

"*Buena idea,*" she said. She reached for the purple oven mitts and began removing the chickens from the oven. As she sliced them, Lili plated the golden slices with beans and rice and the student caterers served.

Chatter at the table of special students got more animated. Maria and Raquel were arguing with John and Ken Gould was paying close attention to what they were saying. I hoped it wasn't about politics. There was plenty to discuss about ingredients and means of preparation. Lili had very strong opinions about Cuban cooking, among many other things. I recalled a visit to a Cuban restaurant in Brooklyn where she criticized every dish. By the time we finished eating I was glad to get out of that place.

I didn't want that same feeling to overshadow what was sure to be a delicious dinner. I quickly carved a piece of chicken and fed it to Rochester, who wolfed it down as Lili joined me and our guests.

"Good call directing Yesenia back to the chicken," I whispered to her.

"I wanted to whack her with a spatula," she said. "This class is supposed to be about cuisine and culture, not the Castros."

She smiled at the table. "Has anyone tried the chicken yet?"

"This is delicious," Mrs. Babson said. "I want to stay for the whole class now that I've had a taste of what you're delivering."

I'd only met her a few times in the past couple of years, but she was a good match for her husband. She had a doctorate in early childhood education and ran a pre-school in Leighville, and she demonstrated the same joy I saw in him.

It wasn't often that you saw a couple so perfectly matched. I liked to think that Lili and I were different in many ways, but also similar in our approach to life. We'd only been married for a couple of months, after two additional years together, and we'd easily adapted to each other.

"This is going to be one of the stars of our intersession," Babson said. "With Dr. Chigwe's of course as well." He nodded toward Gracious.

"What are you teaching?" Mrs. Babson asked, as I slipped another piece of chicken to Rochester.

"I come from Botswana in southern Africa," she said, in her gentle accent. "And I generally teach introduction to sociology. For the intersession, I wanted to explore why my country is so peaceful compared to many of its neighbors. Is it because most of us come from the same ethnic group, the Batswana? Or because we have been blessed with the richness of diamond mines? Money often smooths over problems."

"What's your determination?" Joey asked.

She laughed. "That will be decided by my students. We're reading about ethnicity and geology and international finance, as well as a novel set in my country, *The Number One Ladies' Detective Agency*."

"I loved that TV program," Mrs. Lazerow said. "But I've never read the books. Do they really represent your country?"

"I think they do," Gracious said. "Though I don't have any experience of detective work myself."

I looked down at Rochester, and smiled. We had a lot of experience as amateur detectives.

Back at the special student table, the argument between Maria and John had gotten louder and angrier. Suddenly he stood up and started yelling.

A lot of it was in Spanish, and I was pleased with myself that I'd figured out he was Hispanic despite his Anglo name. Then I began to understand what he was saying. I caught the words "Cuba" and "*¡Patria y vida!*" He picked up his dinner plate and hurled it at Yesenia. It hit the island and then clattered to the floor as he stalked out the back door of the kitchen.

Chapter 13
Murder Most Foul

Lili jumped up to comfort Yesenia, quickly followed by Rochester, nosing at the food spilled on the floor. Deepti stopped filming as people began talking to each other.

Yesenia hadn't been hit by the plate, but by some of the tomato-based sauce, which dripped a red stain down her white blouse.

The room still smelled of the roast chicken. "I'll take care of this," Dan Lazerow said, and he hurried out the door behind John. Fortunately he was a quick eater and had already finished most of his food.

I stepped up to the kitchen island and waited for people to calm down and pay attention. "I'm sorry for the disruption, but I'm sure Dr. Ubeda and Dr. Weinstock will talk about the divisions between people throughout the Caribbean, and how they can be unified by their food." I waved at the room. "Please, continue eating, and we've got a beautiful flan for dessert."

Yesenia left for the restroom, and Deepti began cleaning up spilled sauce around the area where she was filming. Lili and I returned to our table, with Rochester by my side. "I guess that explains who sent the threatening notes," I said to Lili under my breath.

I noticed that several of the students had left the room also, including Ken, Maria and Raquel. At least one of the women had been crying as she left.

"But I saw him arrive this afternoon," Lili said. "He wasn't here Tuesday night." She stopped herself. "I suppose he could have been."

"I'm sure Dan will find him and cool him down. I want to ask Potter to drop out of the class. We can't tolerate that kind of behavior."

"That's a good idea," Lili said. "Even visitors and special students have to adhere to Eastern's code of ethics. I made sure that was prominent on the registration form."

Maria and Raquel returned separately. From their damp hands, they looked like they'd been to the restroom, perhaps to help Yesenia. The rest of the students came back in, including Ken, and finished eating. Rochester prowled under the tables for any dropped food but I couldn't rein him in because Dan joined us. "I couldn't find him," he said to the table. "But I called in two of my guards from campus to come over and keep looking."

The catering students cleared the tables, and Lili and I struggled to generate polite conversation among the group. When they were finished, they began to serve the flan, which had been chilling in the refrigerator. Yesenia returned in a clean blouse and stepped up to the island station, and Deepti began filming again.

"Flan's history can be traced back to ancient Rome when egg surpluses were transformed into custards. Most of the flan made then was savory, to accompany dishes such as meat or eel."

I'd never eaten eel, and had no desire to do so. I was glad that wasn't on that night's menu. Rochester didn't like the smell of the flan, so he slumped on the floor by my chair.

"The Spaniards added caramel sauce, and the Moors added some of the flavorings we still use, including citrus fruits and almonds," Yesenia continued. "The flan you're eating this evening is a Cuban version of the dish, topped with caramelized sugar. Enjoy."

She walked to the table where her Facebook fans awaited her, and I saw both Raquel and Maria reaching over to comfort her.

Deepti stopped filming and moved over to the table to eat but she didn't seem to engage with anyone else. Had she been traumatized by John Potter's actions? Had she captured them on film?

The atmosphere in the room relaxed as everyone enjoyed their dessert. Our guests all made their goodbyes, and Yesenia dismissed the students to their rooms, with a reading assignment for the next morning.

Lili and I walked over to the kitchen island with Rochester by my side. Yesenia leaned back against the counter. "I think it went well," she said. "Aside from that crazy man. He looked familiar – but his beard threw me. Do you know who he is?"

"His name is John Potter," I said. "But we don't know anything more than that."

"That's not a Cuban name," Yesenia said. "I'll bet that's not the one he was born with."

The two catering students finished loading the dishwasher and wiping down the tables. The blonde held out a leather messenger bag. "Someone left this under a table," she said.

I took the bag and noticed the name tag on the handle. Max Abraham. I knew he'd be back the next morning. I told the students I'd handle emptying the dishwasher when it finished and I dismissed them. They walked out the back door, chatting together. A moment later, though, we heard one of them scream.

When we rushed out, we saw John Potter's body on the ground, a gaping wound in his chest. His eyes were wide open and he wasn't breathing.

Chapter 14
Crime Scene

Lili pulled the two girls away and spoke to them in quiet tones, and I called 911. "A man has been knifed at the Friar Lake Conference Center." I gave the dispatcher the street address for the property. "We're at the top of the hill, behind the third building on the left. Can you notify Lieutenant Rinaldi?"

I'd met Tony Rinaldi a couple of times in the past, and though I wouldn't consider him as good a friend as Rick was, he'd been receptive to my helping him. I hoped he'd be in the first group of people to arrive.

Rochester stayed by my side, and I was glad I didn't have to tug him away from Potter's body. This was a crime scene and I didn't want any of us to disturb it. After the scene of crime team left, though, I might let him loose to nose around and see if he could discover anything the police couldn't.

The girls were both shivering, even though they were in winter coats. Lili led them back inside and I followed, though I kept an eye on Potter's body through the open back door. I called Dan Lazerow then.

"Found John Potter," I said. "But you aren't going to like the circumstances."

"I just got home. What's up?"

"Someone stuck a knife in his heart. He's on the ground behind the refectory."

"Let me drop my wife off and I'll be right back. I knew I should have stationed a security guard on the property but I thought my presence would be enough."

I ended the call and turned to Lili, who said, "I'm going to make everyone some hot chocolate. We were planning to use it for a break tomorrow but I think we could use some tonight."

"Great idea." Lili had made us that hot chocolate on occasion, with chopped dark chocolate, whole milk, cornstarch, and a little bit of sugar. It would go a long way toward making people feel better.

Max Abraham came in then, and Rochester rushed over to the door to greet him. "Sorry, forgot my bag," he said. "I was halfway home when I remembered. Has my phone in it so I had to come back."

He looked around. "What's wrong?"

"One of your classmates was assaulted," I said.

"Which one?"

"Mr. Potter."

His face turned pale. "I don't think he recognized me, but I know who he is," Max said. "He wasn't wearing a beard the last time I saw him, but as an actor, I'm accustomed to looking beneath the surface because most of my colleagues are in costume. That man's a Broadway stagehand named Juan."

"How do you know him?"

"I was in the fourth revival of *Fiddler on the Roof* in 2004," he said. "In the ensemble. Juan was one of the crew."

Through the front window of the refectory, I saw a police cruiser pull up, its red and blue lights flashing. "You think you could stick around until the police get here?" I asked.

"I'd really rather not," he said. "It's already late, and I need to get back to the café and get some sleep. I'm up at five every morning to start baking."

He looked at me. "I'll be here tomorrow. I promise."

"Sure. Sleep well," I said.

He walked out as the two officers came in. Rochester circled around them, sniffing, but they paid him no mind. I explained what had happened and led them to the back door. But I grabbed Rochester's collar so he couldn't follow them outside.

The fire company paramedics arrived a few minutes later, and then Tony Rinaldi. I'd first met Tony a few years before, when a mentor of mine had been killed at Eastern during the launch party for our capital campaign.

As Tony approached, I recognized our similar builds - both of us had to work to keep middle-age spread at bay. Though he carried himself with a cop's practiced authority while I still moved with the slight awkwardness of someone more comfortable behind a computer screen than in face-to-face confrontations.

His curly black hair showed no sign of gray. His family was originally Sicilian, so like me, he had a slightly darker Mediterranean complexion. He wore a sheepskin-lined coat over wool slacks and clunky boots.

He waved a hand in my direction and I had to hold Rochester back from greeting him. He walked through the back door to where the uniforms had already started staking out the crime scene. A woman with a camera and a big flash attachment began taking pictures of John Potter's body, and I stepped back into the kitchen.

Dan returned and came over to me. Rochester went down to the floor, but kept looking up at us. "I called President Babson to let him know what's going on and I promised to keep him in the loop. I don't suppose you have any surveillance cameras out there?"

"Never thought we'd need them," I said. "The only ones we have are out front in the parking lot."

"We'll have to talk about your security setup when this is over," he said. "You're out here in the middle of the country, but that doesn't mean you won't have vandalism or other problems."

"I know. But I've tried to keep our budget lean. You've probably heard that there's a group of faculty members who are opposed to Friar Lake. They think we're diverting funds that ought to go to academic instruction."

"And are you?"

I shrugged. "Babson used endowment money to purchase the property and fund the renovations," I said. "Since then, we're self-supporting. But if Eastern was able to sell Friar Lake off, that money could go back to the endowment, and the income could fund scholarships and faculty salaries."

Dan walked outside, where I saw him in conversation with Tony Rinaldi. Lili was in the corner, still comforting Yesenia and Deepti, and I was torn between going over there and waiting for Tony to talk to me. He saved me the trouble by coming back into the kitchen. He took off his heavy coat and rested it on a chair.

"Steve," he said, reaching out to shake my hand. "We've got to stop meeting like this."

"I agree." Rochester stood up and nuzzled him, and Tony petted his head. Then Rochester wandered over to Lili, probably hoping for a handout.

"I've got a team out there combing for evidence, though so far we haven't found anything," Tony said. "Tough to do in the dark and the cold." He pulled out a notepad and pen, and we sat at the table. "What can you tell me about the victim?"

"Almost nothing. He registered for the class under the name John Potter, but he didn't provide any personal information at the time. I think that might not be his real name, though." I told Tony that Max had recognized him and that his real name might be Juan.

Lili came over to join us then. "Rochester pushed this little pot to me, and that gave me an idea." She held up her phone. "Since Juan switches so easily to John, I wondered if he'd translated his last name, too. The Spanish word for potter is Alfarero."

That was just the kind of clue Rochester usually gave me, and I was jealous that he'd gone to Lili instead. He kept his head down as he slid behind my chair. "Juan Alfarero," I said, making the connection in my head. "One of the angry posters on Facebook."

"Exactly."

I turned to Tony and explained that Yesenia had a profile on social media, and that someone named Juan Alfarero had posted nasty messages against her.

"I can clarify that," Tony said. He held up an evidence bag. "Victim's wallet was in his pocket. ID for Juan Alfarero of the Bronx. Union card with membership in the International Alliance of Theatrical Stage Employees."

"So Max Abraham was right," I said.

"Tell me more about the comments this guy posted," Tony said.

Lili and I alternated telling Tony what we'd read. "He got angry several times during Dr. Ubeda's presentation," I said, and I relayed the comments he'd made.

Tony took notes. "I'd like to talk to your speaker now."

We walked him over to where Yesenia sat and introduced him, and he sat beside her and talked.

Dan joined Lili and me. "I'll leave this in Tony's hands," he said. "Call me if anything else happens."

He left, and Deepti finished shutting down her equipment. "Did you get any of that on film?" I asked.

"I was focusing on Yesenia. I got the plate coming at her and crashing, and I might have his voice in the background. I'll have to check later. Do you think it's important?"

I shrugged. "I don't know. Would Yesenia want to use it for publicity?"

"I doubt it. The Food Network people are pretty conservative. I don't think they'd want to hire her if they had to worry about people in the audience throwing things."

That made me less likely to consider that Yesenia had been generating the threats, but only a bit.

The cops were still working outside, but Lili, Rochester and I were the only ones left in the kitchen with Yesenia and Tony.

Rochester kept wanting to go outside and see what was going on, but I found a piece of rope in the cabinet and tied it to his collar, and kept a firm hand on it. I was sorry I'd left his leash in the room we were staying in.

Eventually Tony got up and came over to us. "I've told Dr. Ubeda she can go back to her room, and you guys can, too. I'll finish up here and talk to you tomorrow. We'll need to stake out the area where the body was found so we can come back in the daylight to look for evidence. I'd appreciate it if you would tell all your students to stay away from that area until we're finished."

"We have their email addresses," Lili said. "We can send them a message."

"Did you find a weapon?" I asked.

He shook his head. "The ME's techs suggest a long, sharp blade. We'll widen the search area tomorrow. So far we haven't found any trace evidence—fibers, fingerprints, that kind of thing. But we'll keep looking."

It was awkward leaving Juan Alfarero's body behind, but the medical examiner's van was already there, ready to take him away when the police were finished. As we walked back to our room, I caught Lili watching Yesenia disappear into the darkness ahead of us.

"Do you think she knew he would be here?" Lili asked quietly.

"You mean, did she know John Potter was really Juan Alfarero?" I glanced back at the crime scene, where the police lights still painted the stone walls in alternating red and blue. "Right now, I'm more worried about what President Babson will say when he finds out someone's been murdered at our brand-new intersession program."

"Or what Elena Salazar will say," Lili added. "She warned everyone this would end badly."

And she wasn't the only one who might use this death to shut us down. I just hoped we could salvage something from this disaster before the whole program collapsed around us.

Chapter 15
Great Questions

We went out through the front door of the refectory, and I kept Rochester on the makeshift leash. I didn't want him running through the crime scene and disturbing any evidence. We'd have plenty of time to walk around the next morning in daylight and let his nose do its work.

"Why do you think Juan Alfarero came here?" Lili asked. "Just to cause trouble?"

"I don't know. Now that we know his real name, I'd like to do a search on him. But I'm exhausted and I'll think better tomorrow."

Rochester did his business on the way back to the room. When we renovated Friar Lake, I made sure that one room was large enough for the three of us when we needed to stay over. A king-sized bed with an excellent mattress, good lighting in the en-suite bathroom, and a rag rug on the floor for Rochester.

We quickly settled down to sleep. Friday morning, I woke first, confused for a moment about our surroundings. It wasn't the first time I'd stayed overnight at Friar Lake, but it was the first time I'd done so with Lili.

Rochester came over to nose me, and I got up, pulled on sweats and a coat, and took him outside. He hurried along, sniffing and peeing.

As we approached the area behind the refectory, I put on his leash. Tony's team had set up a white tent, and there were already two techs there doing important-looking things with magnifying glasses and tweezers. Rochester wanted to go over and greet them, but I kept him close to me. He didn't look pleased. Friar Lake was his domain, and he felt entitled to know everything that was going on.

Then he decided he wanted to head toward the parking lot. He's about 90 pounds these days, so I let him take the lead. Sometimes you're the dog, pulling the sled, and sometimes you're the sled, letting the dog pull you.

Most of the time, the lot is relatively empty. My SUV and Joey's truck are there regularly. But that morning, there was a police van parked to one side, as well as a row of cars that belonged to Yesenia and the special students. A few others had Eastern parking stickers so I figured those cars belonged to regular students.

Rochester paid special attention to one beat-up Toyota sedan with a New York plate and an EZ Pass transponder on the windshield. There was a new bumper sticker on the back that read "You Will Be Found." I had no idea what that meant, but it was kind of creepy, and I tugged the dog away.

When we got back to the dormitory, Lili was already awake and using the bathroom. "I promised Yesenia I would help her with breakfast this morning," she said. She wore an Eastern sweatshirt over wide-legged black slacks, and had her auburn curls tied up in a ponytail.

"What are we having?"

"Plantain and egg frittata," she said. "It's easy to make a bunch of them to bake in the oven at the same time. I'd better get moving. I said I'd slice the vegetables."

"You're doing a lot of cooking, aren't you? Is that your contribution to the course?"

"Yesenia's doing the bulk of the lecturing, and she'll be grading the presentations at the end. I'm going to help where I can, including at a couple of question-and-answer lectures."

She left, and I opened my hacker laptop. It was too early to go over to my office, which I wasn't ready to face without breakfast, so I began a search on Juan Alfarero.

His was still a very common name, but by using a very illegal program that could dig up social security numbers, and adding a few terms to my searches, I was able to dig up some information on the Cuban-American man who lived in the Bronx and worked on Broadway.

The most interesting was his arrest record. He had been pulled in three times after domestic abuse complaints. The first two women had declined to press charges, but the third, who was at the time his fiancée, had the backing of a women's center, and eventually he was sentenced to six months' probation and a year of mandatory anger management courses.

That was all I could find in the public record; I couldn't tell if he had completed that requirement or not.

He had also been arrested several times at anti-Castro demonstrations in Manhattan, including one at the New School. I'd have to check with Yesenia to see if he'd been there when she was.

I wanted to do a deeper dive into his social media background, but that required more time. I set up the search but before I left the room I did a quick look for the phrase "you will be found." It was the title of a song from a new Broadway production called "Dear Evan Hansen."

So that was probably Juan's car, because of the Broadway connection. I'd have to mention that to Tony, because he'd need to arrange with Juan's next of kin to get the car.

Then Rochester and I walked over to the refectory to see how breakfast was coming. Lili had brought her coffee maker and bean grinder from home, along with a bag of El Pico coffee beans, so she could have her café con leche.

I had to unload the dishwasher from the night before, and

without the catering students there to help, I laid out silverware and dishes for everyone. Joey had volunteered to help clean up.

It was barely eight o'clock, so I wasn't surprised that most of the regular college students hadn't arrived yet. As Lili brewed coffee, the aroma filled the room. I took two paper cups of the inky brew out the back door. Leaving Rochester inside, I called out, "Anyone want coffee?"

The two techs, both in white Hazmat outfits, stepped out of the tent. "Thanks," the male tech said. "It's cold as a heart of stone out here." He took the two cups and passed one to the female with him.

"Yeah, the wind really whips around up here, especially before the sun is fully risen. You guys find anything yet?"

He shook his head. "Nothing to write home about. But Lieutenant Rinaldi can answer any questions for you."

I went back inside, where most of the special students were clustered around the prep island as Yesenia talked about plantains as she worked and Deepti filmed. Rochester was on the floor in front of the prep island and I wondered if he was in the shot.

"Green plantains are firm and starchy, and they're often used in savory dishes," she said. "Twice-fried plantain slices are called *tostones*, the Caribbean equivalent of potato chips. As plantains ripen, they turn yellow and become sweeter and softer. Like green plantains, they can be boiled, mashed, or fried and used in a variety of dishes like *mofongo*, mashed fried plantains, and *platanos maduros*, which are fried sweet plantains."

Maduros were my favorite Cuban side dish, especially when Lili made them. Rochester hovered around between Lili and Yesenia, hoping for a tidbit, though I knew he wouldn't be happy with any of the vegetables.

"Black plantains are very ripe and sweet, with a soft texture," Yesenia continued as I worked in the background. "They are often used in desserts or as a sweet side dish. Plantains can also be dried and ground into flour, which is gluten-free and used in baking."

Lili was at the stove, managing several skillets in which she was sautéing olive oil with vegetables. Yesenia had already prepared a big bowl of an egg and cheese mixture, and she and Lili worked together to coat the vegetables and then stick the pans in the oven to bake.

By then the rest of the students had joined us. After all the pans were in the oven, Yesenia returned to the prep island. "In addition to their culinary use, plantains have several health benefits," she said. "They are a good source of fiber, potassium, and vitamins A, C, and B6. Plantains are also used in some traditional medicine practices for their supposed healing properties."

I started laying out plates, and Zenobia stood up to help me. "It's interesting to be on the other side of this," she said. "Listen, I wanted to tell you about something strange. It's probably not related to that poor man's death, but..."

"Go ahead."

"Well, I was talking to Ken yesterday at dinner and... he was odd."

"In what way?"

"He doesn't seem to know anything about cooking. He kept asking me very simple questions like what kind of pan Yesenia was using and why she had put the chicken in brine. And then he was very interested when John was talking about politics."

"Maybe he came here expecting this to be a political course, and he was surprised by all the food emphasis," I said. "He told me when he got here that he didn't know much about food."

"That would mean he didn't read the course description," Zenobia said. "Everyone else seems to be here for the food, even the college kids who don't know how to cook."

"Thanks for letting me know. I agree, it's curious."

As Zenobia and I worked, Yesenia smiled at the crowd. "How did everyone sleep?"

There was a general positive murmur, but one of the Eastern students asked, "What happened to that man last night?"

Yesenia looked to me, and I stood up. "I'm afraid that John Potter died last night," I said. "It's a police matter, and the detective in charge will be here this morning to question everyone. We'll try and minimize the disruption to your class."

"I have a research assignment set for the second half of the morning," Yesenia said. "Do you think the police could talk to people during that time?"

"I'll let the detective know," I said, and pulled out my phone to text Tony Rinaldi.

"Are we safe here?" another Eastern student asked. "Should we go back to the dorms?"

"Of course you're welcome to return to the dorms if you don't feel safe here," I said, looking up when I finished typing. "And if anyone wants to drop the course and leave, we'll understand and make sure you get a complete refund. But the police don't think this incident has anything to do with the course, and that you're all safe here."

Well, that's what I thought. I hoped Tony would second that opinion when he arrived.

"What was he doing here, then, if he wasn't here for the course?" Ken asked.

God bless them. These students asked questions, which was more than I usually got when I taught at Eastern as an adjunct. In a regular classroom I had trouble getting anyone to speak up. Maybe it was the presence of the adult students that spurred that interest.

I was surprised when Yesenia answered. "I'm afraid he was here to make trouble for me," she said. "I don't know how or why he was killed, but he posted regularly in my Facebook group and he had very strong opinions about the Castro regime and my work on the island."

"What does any of that have to do with cooking?" the first student asked.

Yesenia smiled. "That's a great question. As we continue in the course, you'll start to make connections between food and culture, and that's going to include politics as well."

A timer went off, which surprised me and sent a tiny shiver of fear up my spine. Yesenia and Lili began sliding the frittatas out of the oven and slicing them. I brushed off my fear and jumped up to help serve.

As I passed out the plates, it was interesting to observe the dynamics of the students, how the special students kept to themselves as did the regular Eastern students. I hoped that would change the more they interacted with each other, and once the shock of Juan Alfarero's death had worn off.

What I felt was more visceral. That someone had dared bring murder to Friar Lake, my domain. It was a violation so strong I knew I had to do whatever I could to bring the villain to justice.

Chapter 16
Sharp Evidence

After breakfast finished, the students had an hour of free time before the morning lecture. I went to my office with Rochester and pulled up the class roster to give to Tony. I made notes next to the names of the people he ought to concentrate on, primarily the special students like Maria and Raquel who were online fans of Yesenia's and might have some insight into why people were angry with her.

I printed that out and moved on to college business. Around ten o'clock the dog was up on all fours, barking. I looked out the window to see Tony Rinaldi getting out of his car.

He was on the phone as he walked toward us. I hushed Rochester and got my hand on his collar as I opened the door. Tony ended the call and reached out to pet the dog.

I always appreciated people who approached Rochester before they came to me. He considered himself my bodyguard, and besides, he was spoiled enough to believe that the world revolved around him.

Tony and I shook hands. The bags under his eyes and his general posture made it look like he hadn't gotten much sleep the night before.

"The students have a research assignment starting at eleven in the library," I said, as we walked into my office. "Yesenia would appreciate it if you could interview them during that time, rather than while she's lecturing."

"I can manage that. I need to talk to you first anyway."

Tony pulled off his heavy coat and settled into the visitor's chair across from my desk. He opened his notebook. "I did some research last night on the program you're running, and Dr. Ubeda. But I'd like some background. How did she end up here?"

"When President Babson announced the intersession last fall, Lili and I started brainstorming about what kind of programming I could offer here at Friar Lake. Something that took advantage of the residential location and the compressed time frame. Lili was born in Cuba and her cooking is a mix of Jewish specialties and Cuban ingredients, and we got to talking one day about how that would be an interesting topic to explore."

I told him how Lili and Yesenia had met and remained friends. "Yesenia had already contacted her about coming to Friar Lake to research a monk who lived here at the end of his life, and had written a book about the way people in the Caribbean used food to heal sickness. Lili invited Yesenia to teach a course that would touch on their shared backgrounds, and the two of them worked up the syllabus and the assignments."

"You didn't explore her political beliefs?"

"I guess we should have. But since she was a friend of Lili's and we knew her academic credentials we didn't dive too deeply. Neither of us knew how political Yesenia has become in the last few years. It wasn't until she got the threat on Tuesday evening that we realized there might be a problem."

"Threat?"

"Slipped under the door of the room she was staying in on the top floor of Fields Hall." I told him about the contents of the note, the way she'd mentioned online where she was staying, and the security at Fields Hall.

"I'd like to see that note."

"Yesenia says she threw it away."

"So you have only her word that the threat existed?"

"I didn't think of that," I said. "But there was a second threat, and we all saw that."

I explained about the note slipped into her grocery bag and how we'd seen it in the refectory. "Printed out from a computer on plain white paper," I said.

"Do you think she could have put it in the bag herself?"

I sat back in my chair. "I did wonder about that. That maybe she was trying to drum up controversy over the program here."

"Why would she do that?" Tony asked.

"She has a social media profile. The more controversy she generates, the higher her profile becomes."

Tony nodded. "Why was that girl filming her last night?"

"Yesenia wants to get her own program on the Food Network, or something like it. She's having her lectures filmed as a kind of demo reel."

"Is she going to put them on YouTube?" Tony asked. "You know, after you get a certain number of views from your videos, you can start getting advertising revenue."

"And death threats would incite her audience to keep watching," I said. "But how does that factor into Juan Alfarero's murder?"

"Killing someone amps up the stakes," Tony said.

I couldn't believe it. Could someone as smart and charming as Yesenia be a cold-blooded murderer, who'd kill to amp up her YouTube ratings? The last few years with Rochester had shown me to never underestimate what a desperate person would do.

Was Yesenia desperate enough?

"Walk me through what happened yesterday," Tony said. "Say, from the time Dr. Ubeda arrived here."

I did. At every step of the way I kept returning to the idea that Yesenia might have orchestrated everything.

"She seemed genuinely surprised and angry when she found the note in the grocery bag," I said.

"Someone who wants a show on the Food Network has to be a good actress and communicator as well as a good cook," Tony said.

"You watch those shows?"

"Some of them. Tanya likes the competition ones, but I prefer the ones where the guys are barbecuing or doing outrageous challenges."

"When the weather warms up you'll have to invite us over for a barbecue," I said.

"I didn't say I was any good," he said with a smile. "And honestly I'm more likely to fail miserably when I try and recreate something I've seen on TV. We had to call the fire department once."

I laughed. "I wish I'd been there to see that. No real damage, though, right?"

"Just to my self-esteem. But let's get back to Dr. Ubeda. What happened after she pulled the threat out of the grocery bag?"

I walked him through everything, from her cooking lessons to the dinner, and then Juan Alfarero's outburst.

"Any indication that the two of them knew each other before yesterday?" Tony asked.

"Not that I saw. They're on different ends of the political spectrum. She visits Cuba regularly, eats at home restaurants, collects recipes. She cooked for a political dinner once when she was there. Juan was on the other extreme, very opposed to any interaction with the regime. She did say that he looked familiar, but his beard was throwing her."

I remembered the Broadway decal on Juan's car. "There's one thing I wanted to mention to you. This morning Rochester dragged me over to the parking lot and I spotted a car I think belongs to Juan Alfarero. Will you be in touch with his next of kin about getting that car out of here?"

I described the car to him. "I wonder if he was in Leighville on Tuesday, when Yesenia got that threat," I said. "Can you check a couple of local motels to see if he stayed over before he came here?"

"I can."

I remembered a detail I'd learned a few months before when

helping Rick with a case. "There's an EZ Pass transponder on the windshield. The New Hope toll bridge has electronic records of cars that pass through, so you could check with the Bridge Commission and see when he crossed."

He made another note, and then looked at his watch. "It's getting close to eleven. Where can I talk with these students?"

"They'll be in the library doing research," I said. "You can walk around and talk to each one quietly. I doubt they'll have much to say, except for the special students."

He tilted his head. "What makes them special?"

I explained about the difference between the students seeking degrees from Eastern, and the community members who had joined us for the month. "Some of them are Yesenia's Facebook followers."

I handed him the printout I'd prepared of the class, with my notes attached. "Thanks," he said. "This will be very useful. Now can you point me toward the library?"

Rochester and I walked over there with him. Inside, shelves lined the walls and desks and chairs were placed in the light of the windows. The students were already there, using their laptops or books they'd found on the shelves. Raquel and Maria were sharing a laptop, and I suggested Tony start with them.

Then Rochester and I went back outside. It was cold, and I wanted to hurry back to my office, but the dog had other ideas. He headed quickly toward the refectory. I was curious to see if anything remained of the crime scene so I followed him.

A chalk outline and a few spots of blood on the ground marked the area where Juan's body had been found. It was surrounded by low wooden stakes linked together with yellow crime scene tape.

I worried Rochester might disturb the area and was sorry I didn't have him on a leash, but he surprised me by nosing his way along the ground toward the trees.

It was possible that a deer or a fox had come over to sniff the blood, and then left a trail that Rochester was following. The property was ringed by stands of oak, maple and Scotch pine, with low vegetation growing beneath the leafless trees. He had his nose to the ground, moving ahead slowly.

Then he stopped in front of a cluster of rhododendrons. In the spring, they'd sprout beautiful pink and white blossoms, but in January all that was visible were their long, leathery leaves, which formed a kind of thicket around the base of a couple of pine trees.

Rochester sat on his haunches and barked, which was usually a signal for me to get closer. I did, and through a gap in the leaves I spotted a piece of wood with an intricate pattern. I leaned in closer.

It was the knife Yesenia had been using the evening before to slice the malanga. But was it also the weapon that had taken Juan Alfarero's life? Who could have used it – and why?

Chapter 17
Fusion Cuisine

I petted Rochester and told him what a good boy he was, then turned to go back to the library and get Tony. Rochester didn't want to leave.

"Stay there if you want," I said. "I'll be right back."

He went down on all fours and stared at me. "Don't give me that look. You know I can't touch that knife."

I hurried back toward the library, and a moment later the dog was racing along beside me. Though the abbey buildings were not connected to each other, except by a couple of covered walkways, they formed a loose quadrangle. The library building was at one corner, another structure of the local stone with a series of tall, vertical windows.

I walked in the front door with Rochester and saw that the students were for the most part watching Tony interview their classmates instead of doing their assignment. Bobby was on his phone in the corner, speaking in what sounded like Spanish. Budding actress Claudia and Bradley, who was taking the course for fun, were giggling together about something, while Iowa Emily and pre-med Matthew sat together, apparently both engaged in their homework.

Tony sat at a large table in the middle of the room with Ken

Gould, who looked anxious to get back to his work. I went up to them. "Sorry to interrupt you, but I have something to show you," I said to Tony.

Rochester sat beside me, staring at Tony, who looked up. "I'm in the middle of interviews here."

I nodded. "I know. But you'll want to see this."

He blew out a breath. "Fine." I noticed that he had been making his own notes on the roster I'd given him. He turned to Ken. "I'll be back to follow up with you later."

He pulled on his coat and followed me and the dog outside. I said, "I hope you have an evidence bag with you."

"Always do. What did you find?"

"Rochester found it. I think it might be the murder weapon."

The dog romped gleefully ahead of us, and Tony and I followed, walking quickly. The stand of oaks was directly behind the refectory, a few hundred yards from the building. When we reached the rhododendrons, Rochester was back on his haunches, a doggy grin breaking his face.

"Right there," I said, leaning down and pointing.

"Jesus," he said. "The dog."

"I know."

He pulled an evidence bag from his pocket. I carefully moved the leaves aside so he could grasp the knife, glad I was wearing my gloves so I wouldn't leave fingerprints.

He pulled the knife out. Someone had attempted to wipe it down, but that left streaks of dried blood on the blade. He stuck it in his bag. "Do me a favor and hang out here for a minute? I've got some stakes and crime scene tape in my car."

I knelt down and petted Rochester while we waited. "You are such a good boy," I said. "Such a good crime-sniffing dog."

I went through a range of endearments until Tony returned and staked off the area around the base of the oak tree. "That's a pretty fancy knife," Tony said. "Does it match any of the ones you use here?"

"I think it's one that Yesenia used last night," I said. I described how she'd sliced the malanga for Lili to fry. "But I didn't notice what happened to it after she finished."

"I'm glad I waited to interview her. I'll be curious to hear what she says about the knife."

He went back to the library to continue his interviews, and Rochester and I returned to my office. We had ordered platters of sandwiches from a deli in Leighville, and when Rochester alerted me to the delivery van, I led the guy with platters to the refectory, where students were already gathering.

Yesenia had instructed the deli on how to make two types of Cuban sandwiches. Before she let the students at the food, she had them all sit down. "We've got two types of traditional Cuban sandwiches here," she said. "How many of you have had a medianoche?"

About half the students raised their hands. "Who can tell us what goes into a sandwich like that?" Yesenia asked.

Enid was the first to raise her hand. "The medianoche is a pressed sandwich, like an Italian panini, with sweet egg bread stuffed with roast pork, ham, cheese, and pickles." She smiled. "The name supposedly came because clubs in Havana began serving them to customers at midnight after a long night of dancing."

"Very good," Yesenia said. "And the other sandwich is an Elena Ruz."

This time it was Maria who raised her hand. "I know about that one. There was a Cuban socialite named Elena Ruz Valdés-Fauli who used to go to this El Carmelo restaurant in Havana. She asked them to make her a sandwich with turkey, strawberry preserves and cream cheese in a soft medianoche roll so often that eventually they named the sandwich after her."

"That's correct," Yesenia said.

"She left Havana after Castro came to power," Maria continued. "Went to Spain and Florida and eventually Costa Rica. I met her once when she was in New York. Her family was very rich in Cuba and they lost everything when they left, but they worked hard in the US and her relatives are now wealthy and powerful again."

Yesenia encouraged everyone to get up and try both sandwiches, and I fed pieces of turkey to Rochester. There was a lot of conversation, and I noticed that there was more blending of the regular Eastern kids with the special students.

"What are you doing this afternoon?" I asked Lili as we ate.

"Yesenia is lecturing about fusion cuisines in the Caribbean," she said. "Starting with Cuban-Chinese, then *Chifa*, which is Peruvian-Chinese, then Jamaican-Chinese. I'm going to talk about how my mother cooked, bringing the Eastern European flavors to the table."

"That sounds interesting. Do you think Yesenia would mind if Rochester and I sit in?"

"Not at all. We'll be in the big classroom."

I took Rochester out for a run around Friar Lake, then we stopped back at my office to make sure I wasn't missing any important emails or phone messages. I was curious to see what Yesenia was posting online about the course, so I opened Facebook.

Though we had cautioned her about making too big a deal over the paperwork we'd found, she had posted several photos of the documents. She'd also listed the family tree she had told us about, which made her the heir to the land in Havana.

"Stupid move," I said to Rochester.

He looked up at me with an expression that conveyed he was accustomed to humans doing dumb things. "This is just going to cause more trouble."

I sat back in my chair and thought about what Tony and I had discussed. Perhaps Yesenia was manipulating everything to generate more social media attention. The higher her profile, the more speaking engagements she could get, and perhaps leverage herself into a full-time faculty position somewhere.

But did that include murder? It was hard to consider her knifing Juan Alfarero for such an indeterminate goal. And she hadn't mentioned anything about the death on her page. It was a logical step

—see, someone has been threatening me, and now they've killed one of my students. That would certainly get attention online.

On the other hand, if she had killed Juan, she was smart enough not to say anything that might come back to incriminate her. For example, if she revealed something about the crime that only the murderer would know, that would be a big mistake. So she might have a strong reason not to mention Juan Alfarero, even if he'd been a member of her group.

Neither Maria nor Raquel had mentioned him either. Maybe because they didn't approve of his posts, but still, he was a member of the group and other members might have liked him or would want to know about what happened to him.

At two o'clock Rochester and I walked to the infirmary, to the room where he had found the box of cigars and documents.

Yesenia stood beside the teaching podium, with a computer screen beside her displaying the start of a PowerPoint presentation. She wore a Chinese-style dress in red with gold embroidery. I noticed Ken Gould at the back of the room with his laptop open and wondered if he was doing his own work, or planning to listen to the lecture.

"Today we're going to talk about fusion cuisine," Yesenia began. "Who can give me a definition of that term?"

Enid, the culinary student, was quick to raise her hand. "It means bringing together ingredients from different cultures and merging recipes."

"Exactly," Yesenia said. "Today we're going to focus primarily on Cuban-Chinese or Chino-Cubano. As the slave trade began to slow in the middle of the 19th century, plantation owners needed a new supply of workers, so they began importing Chinese men, primarily from Guangdong province. These men also went to work building railroads throughout the island."

She popped up a black and white image of laborers cutting sugar cane.

"Most of the immigrants were men, so if they couldn't afford to bring over Chinese brides, they married native women, who blended their own cooking style with requests from their husbands. As well, as the Chinese community grew in Cuba, Chinatowns emerged in Havana and other cities. Chinese restaurants began to open, catering initially to the Chinese community."

The next slide showed a photo that read "Barrio Chino" over a Chinese pagoda spire. "Chinese chefs began to incorporate Cuban ingredients and flavors into their dishes to appeal to the local palate. They used ingredients like plantains, cassava, and black beans, which were not typically found in traditional Chinese cuisine."

She flipped through a few images of produce. "Over time, distinctive Cuban-Chinese dishes emerged, such as *arroz frito*, Cuban fried rice, and *pollo al sésamo*, sesame chicken."

Raquel said, "I worked for a couple of years at a Cuban-Chinese restaurant in Morningside Heights. My favorite dish to make was chop suey Cubano."

When she spoke, her hands moved in precise, controlled gestures, like she was still directing line cooks during a dinner rush, and her voice carried the calm authority of someone used to being obeyed in high-pressure situations.

"That's the essence of fusion cuisine," Yesenia said. "It's a testament to the cultural exchange and adaptation that can occur when different communities come together, resulting in a unique and flavorful fusion of culinary traditions."

"Are we going to eat any Cuban-Chinese food?" one of the Eastern students asked.

"Dr. Weinstock and I are putting together our menu for Sunday dinner, before we move to the campus. We can certainly add something there."

She clicked through to her next slide. "Wherever Cubans went, either after Batista fell or as people started to chafe under Castro, they blended their cuisine with local ingredients. We'll be talking about Peruvian-Chinese cuisine, also called *Chifa*, and a Cuban-Caribbean, with influences from Jamaica and other islands."

"What about Cuban-Spanish?" Maria asked. "When I go to a Cuban restaurant I'm often surprised at how many of the dishes are similar to what I'd see in a Spanish restaurant."

"That's a great point," Yesenia said. "Certainly dishes like *ropa vieja* and *arroz con pollo* have roots in Spanish cooking. And a dish like the Tortilla Española, much like the frittatas we made this morning only with potatoes rather than plantains, is a very Spanish dish that you'll find on a lot of Cuban menus."

She flipped to her next slide. "African influences can be found in Cuban cuisine, particularly in the use of certain ingredients like plantains, yams, and okra. And as with any immigrant cuisine, American tastes have influenced Cuban food, and vice versa."

Enid raised her hand. "There's something I've noticed too, in my cooking classes. We've learned how to make a French mirepoix, a combination of onion, carrot and celery generally cut to the same size. And in Cuban cuisine we use a puree of onions, peppers, cilantro, and garlic, called a sofrito. Are those related?"

"They are," Yesenia said. "That's a great example of the French influence on Cuban food, which may be less pronounced than others but still present."

She flipped to another slide. "These fusion cuisines demonstrate the diverse cultural influences that have shaped Cuban culinary traditions over time, as well as the adaptability and creativity of Cuban chefs in incorporating new ingredients and techniques into their cooking."

The hour-and-a-half program flew by, and the students returned to their rooms to read or relax, and Yesenia and Lili huddled together to discuss their progress. I went back to my office with Rochester.

I was getting ready to wrap up for the day when Tony arrived. "I've interviewed everyone who was at the program last night except Dr. Ubeda," he said. "I'm meeting her in the library in a few minutes."

"Anything unusual stand out in your conversations?"

"The people at Mr. Alfarero's table noticed him getting increasingly agitated during the evening," he said. "There's general agreement on that. He fiddled with his place settings, he pushed the food around on his plate, he muttered things in Spanish. The two older women were frightened of him, and they were planning to complain about him to Dr. Ubeda after dinner."

"That's not surprising, now that we know he was an anti-Castro activist."

Tony nodded. "I'm still trying to understand what he was doing here. He lived alone in the Bronx, and his last job on a Broadway show was about six months ago. So far I can't find anyone who knew him more recently."

"I can do some searching," I said. "All legit, of course. I've been working with Rick Stemper on finding legal search tools that can dive into peoples' backgrounds."

"Yeah, I'm sure those exist. But we don't have access to them in Leighville, and the state police are always backed up. So I'd appreciate your help. As long as anything you find can be part of evidence in a legal case, once we have a suspect."

"Absolutely." I could already feel my fingers tingling and I was eager to get back to my hacker laptop and see what I could dig up.

Chapter 18
Marriage and Murder

Rochester and I took a quick walk, and ended up at Joey's office. "How's the program going?" he asked.

"Yesenia's doing her best to keep things on track," I said. "Great lecture this afternoon, and Tony Rinaldi managed to get most of his interviewing done while students were in the library researching."

"How are you holding up?"

"Last night wasn't really the way I wanted the program to start, and I wish I knew more about Juan Alfarero and what he was doing here. But so far I'm keeping my head above water."

"You'll be able to hold down the fort over the weekend?"

"I'm sure. I'll have Lili for support. And if anything breaks I'll just jury-rig it until you come back on Monday."

"That's not very reassuring," he said with a laugh.

He started packing up to go home, and I returned with Rochester to the room Lili and I were sharing, where I settled down with my hacker laptop and Rochester at my feet. I may have exaggerated a little when I told Tony about the legitimacy of my search tools. Yes, most of them were legal, though I may not have paid for subscriptions. And a few others were of murkier status.

It took me a while to get each program going. In some cases I had to update the program, and I was always very careful to do that. I may want to break in somewhere, but I don't want to leave an open door to my own computer.

I wanted to take a deep dive into Juan Alfarero and find out as much as possible as I could about him. Where he was born, educated, and lived. Where he worked and what happened at the places where he did. The artificial intelligence behind these programs was good at teasing out that kind of information. Suppose Juan worked at a theater and while he was there, the police were called because of a theft, an assault, or something else. There might be no formal charges, but the program could put the data together for me in a way I couldn't myself.

I sat back and let the program work. People don't realize how much information is available about them online. Sure, they might Google their name or check the licensing of a medical professional or attorney. They know how to look up property records and sometimes mortgages.

But there's so much more out there, buried in databases on what's called the deep web. Your bank information is locked up in a site that you need password access to. But if someone gets hold of your ID and password, they can dive in and move your money around.

The same is true for insurance companies, credit cards, even your college alumni association. Any site where you need a password is considered part of the deep web.

Now, the deep web isn't the same as the dark web, though sometimes people get them confused. The dark web is where the script kiddies, the hackers, and the criminals hang out and sell or trade information they've gained from forays into the deep web, or programs used to break into them. That's also where pedophiles hide sexual photos.

There is a lot to worry about online. Most people knew about phishing, where someone gets hold of your email address and manipulates you into doing something that compromises your bank account, your credit cards, or some other financial product.

Lately I had been reading about another form of social engineering called pretexting. A criminal creates a fraudulent narrative, a convincing story, to deceive a target. A bad actor pretends to need your help to access a million-dollar bank account, and promises you part of the money for your help. Or someone pretending to be your grandson says he's in trouble and needs you to wire bail money.

Sometimes cybercriminals register domains that appear to belong to official charities, prompting visitors to those sites to input their personal and financial data to make a donation. Maybe there's a spelling difference in the name of the charity, or an extra word added, or a different domain. Someone impersonating the Boy Scouts might grab the domain for boysscouts.com, adding an extra S that most people wouldn't notice.

Corporations were as vulnerable as individuals. I read about a case where a group used LinkedIn to find employees of a company, then called the company IT helpdesk impersonating one of those employees and requesting a password reset. Eastern College had a whole set of steps you had to go through to reset your password, as well as instructions on how to set up unique, hard-to-crack passwords for each of your personal accounts. And never keep them in writing!

That was good advice, in principle. But if you trust everyone you share your home with, then writing your passwords down and keeping them together in one safe place is more secure than reusing weak passwords you have memorized. However, if you have a child in the home with a drug problem, for example, he or she could use your password to empty your bank account.

I was sitting there, staring at the screen without really focusing, when Rochester barked. He was sitting on his haunches right next to me, as if he was looking at the display.

I snapped out of my fugue state. "What's up, boy? Did you hear something?" The program often made a pinging sound when it found a result.

I rubbed his head and then looked at the screen. The program had accessed some records from the City Clerk's office in Manhattan, where it had found Juan Alfarero's name.

Three years before, he had applied for a marriage license. His intended? Yesenia Ubeda Goldstein.

Chapter 19
Awkward Dinner

My phone beeped with an incoming text message from Lili. "Where R U? Dinner about to start."

I looked at my watch. I'd gotten so caught up in computer work that I'd lost track of time. Rochester and I had to hurry over to the refectory, where Deepti was already filming Yesenia's introduction.

"Tonight we're going to share a dinner to celebrate the Jewish Sabbath," Yesenia said, as I walked in. The projector was on, showing the introduction for a PowerPoint. The illustration was of a dinner table, set with fine china and wine glasses, with a pair of silver candlesticks.

"As you know, Dr. Weinstock and I both share Jewish roots, and Shabbat dinner is one of our most hallowed traditions. Families assemble around the table all around the world as evening falls, to welcome the Sabbath queen and share a meal."

Rochester and I settled into a table by the wall.

Yesenia turned to Lili, who stepped up to the podium. "All four of my grandparents were Jews from eastern Europe who fled persecution and pogroms at the turn of the twentieth century."

She popped up a photo I'd never seen, of one of her grandmothers in a Havana kitchen. "My grandmothers learned to use the ingredients available to them to make their traditional dishes, and they also learned about different kinds of produce from their Cuban neighbors."

She smiled. "They didn't observe kosher dietary laws, but they never ate pork, either, which made them a very strange kind of Cubans."

The audience laughed. "My mother and father were both born in Havana, and considered themselves Jubans, or Jewish Cubans." She walked through a number of dishes her mother had made, many of which Lili still prepared.

I'd attended events where she introduced speakers, and where she participated in panel discussions, but I'd never seen her teach a class before. For the most part, she taught hands-on studio art courses in photography, rather than lecture-based ones, but she was a terrific lecturer.

She commanded the room effortlessly, her tall frame moving gracefully between the prep station and the students. Unlike many professors who stayed rooted behind a podium, Lili used the whole space, her photographer's eye evident in how she positioned herself to best demonstrate techniques. Her voice carried clearly without ever rising to a shout, and students found themselves leaning in to catch her words, drawn in by her natural storytelling ability.

I was affected by her examples, the cadence of her speech, and the way she engaged the audience with questions and humor. I had been teaching off and on for twenty years, and I recognized I could learn from watching her.

Lili had brought her own silver candlesticks, which stood on the prep island beside her. "The meal always begins with the blessing of the candles." She lit a match, then illuminated both candles. She put her hands over her face and recited the blessing. Then she put her hands down and said, "Shabbat Shalom."

The audience responded, "Shabbat Shalom," even though some of them probably didn't know what it meant. Rochester woofed in agreement.

"We've already prepared the meal, so without further ado, our catering help will serve everyone, and then we can take questions after the meal," Lili said, and then she joined me at a table with a group of students.

The special guests were gone, so we mingled with the students, and I didn't get a chance to pull Lili aside and tell her what I'd found about Juan and Yesenia. I could barely concentrate on the food, the same meal Lili had often prepared for us at home, because my brain was racing.

Why hadn't Yesenia told us about the marriage license? As far as I could tell, that was as far as she and Juan had gone. There was no record online of an actual marriage, nor had she added Alfarero to her name anywhere.

Lili carried on a spirited conversation with the students at our table, and I answered when necessary. Rochester kept nuzzling me to remind me to give him some chicken.

Finally the catering students cleared the plates and Lili stepped up to the prep island again, with Yesenia beside her. "We have slices of a honey cake for you, and Dr. Ubeda and I can answer any questions."

I had a question, all right, but I couldn't ask it in front of the students. Fortunately Maria had one.

"How did your families reconcile Jewish dietary restrictions with Cuban cuisine? In my family, you weren't considered Cuban if you didn't eat at least three different cuts of pork."

"It required creativity," Lili said. "Fortunately, Jews in Eastern Europe were accustomed to food shortages and substitutions. My mother found many different ways to serve chicken, for example."

Rochester must have recognized the word chicken, because he nuzzled my leg. "Sorry, nothing more for you, puppy," I said.

"The same is true for traditional holiday foods," Yesenia added. "Potatoes are not in season in the winter in Cuba, so we made our Hanukkah latkes with malanga. On Purim, hamantaschen are made with a guava filling rather than the typical poppy seed, prune, apricot, or raspberry."

They answered a few more questions, we ate our cake, and then finally the students left. I waited until the catering students had cleared the tables and loaded the dishwasher, and Deepti had taken down her equipment. Finally it was just me, Rochester, Lili, and Yesenia in the refectory.

I would have rather spoken to Lili privately and then approached Yesenia, but the clock was ticking on Juan's murder and we needed to know the truth. I decided to start carefully.

"You mentioned recognizing something familiar about Juan," I said to Yesenia. "Was it just his accent, or was there more?"

She shifted in her chair. "His manner of speaking, perhaps. Many Cubans from Cienfuegos have a similar way of expressing themselves."

"And you've spent time in Cienfuegos?" I asked, watching her face.

"For research, yes. The Spanish influence is very strong there." She lifted her chin slightly. "Why are you asking about this now?"

I glanced at Lili, who was watching us both intently. "You know, it's interesting - Juan registered under a false name. That suggests he knew you would recognize his real one."

Yesenia's fingers tightened around her coffee cup. "I meet many people in my work."

"You knew Juan Alfarero before the program," I said finally, and watched the color drain from her face. "You registered for a marriage license with him. I found that online."

Lili gasped.

Yesenia cocked her head. "Marriage license? ¡Dios mío! I never did."

"Maybe you should explain more about your connection to him," I said, and I pointed toward a table. She and I sat down, while Lili moved to make us cups of café con leche. Rochester settled himself beside Yesenia.

While the bean grinder worked, Yesenia composed herself. "This is a difficult story. I'd rather wait until we have the coffee."

"That's fine," I said. "Take all the time you need."

After a couple of minutes, Lili brought us big mugs of steaming coffee, mine sweetened with chocolate powder as I liked. Both Lili and Yesenia took their coffee black and strong.

"*Ase cinco años*, I got an email from a guy named Juan," Yesenia began. "He was a fan of my work, and wanted to get to know me better. He wrote a lovely letter about the food his mother cooked when he was growing up in Cienfuegos, and I answered."

Lili and I looked at each other, but neither of us said anything.

"We started a regular correspondence," Yesenia said. "I was doing a lot of traveling, so it was hard for us to find a time to meet." She looked down at the table, then back up. "After about two months of email, we agreed to meet for coffee."

She smiled. "I'm not a total fool. He sent me his photo and I knew that he was a stagehand on Broadway. We met at a Starbucks one evening before he had to be at work."

She looked at Lili. "You didn't get a chance to talk to him, but he could be very charming. And his accent reminded me of people I knew in Cuba, people who had been kind to me."

Rochester sat up and rested his head on her leg, and she stroked his fur.

"*Era guapo*," Lili said. "I can see how he'd charm you."

"And he did. Because of his work schedule, and mine, it was hard to get together too often, but we started to date, first for lunches, then on Sunday night and Monday when his theater was dark."

"I'm confused about something," I said. "You said there was a demonstration when you spoke at the New School, and police records show that Juan was arrested then. Didn't you see him?"

She shook her head. "He must have been careful to stay out of my line of sight. But gradually, he wanted to talk about Cuba more and more, not about us. He tried to convince me that I was wrong to engage with the Castros, and I tried to present my view."

She sighed. "My parents always wanted me to marry an educated man, even more than a Jew. They said if I was smarter than my husband the marriage wouldn't last." She wrapped her hands around her arms. "I understood what they meant after a lot of arguments with Juan. One of the things I think education gives you is the ability to carry two competing beliefs in your head."

"Like supporting Castro is wrong, but believing in the Cuban people is right," Lili said.

"Exactly. And that's what Juan couldn't grasp. He had one narrow view. Admittedly, his family came out of the revolution much worse than mine did. My father was a doctor, and he went to a medical convention in Florida and got a hospital job while he was there."

She looked at me. "Back then, they didn't have all the restrictions they have now on foreign-trained doctors. If you had an MD, they gave you a white coat and a job. So he was able to bring my family here, and we had almost as good a life in New York as we had in Cuba."

Rochester gave up being petted and settled down on the floor.

"How did Juan come here?" Lili asked.

"He was a *balsero*," Yesenia said. She turned to me. "Thousands of people wanted to leave Cuba after Castro took over. Families that had money were able to get out relatively easily, like Lili's family and mine. For the poor, it was much more difficult. Visas and airfare were expensive. But the Cuban people are accustomed to being inventive."

She sipped her coffee. "There was a period in the early 1990s when people got very inventive about building rafts, called balsas. Thousands of people made rafts out of old car parts, tree trunks, and palm fronds. As people learned the US was admitting the rafters as refugees, they even started hijacking boats."

"Thousands of people died trying to make that crossing," Lili said. "One of our next-door neighbors in Havana died of dehydration, and another woman I know barely survived."

"It was a terrible time," Yesenia said. "Castro tried to crack down on the rafters, but there were big protests, and finally in 1994 he announced that anyone who wanted to leave could do so. Juan told me that he got out on one of the boats then."

"Over thirty-thousand people left from all parts of the island," Lili said. "Some washed up on the beaches in Key West and Miami, and if they were lucky, people helped them avoid the police and connect with families and friends who were here."

"Juan was sent to the US Naval Base at Guantánamo Bay, where he stayed until he was finally admitted a year later. While he was there, he met a guy who had family in New York, and he followed his friend to the city. His friend's cousin got him a job as a stagehand."

"What about his family?" Lili asked.

"His father owned a shoe store, and they were well-off. But he died when Juan was a boy and the store was confiscated by the state. Juan blamed Castro for destroying his family. His mother was never well, and the stress of raising four kids in poverty made her sick all the time. She was glad to see him go because she thought he'd have better opportunities in the US. One of his sisters died after he left, a car accident, I think. The other two ended up in Miami. He said something about wanting to get to know his nieces and nephews but his sisters didn't agree with his politics so they were estranged."

"Let's get back to the two of you dating," I said. "What happened? Did he propose?"

She shook her head. "I had no idea he ever registered for a marriage license. He must have forged my signature."

"Were you still seeing him?" I asked.

"No, no. A little over three years ago, I was invited to go to Cuba and give a talk about food traditions, and I would have the opportunity to visit a lot of local cooks and get recipes. Juan was very opposed to my going, and I told him that if he couldn't accept our difference of opinion, we were done."

"How did he react?" Lili asked.

"He ghosted me. And honestly, I was glad. I was ready to move on and didn't want a lot of arguments."

"Did you recognize him when he showed up here?" I asked.

"I thought he looked familiar," she said. "But the beard was new, and it confused me. Then I was on stage talking and cooking, so I didn't think about him. Then he jumped up and started yelling, and threw his plate at me, and then he ran out."

"Is that the last time you saw him?"

She looked at me. "You think I tracked him down and killed him?"

"Your knife was the murder weapon," I said.

The color drained from Yesenia's face. Her hand flew to her mouth. "No," she whispered. "*No es posible.*"

She rushed to the prep island where her knife roll rested, her trembling fingers fumbling with the ties. She unrolled it quickly, counting her knives. "*¡Dios mío!*" she said, her voice breaking. "It's gone."

The one with the distinctive carved handle - her favorite for demonstrations - was missing from its usual spot.

Rochester pressed against her leg as she sank into a chair, but she barely seemed to notice him. Her eyes were wide with shock as the implications sank in. Not only had Juan been killed, but someone had used her own knife to do it.

Chapter 20
Damage Control

"When you spoke to Detective Rinaldi last night did he ask you anything about your knives?" I asked.

She shook her head.

"He's going to find out tomorrow," I said.

She returned to the table and put her head in her hands. "*Que horrible*," she said. "I'm embarrassed about what happened with Juan, but I never wanted to see him dead. And now the police will suspect me!"

"It's all right, *mija*," Lili said, stroking Yesenia's arm. "Steve and I will be here for you."

Lili walked Yesenia back to her room, and I took Rochester around the grounds. He stopped beside the door of the dormitory and sniffed the base of a rhododendron bush and then looked up at me and barked. Then he sat on his butt.

It was the same behavior he'd demonstrated when he found the knife. It was his signal that there was something he wanted me to look at. I looked down but didn't see anything, so I squatted down to his level. There, caught in the bush between branches was a plastic card. I used a tissue from my pocket to extract it.

It was a library card from a facility in a Virginia suburb of Washington, DC. I figured one of the visitors to Friar Lake had dropped it in the past, and wondered why Rochester wanted me to pick it up. "You on trash collection detail now, boy?" I asked.

I slid the card in the pocket of my coat and stood up. "Let's get back to the room. It's cold out here."

When we returned to our room, Lili was there. "What are we going to do about discovering the knife belonged to Yesenia?" she asked.

"I already told Tony Rinaldi that I recognized the knife. And it looks like she has a very strong motive to kill Juan."

Lili put her hands on her hips "Over an outburst at dinner?"

"Not just that. But they dated, Lili. And they broke up over political differences. You know yourself that she's a very passionate woman when it comes to Cuba. Juan was probably just as passionate on the other side of the issue. Maybe all that boiled up when they saw each other again."

"I can't believe she would kill someone."

"She ran out of the refectory right after Juan did. So she had means, motive and opportunity. Tony's a good cop, so I don't think he'll railroad her. But you've got to admit the stars are aligning against her."

"Then we have to do something. Can't you do more searching online? Find someone else who had all those things?"

"I can try."

Rochester jumped up on the bed and looked at both of us. "But I'm tired, and I'm sure you are, too. We'll sleep on it and get started in the morning."

Lili used the bathroom first. I tried to remember a time when we'd had a strong disagreement, and couldn't recall one. We were usually on the same page with major decisions, and it was easy for one of us to convert the other on small ones.

Yes, it was time to have the inside of the townhouse painted. Yes, we'd stay in an elegant hotel in El Salvador when we went there for Talia's wedding, and make the trip into an additional honeymoon.

If I wanted Italian for dinner and she wanted Mexican, we compromised. We'd go to Tequila Mockingbird first, and then Pasta La Vista the next night. If she wanted new blue towels for the guest bathroom, I didn't have an opinion.

But thinking about her friend as a murderer? There we were of two different minds. I wasn't ready to close the book on Yesenia, but the evidence against her was mounting up. Lili knew her better and was entitled to her doubts, but as I reminded myself they weren't best friends, and had hardly spent much time together since they met. It was more a case of an instant connection.

My loyalty was to Lili. If her friend was a murderer, then I had to protect my wife. And if her friend was innocent, then I'd do what I could to prove that.

Saturday morning I woke early, took Rochester for his walk, and opened the refectory for a delivery of breakfast foods from Eastern's kitchen. Muffins, croissants, cereal, yogurt and fruit were laid out on the prep table Yesenia lectured from, and I got our big coffee maker going, along with hot water for tea or cocoa. Lili arrived to grind her beans for café con leche.

Students began filtering in around eight-thirty, grabbing their food and settling at tables to chat. I picked up a copy of the class handout and looked at the agenda for the morning.

Lili and Yesenia had designed a game they called Test Your Taste Buds. They had selected twenty items, from sweet to salty to spicy. Each student would come up, be blindfolded, and then given five of the items at random to identify. After a winner was crowned, Yesenia would lecture about the origins of the ingredients and their uses.

Lili came into the refectory a few minutes before nine and came right over to me. "Yesenia is going to talk to Tony Rinaldi this morning, and she doesn't think she'll be up to running the contest. I said you and I would take care of it for her."

"I don't have to taste things, do I? You know I don't have much of a palate."

"No, the students will do the tastings. You'll just be my little helper." She smiled.

I leaned over and kissed her cheek. "Anything for you, *mi amor*," I said.

While a group of students fawned over Rochester, I helped Lili set up the challenge. As she fed an item to the taster, I held up a card with the item identified, so students could laugh and play along as the tasters made outrageous guesses.

That took over an hour and a half, and then students had a break. "Can you do the lecture part?" I asked Lili.

"Yesenia gave me her PowerPoint. I'll follow along with it."

My wife was a champ, of course. She kept the students engaged for an hour, adding her own off-the-cuff stories about the foods. "My family lived in Mexico City for two years after we left Cuba," she said. "And then we moved to Kansas City. I remember taking my little brother into an ice cream shop and he wanted guanábana, and the girl behind the counter had no idea what we were talking about. She said they didn't make ice cream out of iguanas and bananas!"

The audience laughed, and Lili told another story I'd heard before, about a neighbor who thought her mother's kitchen was spick-and-span. "My mother only heard the word 'spic' which she knew was negative, of course. I had to have my second-grade teacher write an explanation for her."

When I was growing up, occasionally I heard stories from my elderly relatives about discrimination they'd experienced in the US. But hearing Lili's stories reminded me that such discrimination still existed. There had been complaints muttered around Stewart's Crossing, for example, when a Thai couple took over the Italian sub shop in the center of town. I'd been fortunate to experience very little of that myself, though occasionally I'd found myself the only Jew in the room, explaining why some of us wore skullcaps and others didn't.

I ducked out of Lili's lecture a few minutes before it ended to accept the delivery of sandwiches for lunch. I signed for them and carried the platters into the refectory. On my way back to the classroom in the infirmary, I spotted Tony Rinaldi in the parking lot and went up to him.

"How's it going?" I asked.

"The knife was wiped clean of fingerprints, but Dr. Ubeda confirmed it belonged to her."

"There were at least a half-dozen people out of the room between the time of Juan's outburst and the discovery of his body," I said. "Have you spoken to each of them and gotten their whereabouts?"

"I have. And none of them have anyone to back them up, except Bradley and Claudia, who say they were together."

"Would you be comfortable sharing those names with me? Then I can do some research for connections?"

"I already thought of that. Here's a list." He opened his notebook and tore out a page. He handed it to me. Several of those on it were special students, but others were Eastern college kids.

"Did Yesenia tell you about her relationship with Juan Alfarero?"

"That they dated?"

I nodded. "He felt more strongly about her than she did about him, because he applied for a marriage license for the two of them."

"She mentioned that, but said she didn't know about it until you questioned her. Why didn't you tell me first?"

"It was her story to tell," I said. "If she hadn't told you this morning I was going to."

"In the future, when you learn something about a suspect, I'd like to hear it first."

Though the words were pleasant enough, there was iron in his voice. I'd gotten too used to working with Rick Stemper, who tolerated my amateur sleuthing because we were friends and because I often turned up useful information. But Tony was different - more by-the-book, and rightfully protective of his investigation. The kind of detective who believed in proper procedure rather than hunches from civilians and their dogs.

"Absolutely." I held up the sheet of names. "I'll do some digging and see what kind of connections I can make."

I couldn't do that until after lunch, though. Today's sandwiches were from a shop in Leighville, ordinary American ones with turkey, roast beef, and tuna salad, along with chips and drinks. It was important for me to be there, to support Lili and help create an atmosphere that would stay focused on the course, not on the crime.

I was worried about the cost of all the food. We'd budgeted everything based on the tuition revenue we were bringing in, and I had a small profit margin, in case of unexpected expenses. But what if Yesenia was arrested and we had to cancel the class, and refund the tuition money? It would destroy my budget and put Friar Lake deeply in the hole for the rest of the year.

If Yesenia was guilty, maybe it would take Tony a month to prove that.

But I wasn't counting on it. I had to hope that she was innocent, and that I could salvage the program, Friar Lake's budget, and the reputation of the intersession.

Chapter 21
Library Card

As Lili and I sat down with the students to eat our sandwiches, I saw Yesenia at the next table. She seemed awkward and brittle, taking extra time to answer questions. I understood how she might feel. A man she had dated had been killed only a day before, and Tony Rinaldi had questioned her that morning. I'd been shaken, and I'd only met the man briefly.

We watched her for a moment, and then Lili said, "Yesenia says she can handle the afternoon session, but I'm going to stay with her. I'm afraid if someone asks the wrong question she could break down again. She's that close."

So Lili sensed it too. That was good. I didn't want to admit my mixed feelings, though. If Yesenia had killed Juan, then she ought to be upset, and on the brink of collapse. A breakdown could lead to a confession.

But if she was innocent, then she was in bad shape and deserved our sympathy. The only way to get around my conundrum was to jump back into research. When the students finished their lunch, Yesenia and Lili led them back to the classroom to continue. The catering students would be back that afternoon, but I didn't want to leave a mess for them, so I packed up a big black trash bag with paper plates, plastic silverware, and chip bags. When I could I gave Rochester bits of leftover food, but not too much.

After I finished, I took Rochester for a walk around Friar Lake and then back past the parking lot. As he trotted beside me, I saw he was confused. Why weren't we going home? Would we ever?

It wasn't like it had been on our honeymoon, when we all got in the car and drove hours to Vermont. Rochester could tell the difference between a house and a hotel, so he knew that eventually we'd return to Stewart's Crossing. But this was the first time all three of us had stayed over at Friar Lake. Even though we brought some of his toys, every time we passed my car I could tell he was straining to go home.

Joey and Mark were going to be staying at Friar Lake with the special students each night until the weekend, when Lili and I would take over again. "We're going home tomorrow night, puppy," I said to him. "Hold out another day, all right?"

He gave one last tug toward the parking lot, then followed me into the office. He slumped down by the wall in the office as I took off my coat.

The plastic library card Rochester had found fell out of my pocket as I hung the coat up. I looked at it more closely in the light and recognized the face on it. It was Ken Gould, but the name on the card was Richard Givens.

"Well, that's weird," I said. "Why would Ken have a library card in another name?"

I got out my hacker laptop and typed in Richard Givens, and set the search program going. Then I looked at the list of potential suspects Tony had given me.

Maria Cabrera had gone after Yesenia, to comfort her, but hadn't been able to find her. She'd ended up back at her room to use the bathroom, where she had met up with Raquel Jaceldo. Then they returned to the refectory together.

I'd already seen that Claudia, our theater student, had outsized emotions, probably accustomed to emoting on stages, and she had jumped up and run away, followed by Bradley, who had attached himself to her. Bobby had gotten up a moment later, and I wondered if he was vying with Bradley for Claudia's attention. Ken Gould had followed Bobby but said he stayed around the front door, getting fresh air. Neither of them had seen the other.

Dan Lazerow had gone after Juan but had been unable to find him. He'd been on his own while he searched.

That left eight people out of the refectory during the time that Juan had been stabbed. Though I wanted to eliminate Dan immediately, because he was the head of campus security, I had to be methodical. I added his name to Yesenia's and those of the six students.

All eight needed consideration. Dan Lazerow had no obvious connection to Juan, but could he have some ulterior motive for disrupting the intersession? Some faculty members opposed the program - could Dan be working with them?

Yesenia and Juan had dated until they clashed over Cuban politics. Claudia had been involved with him during her theater internship, though she claimed the compromising photos he took didn't bother her.

Bobby Cruz was Cuban-American, from Miami's tight-knit émigré community. Maria and Raquel were both active in Cuban exile politics and fervent supporters of Yesenia.

Ken Gould remained a mystery - his story about working remotely didn't quite add up. And Bradley had followed Claudia out, but was he concerned about her, or did he have his own agenda?

I plugged all the names into a series of programs and let them work while I continued to think.

Past statistical research had indicated that men committed ninety percent of murders in the United States, and that guns were their weapon of choice. As for women, they used guns as well, but their second choice was the knife. Beating the victim, or striking with a blunt object, came next, then poison.

The medical examiner would be able to tell Tony things like the angle that the knife entered Juan's body, and what that implied for the relative height of assailant and victim. Juan had run out of the refectory without his coat, so the knife only had to penetrate his shirt before reaching his skin.

I grabbed a pen in my right hand and practiced swinging it up and into someone's chest. Rochester didn't like that; he jumped up and started barking at me. I stopped, but it made me realize that a killer would need a lot of force, as well as a very sharp knife.

If Yesenia was anything like the chefs Lili and I watched on TV competitions, she probably kept hers sharp, both at the point and on the blade. I saw how easily she sliced through the malanga root at her demonstration.

The killer was probably frenzied, which would add to his or her strength. This was a crime of passion, of opportunity, rather than one that had been planned in advance. It was possible that the killer had arrived at Friar Lake planning to kill Juan, but I doubted that. He'd registered under a false name, and even his ex-girlfriend didn't know he would be there.

The killer saw Juan leave on his own, and in the hubbub that followed the killer grabbed the knife from the counter and went after him.

It was likely that the killer had a previous connection to Juan. You didn't generate that kind of anger on the first day of a program. Even if Juan had said shoved another student, or said something nasty, that wouldn't be enough to strike out so quickly. That kind of anger needs to bubble up and burn.

Did that eliminate Bradley? He wasn't Cuban and he was from Pittsburgh, which made it less likely he'd have encountered Juan somewhere.

I looked over at my laptop. All the programs were up and running, and it was late afternoon. As I waited for results, I glanced out the window and spotted Ken Gould walking along the perimeter of the property. He had his phone out and appeared to be taking photos - not of the historic buildings or the scenic view, but of the access roads and the security cameras.

Rochester raised his head and growled softly. In all our time together, I'd learned to trust his instincts about people. And right now, those instincts were telling me that Ken Gould wasn't just here to learn about Cuban cooking.

Chapter 22
By Any Other Name

I roused Rochester and walked back to the refectory to see if the catering students had arrived, and found Max Abraham there, working at a laptop. "I don't want to waste time driving to Potter's Harbor and back before dinner," he said. "I thought I'd hang around here."

"You can go to the library if you like," I said. "The wi-fi works all over the property."

"I'm more likely to doze off there," he said with a smile. "I didn't get much sleep last night before I had to get up and start baking."

"This must be tough for you," I said. "Keeping up your day job and coming up here."

"It'll be easier during the week," he said. "Fewer customers at the café means less baking, my husband can keep things humming during the day, and I'll be able to leave here as soon as class ends in the afternoon since there won't be evening dinners. I'm eager to expand my repertoire of Caribbean pastries. Something different to offer the customers."

I sat across from him. "You said you recognized Juan from a theater where you worked. Did you know him well?"

"I suppose so. I only had a small part so I was backstage a lot, and we talked now and then."

"What can you tell me about him?"

"He had a quick temper, I'll tell you that. Any time anything went wrong, he was quick to blame someone else, and start yelling. But he could also be very charming. He set his sights on one of the actresses and he was always chatting her up. She was in her early twenties, new in New York, and he volunteered to show her the city. There was a buzz around them, but then the show closed and I doubt they kept in touch."

"Anything else? I understand he was passionate about Cuba."

"I'd say politics in general. But maybe he was focused on Cuba and I didn't catch that. He talked about immigration, for example, how the US needed to open its borders more. Apparently it was very difficult for his sisters to come to this country, and that drove a wedge between him and them. And he was fervently anti-Communist."

Yesenia and Lili came in to start dinner, and Max offered to help with prep. He did some rinsing and chopping while the chefs laid out their tools and ingredients.

The catering students arrived as I was emptying the dishwasher, and they set the tables and put out bottles of wine and fresh-baked rolls that arrived from a bakery in Leighville.

"You guys are really cooking up a storm," I said to Lili when she took a break.

"When Yesenia and I put together the budget and the syllabus I didn't realize we would be catering so many big meals," she said. "During the week at home we're eating take-out or at restaurants. Thank God the dining service will be open during the week so everyone can eat their meals there."

Dinner went smoothly. Yesenia did less on-screen cooking, mostly talking about methods and ingredients while everything simmered or stewed in the background. "Cubans say that their cuisine provides a very large part of their cultural identity," she said. "For me, growing up in a Cuban household, aromas of garlic soup, roasted red peppers, spicy picadillo, flaky empanadas, fruity *batidos* and luscious baked flan are some of my earliest and most pleasurable food memories."

She seemed less brittle than she had been earlier in the day, but maybe she'd taken something to calm down. There was less energy in her speech than there had been.

"The first documented introduction of pigs into the Americas was during Columbus' second voyage in 1493 where he released pigs on to several Caribbean islands. More expeditions brought more pigs and often intentionally left them behind so there would be food sources for future expeditions. By the mid-1500s, there were so many pigs in Cuba that explorers picked them up to carry to other islands. And now, Cubans love pork, which can be roasted, fried, or sliced up and served in sandwiches."

She looked up at the students. "Who can tell me some of the most common pork dishes?"

Students fired terms at Yesenia and she returned quick descriptions for the benefit of the rest of the class. Bobby Cruz said his mother made a great lechon asado, roasted in her homemade mojo sauce. Raquel Jaceldo loved croquetas with Spanish ham, while Maria Cabrera was a fan of Jamon Serrano, a Spanish-style slow aged ham made from a pig's hind leg. Ken Gould loved chorizo, a smoky, deep red Spanish sausage, and several of the college students ate pork rinds.

It was fun to watch, and I could see Yesenia interacting with a live audience at a Food Network broadcast. Dinner was delicious, as expected, and after a dessert of a three-milk pudding called tres leches, everyone was full and groaning. I was happy to let the catering students clean up and lock up.

Rochester and I went for a quick walk and then met Lili back at the room. I was eager to see what my hacker programs had brought up.

There was a lot of information on Richard Givens, the name on the library card with Ken Gould's face, but I couldn't match any of the faces that showed up to his. I went back to my notes and saw that Ken had left the refectory after Juan Alfarero's outburst. I decided to have a chat with him the next day and see if I could learn anything more about his background, and a possible connection to Juan or Cuban exile politics.

I wasn't surprised that there was little to find online about Dan Lazerow. Because of his police and security background, he was smart enough to keep his information safe. Good for him, though it made it harder to see if he had any previous connection to Juan Alfarero.

There also wasn't much we didn't already know about Yesenia. Everything my programs found was from public information such as her biography, her teaching vita, and her trips to the island.

I found one curious connection between Claudia Monson and Juan Alfarero. The previous summer, she had a dramatic internship at a theater where he worked. It wasn't much of a tie, but it was something that Tony would have to explore.

Because Bobby Cruz had come to the United States as a refugee, his family paperwork was in an immigrant database that wasn't as secured as it should have been. His full name in the Spanish style was Roberto Desiderio Cruz Alfarero, and his mother, who had accompanied him, was Lucia Elena Alfarero Rienda de Cruz.

Lili had to help me figure out those names. "It's simple," she said. "Roberto is his first name, and Desiderio his middle name."

"Like Desi Arnaz," I said.

"Exactly. And his last name is Cruz, and his paternal grandfather's last name is Alfarero."

"Or his mother's maiden name."

"If you want to get all American on it, yes."

I sat back. "I knew a couple of very radical feminists when I lived in California. It was fun to ask 'The last name you use. Is that your father's or your husband's?'"

"I'll bet that went over well."

"Not exactly. One woman I worked with had changed her name

twice. She was born as Jill Freeman, but in college she changed it to Jill Freewoman. Then again later she became Jill Freeperson. But eventually she realized that was putting her politics in her name, and she was having trouble getting promoted, so she shortened it to Jill Free."

"And did she get the promotion?"

"She did. Now a senior VP in Silicon Valley."

"So Shakespeare was wrong," Lili said. "A rose by any other name doesn't smell as sweet."

"Not if you're trying to avoid a murder charge," I said.

Suddenly I made the connection. "Juan Alfarero," I said. "A relative? Is it that common a name?"

I did a quick Google search. There were over two million people worldwide with that last name, most of them from the Philippines, Venezuela and Peru. Not Cuba, but it was clearly a name of Spanish origin, and lots of Spanish people had moved to the island.

"You'll have to tell Tony Rinaldi," Lili said. "I didn't notice Bobby connecting with Juan at all, did you?"

I shook my head. "But they only met at dinner, and clearly Juan had more on his mind."

"And Yesenia said that she didn't recognize Juan at first because of his beard. Maybe the same was true for Bobby."

"If they're actually related," I said. "We don't know that for certain."

Rochester came over to us then, but instead of begging for a treat, he sat at attention, staring at the window. A moment later, a shadow moved past the security light.

"Probably just a student," Lili said, but she didn't sound convinced.

Rochester's low growl suggested that whoever was out there in the dark wasn't just taking a casual evening stroll. And given what we'd learned about our suspects, I had a feeling things were about to get much worse.

Chapter 23
Past Connections

Sunday morning, Rochester roused me early and we went outside. A chilly wind swept through Friar Lake and I was eager to get back to the room, but Rochester kept nosing around, eventually leading me to the chapel. We had left many of the original features of the building, including a depiction of Christ on the cross on the side wall.

Rochester plopped his butt in front of the raised image and barked. "I have no idea what you want, dog," I said. "It's cold, and we're Jewish. Yes, it's Sunday morning and if this property were still an abbey, the monks would be coming to the chapel to worship."

He looked at me and barked again, and then he moved up close to the wall and sniffed the bottom of the cross. I couldn't imagine what he wanted, but for fun I made the sign of the cross over my body, as I had learned from Christian classmates in elementary school.

Rochester barked again, and nosed my hand. "Something about the cross?" I asked him.

He barked enthusiastically and circled around me, then took off back to the dormitory.

"The cross," I said, as I followed him. "Cross-stitch. Crossword puzzle. Southern Cross. Cruz del sur."

It hit me as I reached the front door. "Bobby Cruz," I said. "Are you trying to tell me something about him?"

But Rochester was already inside, waiting at the door to the room the three of us were sharing.

I poured some chow in his bowl and refreshed his water as Lili slept. Then I opened my hacker laptop and went back to the report on Bobby Cruz.

We'd discovered the night before that he had Alfarero in his name. It was a big jump, but did that mean he was related somehow to Juan?

Lili woke up. "You're at the computer early," she said. "You haven't even had coffee yet, have you?"

"No, but Rochester was trying to tell me something when we were walking," I said. "Last night we were talking about names. Bobby Cruz's mother's name is Lucia Elena Alfarero Rienda de Cruz. Does that mean her maiden name was Alfarero?"

"It does. But it could be a common name, though I don't know that I've ever heard of someone named that." She sat up. "Hand me my laptop, will you?"

I did, and as I stared at my own screen, she opened hers and started typing. I wasn't coming up with anything.

"In his application he mentioned that he had an uncle in New York, but that when he and his mom came to Miami the uncle wouldn't help him," Lili said.

"Uncle Juan?" I went back to my program that looked for connections between people and typed in as much as I could about Juan Alfarero and Lucia Cruz. It only took the program a few minutes to tell me that when Lucia Cruz arrived in the United States, she cited her older brother Juan Alfarero as a permanent resident of New York, with a green card. She gave his work address as a theater on West 42nd Street in Manhattan.

"Wow," I said. I was impressed at the program's ability as well as the connection we might never have made ourselves. "Do you think Bobby knew Juan was going to be here?"

"That's something Tony is going to have to ask him, don't you think?"

"I do." I sent a text message to Tony with the information and that he ought to talk to Claudia Monson as well about the time she had been in contact with Juan in New York. He replied quickly that he was getting ready to take the family to church, and would come by Friar Lake later.

The three of us went to the refectory, where I accepted another delivery of breakfast pastries, which of course made Rochester very curious. I set up the coffee maker while Lili boiled water for tea and cocoa and made her special Cuban coffee, and eventually the students began to filter in.

When I saw Ken Gould, I grabbed my cup of hot chocolate and stood next to him in the line to grab pastries. "How's the Wi-Fi holding up for you?" I asked.

He looked confused for a moment, then said, "Oh, yeah, it's fine. I'll really need it starting tomorrow when I need to be able to answer emails and work on projects."

"You said something when you got here about shipping software," I said. "I used to work for a software company back in California. You must be at a pretty high level to allow you to work remotely."

He shrugged. "Who knows? Maybe they don't want me in the office."

He flashed a smile that seemed false to me, which only made me want to dig more. "You came here from Virginia, didn't you?"

He put a piece of raspberry Danish on his plate and turned to me. "I was there for a while because my dad wasn't well, and I wanted to keep an eye on him. But he passed a couple of months ago, so now I'm visiting family and friends and doing some house-sitting." He smiled. "I'm great at watering plants."

He picked up the Danish and took a bite. "This is delicious. Catch you later."

He took his plate over to sit next to Claudia Monson. I didn't feel that I knew much more about him, and that was the way he wanted it.

I looked around the room. I thought about talking to Bobby, but he was laughing at that table of students with Claudia and Ken and I didn't want to bother him. I'd let Tony handle the conversation about his uncle. If he didn't know that he was related to the dead man, he might be sad that he'd missed the opportunity to connect.

Or maybe he knew exactly who Juan was, and held a grudge on behalf of his mom and Juan's other sisters. Tony had already cautioned me once about gathering facts before he could, and I didn't want to anger him.

Everyone was there except Deepti, and I wondered if she was a late sleeper or catching up on her other work when she didn't need to be filming Yesenia. Eventually she did come in, but she grabbed a plate of pastries and a mug of coffee and returned to wherever she was working.

Yesenia and Lili had designed another research assignment for Sunday morning, one they could do quickly and then have much of the day to relax. We had a bus coming late in the morning to return the Eastern students to campus, and the special students would have the afternoon to themselves, with dinner either on their own or at the campus dining hall.

As they finished eating, the students dispersed out of the refectory. I noticed that Ken had attached himself to Claudia and her friends, and wondered if it was so that I couldn't catch him and ask more questions.

Lili went to the library to do some work of her own and help Yesenia supervise the students. I cleaned up the refectory, tossing the paper plates and plastic utensils, and I put the coffee mugs and other stuff into the dishwasher and turned it on. The students had picked the serving trays clean so I left them for the restaurant to pick them up later.

Someone had tried to drop a piece of lined paper in the big

plastic trash can and missed, and I only found it when I pulled the can away from the wall. Rochester was very interested in it. "What's up, puppy? Someone spill food there?"

I nudged him away and picked it up. There was nothing interesting there—just some scribbled class notes and a list of products that could be written about for the class paper, including tamarind, a sweet and sour fruit that Lili liked in candy, and a few others. The last item on the bottom, with a question mark, was tobacco.

It wasn't an edible, but it certainly had a connection to Cuban culture. I wondered if whoever had written it knew about the box of cigars we'd found in the wall, and that made me consider the documents Yesenia had identified. We only had her word for what they were. Could she have manufactured a story about that land grant to her family? Maybe the papers were something else entirely, but they had given her the idea of forging something in the future to use as leverage against the Castros?

It was a wild idea, but I'd learned in my dealings with Rochester that I had to trust his nose. I tossed the paper in the trash, but kept the idea in the back of my head. I'd talk about it later with Lili, and perhaps we could get Yesenia to show Lili the papers from the cigar chest and see how she might translate them.

Rochester and I went back to my office, where he snoozed in his favorite sunny spot against the wall. Tony arrived around eleven, in a pair of dressy black slacks and a white shirt under his parka. It looked like he'd dropped his family off at home and come over after his church attendance.

"Anything new?" he asked.

"Just the stuff I texted you about this morning," I said. "Claudia Monson and Bobby Cruz."

"Know where I can find them?"

"Probably at the library. They have an assignment to work on this morning."

About twenty minutes later, he was back in my office, where I was trying to get a head start on the week's paperwork so I could spend time on campus for the classroom portions of the program.

"He says he never met the uncle, and had no idea he was here," Tony said. "I'm not sure I believe him, but he swears his mother and her brother were not in contact, and that there was no picture of Alfarero in their house other than a single family portrait when he was about twelve."

"He's a smart kid, and like almost every college student he can use the internet. There's a possibility that he tracked Alfarero down. But Alfarero registered under a fake name, so it's doubtful Bobby could have known he'd be here. If there's a strong family resemblance, he could have recognized him, but in that case I'd expect him to confront his uncle. Make a scene. But Alfarero's murder happened too soon, and Yesenia said that he had added a beard after she stopped seeing him."

"Shame, because he's got a motive, means and opportunity," Tony said.

"So on to the next suspect," I said. I pulled out the library card I'd found. "Look at this."

He did. "It's a library card. Who's Richard Givens?"

"I don't know. But the photo matches Ken Gould. Rochester found that card outside the dormitory. I looked through my past records and I can't find anyone named Richard Givens who's ever been here overnight."

"So the guy could have been a guest for one of your programs, and lost his library card. That's not a criminal offense."

"But it makes me wonder. Could Gould be here under a fake name, like Juan Alfarero?"

"Didn't you tell me you researched all the special students before they got here?"

"I did. Ken gave us the name of the company he worked for, his address and his email address. I didn't find much information about him online, but his name is a pretty common one."

Tony's expression hardened. "Steve, we've talked about this. I appreciate your help with background research, but I need you to let me handle the investigation. If you have concrete evidence about Gould - or anyone else - bring it to me. But don't go chasing down theories on your own."

I held up my hands in surrender. "You're right. I need to stay focused on running Friar Lake and supporting the course."

Chapter 24
A Little Rope

"Where can I find Claudia Monson?" Tony asked. "She wasn't in the library."

"I can take you to her room," I said. I checked the roster and saw that she was in the same building Lili and I were. I pulled on my coat and hooked Rochester's leash, and the three of us walked over there.

He knocked on the door. "Miss Monson? Leighville Police. Can I have a word?"

She opened the door in an Eastern T-shirt and sweatpants. "My roommate is working," she said. "Can we go somewhere?"

"You can use my office," I said. We waited for Claudia to get her parka and come out into the hallway, where she stopped to pet Rochester.

Then the four of us walked outside. "This is about Juan, isn't it?" she asked. "I mean, not just about him getting killed. But you figured out I knew him, right?"

I looked at Tony. Neither of us had expected her to come up with that so quickly.

"We know you were part of a drama program at the theater where he worked last summer," Tony said. "Did you know him well?"

She blew out a breath, which turned white in the cold air. "Too well."

We walked in silence to the gatehouse. "I'll wait in the lobby," I said.

"No, you might as well hear this too," Claudia said. "My therapist told me that it's important not to keep secrets, because then they fester inside you."

Therapist. Was Claudia just high-strung, or had something happened with Juan?

Instead of going into my office, which would have made our conversation more formal, we sat on sofas in the lobby, Tony and me on one and Claudia across from us. Rochester sprawled on the floor beside her. We all pulled off our coats—well, all of us except Rochester.

"There were about twenty kids in my theater program in New York last summer," she said. "As you'd expect, mostly girls, and the boys were all gay or just weird. So when Juan started to talk to me, I listened."

Tony handled the interview with the skillful touch of a veteran detective. His posture shifted subtly, becoming less threatening - shoulders relaxing, hands open and visible on the table. He maintained eye contact without staring, giving Claudia space to look away when she needed to collect herself.

Even his note-taking showed practiced expertise - he kept his movements minimal, never letting the notebook become a barrier between them or allowing the scratching of his pen to interrupt her flow of speech. I admired how he created an atmosphere where Claudia felt safe sharing difficult details, while still maintaining the professional distance necessary for a criminal investigation.

"He was kind of good-looking, in a rough way, and he was very charming. I loved his accent, and the stories he told about places where he worked. What the theaters were like, the directors and the actors. We hit it off, even though he was like ten years older than I was."

"More like sixteen," I said. "He lied about his age?"

"I'm sure he lied about more than that," she said. She sighed. "I was stupid, and I agreed to do things with him because he was so persuasive and charming.

"Sexual things?" Tony asked gently.

She pushed a few tendrils of hair behind her right ear. "I didn't mind having sex with him. He was much more knowledgeable than any of the boys I knew in high school or college. It was the pictures. Very strange ones at first. Like he wanted to photograph certain body parts. He never included my face, at least not in the ones he showed me. More like a close-up of a nipple, for example. Or he had me pose on the bed with my fingers opening up my, you know."

"How did you feel about that?" Tony asked. I admired the way he modulated his voice to make it seem like he and Claudia were sharing a confidence. His voice carried just the right note of sympathetic understanding, neither dismissive of her experience nor overly dramatic.

She shrugged. "It is what it is, you know? My program finished and I went home for a few days, then came back to college. I never heard from him again, and I was shocked to see him show up for this course. Though it took me a while to recognize him. He added a beard since last summer, and he lost some weight, too."

"He never threatened you? Tried to blackmail you?" Tony asked.

"For a while I was worried he might. But like I said, he never photographed my face, as far as I knew. And when he had his camera right up close to my boob I knew he couldn't get my face in there. So what was he going to do? Send out some random photos claiming it was my ass or my vajayjay? Who would believe him?"

"Did you talk to him at all?" I asked. "I mean here at Friar Lake."

"No, I didn't see him until we were at dinner, and then it took me a couple of minutes to recognize him from across the room."

"Thank you very much for talking with us," Tony said. "I know this kind of thing is difficult."

"My drama coach says everything that happens to us is grist for the mill," she said. "I had to look that up. But she means we can draw on these experiences in our performances. That's one of the reasons I took this course. In case I ever have to play a chef, or someone who knows about food."

She stood up and put her parka back on. "I hope you find out who killed him. He may have been a kind of jerk but he didn't deserve to die."

She walked out, and a swirl of cold air swept through the open door, chilling me.

"Do you believe her?" Tony asked me. "She seems too cool about everything. I've talked to an unfortunately large number of women who've suffered sexual assaults, and most of them get emotional at some point. A few have built up walls and they try and stay cool, so that may be her case."

I turned toward him. "I don't know. I've been teaching on and off for the last few years, and sometimes I've found students are so desensitized to violence and sexual imagery from what they've grown up seeing that it's hard to get a reaction out of them."

"But this is a nineteen-year-old girl having a much older man take weird photos of her—what did she call it? Her vajayjay? And that didn't bother her at all?"

"It's a term from reality television," I said. "I think it came from one of those housewife shows. And maybe she's been trained to remove herself from situations and play a part."

"I was in the drama club in high school and we never learned anything like that," Tony said. "Most of the time it was about moving around on stage, projecting your voice."

"You were in the drama club?"

"Hey, I have unplumbed depths," he said. "Though I agree with some of what she said. In drama we learned to pay attention to what the other person was saying and react appropriately. You know, if someone told a joke, you should laugh, but only in proportion to how funny the joke was. And if another character was sad, you had to use body language to respond, like touching their arm or nodding."

"Which you do as a detective," I said.

"I'm learning all the time." He looked at me. "So where do we stand with the eight people who were out of the room when Juan Alfarero was stabbed?"

"All of them had the means and the opportunity," I said. "In the confusion after Juan threw the plate at Yesenia, no one noticed anyone pick up her knife and run off with it. And all eight were all out of the room when Juan was stabbed. So that leaves us with motivation."

I started ticking them off on my fingers. "Dan Lazerow has no connection to Alfarero, so no motive. Then we have Bobby Cruz. He says he had no idea Juan was his uncle, and because Juan was estranged from the family, he couldn't have recognized him from a photograph."

"Or so he says. I'm going to call his mother and see what I can find out. She's probably next of kin so I should notify her anyway."

"Good point. I don't know that either of us completely believe Claudia Monson. It's possible she's lying through her teeth, and that she resented Juan for the way he treated her, or that he was after her for more photos, or more sex. She sees him, and during dinner her rage rises up. He runs out, she grabs the knife and goes after him."

"Plausible," Tony said.

"Why don't you ask her for the name of someone who was on the theater program with her? That person might have a different view of her, or what happened last summer." I intoned in a deep voice, "I know what you did last summer."

He grimaced, but made a note. "On it."

I sat back. "Where did she say she was while Juan was being stabbed?"

"She and Bradley alibi each other. She was upset at seeing Juan, so she stepped out to compose herself, and Bradley went with her. They went out the front door of the building, not the rear door that Juan left through. They smoked a joint together so Claudia could calm down."

"Convenient. Then we have Ken Gould," I asked. "What did he say?"

"He had an urgent phone call to return and saw the break as a way to slip out and make the call. He went around the corner of the building so he didn't see Bradley or Claudia. When I pressed him, he admitted that he smelled the marijuana and thought about getting closer to the college students so he could share at some point."

"That makes sense. Then we have the two older Cuban ladies, Maria and Raquel. What did they say when you spoke to them?"

"Raquel said she was worried about Dr. Ubeda and went looking for her, to comfort her. But she couldn't find her, and ended up back at her own room. Maria said that she got some sauce on her dress when she was helping Dr. Ubeda clean up, so she went back to her room to wash. She was there using the blow dryer when Raquel came in."

"Maria has been very protective of Yesenia," I said. "I've noticed that in lectures. Whenever anyone challenges Yesenia, Maria tries to shut them down."

"Motherly instinct?" Tony asked. "Or something more?"

"I read through all Maria's posts to Yesenia's Facebook group. She seems very in favor of engagement with Cubans on the island, and she defends Yesenia when anyone criticizes her. But stabbing someone just because he threw a plate at Yesenia seems over the top."

By then we'd gone through almost everyone. "The last person who was out of the room was Yesenia." Though I didn't want to throw her under the bus, I said, "By using a fake name to register for the course Juan passed under her radar until she saw him at dinner. She was upset by his outburst, and maybe by what happened between them in New York. He threw the first punch, so to speak, so maybe that allowed her to respond."

"To grab the knife and go after him," Tony said. Rochester rose from the floor and moved over to Tony, who petted him. "It doesn't feel like we're eliminating anyone. Any one of these people could have done it, except for Lazerow. And I'm not willing to knock him off the suspect list because he could have some secret past with Alfarero."

"He went to a Broadway show and Juan was rude to him?"

Tony shook his head. "You know what I mean. They're about the same age, and they might have crossed paths in the past. Wasn't Lazerow a cop in New York before he came to Eastern?"

"I think so. But he's very careful about what he puts online. I'll see if I can dig anything more up about him."

Tony stood. "Right now, Dr. Ubeda is my prime suspect. I'm going to give her a little rope, and see if she chooses to hang herself."

Chapter 25
Cry Uncle

After Tony left, Rochester and I stepped outside to clear our heads, and he immediately spotted a porcupine nosing around near the walkway. Before I could grab his collar, he went down on his front paws in a play bow, tail wagging enthusiastically. The porcupine, clearly unimpressed by this invitation to fun, backed up against the chapel wall and flexed his quills like a spiky umbrella opening.

"Not everyone wants to be your friend, puppy," I said, finally getting hold of him. He gave me a look that suggested I was ruining his chance at an exciting new relationship.

Gray clouds clustered overhead and I worried that a snowstorm might be approaching. "This could turn into one of those horror movies, Rochester," I said, as he sniffed the ground. "A bunch of people trapped at a remote location with a killer."

I shivered under my parka. That was too close a scenario for comfort. So I snapped on the dog's leash and we hurried back to our room. Our plan was to sleep at Friar Lake that night, with the special students who were staying there. Monday morning, the Eastern cleaning staff would come in and tidy up all the rooms while everyone was on campus. Then Joey and Mark and Brody would stay over until Saturday morning, when Lili and I would come back.

Lili was sitting on the bed, and Rochester romped over to her for a sniff and a lick. "What have you been up to?" she asked.

"Talking to Tony Rinaldi." I sat on the bed next to her. "Do you think Yesenia could be creating the threats against her to jazz up her social media presence?"

"What makes you say that?"

"It's something I've been thinking about with Tony. We have only her word for the two threats against her, the one in the room at Fields Hall and the one in her grocery bag."

She thought about that for a while. "So maybe Juan's murder isn't connected to those threats at all?"

"I don't know. She's been very quick to post about the threats, and the documents we found in that cigar box, but nothing about Juan or his death."

"Maybe she's trying to keep the focus on her," Lili said. "Mentioning Juan and his death would bring up all kinds of other issues." She sat back against the pillows, and after drinking some water, Rochester came back to slump beside her on the floor. "What did Tony say about the other people who were out of the room when Juan was stabbed?"

"We're agreed we can eliminate Dan Lazerow, at least on a preliminary basis. No connection to either Yesenia or Juan that we can establish, and he's a cop by training. If he wanted to kill Juan he'd do it in a much more subtle way."

"That's encouraging," Lili said.

"You know what I mean. This is a crime of passion, and Dan doesn't seem like a passionate guy."

"We'll put that aside for a moment. What about all the students who were out of the room?"

I told her that Tony had confirmed that Juan had been Bobby's uncle. "But Juan hasn't been in touch with his sister since she arrived in the US. Though Bobby has a motive, he didn't have enough time to discover the relationship."

"Okay. What about the others?"

"Juan and Claudia Monson dated last summer, when she was in a summer program at the theater where he worked."

"Really? He's so much older than she is."

"Yeah, she didn't know how much older. And he took some compromising pictures of her, but she didn't seem to mind."

"Were we as dumb when we were students as some of our students are?" she asked. "We talk about the ethics of photography in my classes and no one seems to think there's a problem taking any kind of pictures as long as the subject agrees."

"Do they ever consider what will happen if they break up? And the person with the pictures is angry?"

"We've talked about that, and I've brought up criminal cases. But it doesn't sink in."

"Claudia didn't seem very bothered. She said that because he never included her face in the photos, she was fine." I sat back beside her. "I'm still curious about Ken Gould. There's something shady about him I haven't been able to put my finger on."

"Why?"

I told her about the library card with his photo and another name. And the conversation we'd had, where he was evasive.

"Not everyone wants to tell you their life story over pastries," she said. "I'm sure there's a reasonable explanation for him. Maybe he had outstanding fines on a library card in his real name and he created a fake identity so he could keep taking out books."

"Now you sound like me, making up theories."

"Maybe I've been with you too long," she said. "What about the two older ladies? Raquel and Maria."

"They both have shaky alibis. They were on their own for at least a few minutes, until they met up at their room."

"Is it possible that someone killed Juan to get at Yesenia?" Lili asked. "Maybe someone who knew they dated, and thought they were still involved?"

"Who would that be?" I asked. "The only two people who knew Yesenia before this program are Maria and Raquel. Do you see either of them grabbing a knife and running after Juan, then stabbing him and running off?"

"After living with you and hearing about the people you've investigated, I never underestimate anyone. Do you?"

"You're right. Appearances can be deceiving. And I know firsthand how hot-blooded Cuban women can be."

She smiled. "You're treading on thin ice, Anglo," she said. "Remember I'm the descendant of Ashkenazi Jews and I only spent a couple of years on the island."

"Let's go back to Yesenia," I said. "Let's say she's the one behind the threats. How does Juan fit into this?"

"Maybe he doesn't, and the threats aren't connected to his death. She didn't know he was going to be here, because he registered with a fake name." She looked at me. "Why do you think he did that?"

"Because he dated her?" I asked. "And they broke up?"

"So why come after her again? Yesenia said she stopped talking to him after they had an argument about Cuba, and then he ghosted her."

"He probably heard about the class through her Facebook group," I said. "Maybe he wanted to try again with her. She's a very attractive woman, and maybe he felt a strong connection to her."

"Would you do that?"

"If you and I had broken up before we got married? And I had a chance to try again with you? Of course. You're worth fighting for."

"You're sweet." She flipped her laptop closed. "We have some time before we have to send the regular students back to campus. I told Yesenia and Deepti we'd go out to dinner with them in Leighville after they move back into Fields Hall."

She turned to me. "Think we can occupy some time together?"

I understood. "Absolutely." I kissed her, and we moved on from there. Until Rochester started barking.

"Oh, come on, dog," I said. When he acted up like that, we locked him out of the bedroom. But since our accommodation at Friar Lake was only a single room, we couldn't do that unless we shut him in the bathroom.

Then someone knocked on the door. "I give up," I groaned. "Can we reconvene later?"

"If you're good," she said.

I tugged my clothes back on and opened the door to find Yesenia there. She was trembling, her normally composed demeanor shattered. The bright red polish on her right index finger was chipped, as if she'd been desperately clawing through her belongings. "Someone stole the documents from my room!"

Chapter 26
Irons in the Fire

I let Yesenia into the room and she immediately went over to Lili's side of the bed and sat in the chair there. The silky black pants and emerald-green cashmere sweater that had looked so elegant at breakfast now seemed rumpled, like she'd been pacing and wringing her hands.

Her usual confident energy had collapsed into something smaller and more vulnerable. "I am so stupid," she said, and she put her head in her hands, her silver bangles sliding down her wrists with a soft chime.

Rochester moved over to her side and leaned against her, responding to her distress the way he always did with people who were hurting. "What happened?" I asked.

"I bragged on Facebook about finding the documents," she said. "I know, I shouldn't have. We even talked about it, keeping the secret so it wouldn't affect my ability to visit the island. But I couldn't help myself. I was so excited."

"Where were you keeping them?" Lili asked.

"In the chest, under the cigars, where they were. I stowed the box under the bed. But when I got back to my room a little while ago, the box was open in the middle of the floor, the cigars were dumped out, and the papers were gone."

"We should call Tony Rinaldi," I said. "Maybe whoever did it left fingerprints."

"I don't have much faith in him," Yesenia said. "He's a small-town cop. This could mean that Cuban operatives have followed me here! They're threatening my life, killing off my students, and stealing my property. How can someone like him manage to figure it all out?"

"He's a sharp guy," I said. "I've known him for years and worked with him in the past."

Yesenia turned to Lili. "Do you think I should give up this class? Go back to New York? You can teach the rest of it, can't you?"

"How much coffee have you had today?" Lili asked.

Yesenia looked abashed. "*Mucho.*" Rochester must have figured she was okay by then, because he left her side and sprawled by the wall.

"And you haven't been as active as you would be if you were up in front of the class all day," Lili said. "You need to calm down. I doubt the CIA has sent someone to Friar Lake to make your life miserable."

"Then how do you explain all this?" Yesenia demanded.

Lili looked at me, and I shrugged. But she kept looking.

"Tony has an idea that the threats aren't related to Juan's death," I said, careful not to mention that he believed the threats were part of her plan to generate social media buzz. "He's looking at a number of students in the class who have a previous connection to Juan. One of them may be responsible."

"*Quién?*"

"I don't feel comfortable revealing that," I said. "I've been helping him collect information, but it's up to him to decide what to do with it."

"It's the Cuban boy, isn't it? Bobby Cruz? I'll bet he's not who he says he is. He even looks older than a typical college student."

"Bobby Cruz is exactly who he says he is," I said. "I checked him out. And he's a student at Eastern. Remember, Juan applied to this course under a false name. There's more going on here than we understand."

"Even so, I'm glad I'm moving back to the campus today. There's more security there, isn't there?"

I nodded. "There is. And you met Dan Lazerow, he's the head of campus security. He'll be keeping an eye on you and the students."

It took some more convincing, but eventually Yesenia calmed down. Lili took her over to the library to look at Brother Gervase's book and see how they could incorporate his work into the class.

As soon as they were gone, I called Tony and told him what had happened. "New development this afternoon," I said. "You remember I told you about that box we found, with the cigars and documents?"

"The ones that said Dr. Ubeda owns a chunk of Havana?"

"That's the set. Well, someone stole them from her room."

"She's sure she didn't just misplace them?"

"I know you think she's orchestrating things to generate buzz on social media, but I wanted to let you know. It's possible that all the stuff going on out here is related, including Juan Alfarero's murder."

"You saw these documents?" he asked.

"I found them," I said, leaving out Rochester's part. Sorry, puppy, not everyone believes in your skills. "In a chest that had been hidden between the walls in one of our classrooms."

I explained how we'd had the leak, and Joey and I had taken down the damaged drywall. "There were eleven cigars in the box, but it wasn't until I showed the box to Yesenia that she discovered the layer of papers underneath the cigars."

"You're sure she couldn't have put the papers there herself?"

"I'm sure. I had the box myself."

"But she's the only one who translated them, right? So they don't necessarily say what she says they do."

"That's correct. But whatever they say, someone stole them from her room. Can you come out here with some fingerprint powder?"

He sighed. "There goes my plan to watch the hockey game this afternoon. Sure, I'll be out in a half hour."

"Thanks, Tony," I said.

I went back to my office with Rochester and pulled out the Furminator brush I kept in my desk. Grooming him always helped me think more clearly - and kept golden fur from coating every surface at Friar Lake. As I worked through his coat, I considered what other evidence Tony might find in Yesenia's room. Rochester slumped contentedly against my leg, and I was just finishing up when he raised his head and barked.

Tony took off his coat and hat as he walked into my office, then leaned down to pet Rochester. "I'm starting to get tired of drama around Dr. Ubeda," Tony said, when he stood up. "Especially when I'm trying to solve a murder. Which I might add does not happen that frequently in Leighville, so it kind of demands my full attention."

"I know how you feel," I said. "If I could go back to last fall when Lili first suggested this program, I wish I'd said no. But we're here."

He pulled out his notebook. "Tell me about these papers."

"Joey was repairing a wall in the infirmary last week and we found this box hidden there. He and I opened it, and we saw a layer of cigars. I kept the box in here until Lili and I showed it to Yesenia. She thought something was unusual so she pulled all the cigars out. Under them we found this series of documents."

"No chance she could have put them in the box herself?"

I shook my head. "Joey and I found the box before she arrived, and it was in my possession until then."

"What do the documents say?" Tony asked.

"We didn't look at them very carefully. Yesenia pulled one page out and noticed it had her great-grandfather's name on it. I can't read Spanish, but according to her it granted a piece of land to her great-grandfather."

"Okay."

"We did a little research and discovered the land was commandeered from her family in the 1800s to build a government office. Which is now the home of the president of Cuba."

"I don't understand why this is important, or how it could relate to Mr. Alfarero's murder."

"I don't understand the connection either, but the gist of it is that Yesenia is the legal owner of the presidential palace in Havana. Which could be very tricky for Cuban-American relations, and for her particularly if she wants to keep making trips to the island for her research. At the time we found the papers, she was boasting that she could use her claim as leverage to get more access to information and people on the island, which could elevate her position, maybe even move her into a tenured professorship at a university."

"I thought she wanted to be a food personality on TV."

"She's got a lot of irons in the fire." I sat back. "I can't blame her. She's a single woman in her forties and she told Lili she's tired of jumping from one temporary teaching job to another. A TV gig could give her visibility and a steady income. If the TV job doesn't work out, a tenure-track professorship somewhere would be the next best thing."

He pushed his chair back and stood up. "Can we take a look at the scene of the crime?"

"Sure." We both put our coats on and Rochester was happy to accompany us over to the dormitory. "I can't show you where we found the box because Joey replaced the drywall and painted. I have a master key and we can get into Yesenia's room, and Lili is keeping her busy in the library."

Tony examined the lock. "Who has keys to this room?"

"There's a master key for all the rooms, which we keep in my office, unless Joey or I have it. There are two copies of each room key. As you can see there are two beds, so Yesenia was sharing with Deepti and they each have a key."

When Tony examined the lock he saw that someone with a heavy-duty credit card could flip the bolt, though there was a top bolt and flip lock for extra security once you were in the room. "We were cutting corners when we renovated," I said. "We thought this level would be sufficient."

"That's assuming someone really stole those documents, and not that Dr. Ubeda is trying to create more drama."

I opened the door, and we saw the open box on the floor, with the cigars tossed carelessly beside it. Tony sat down cross-legged beside the box and pulled a pair of rubber gloves and a package of fingerprint powder out of his jacket pocket.

As he worked, he asked, "Did she say where she kept this box?"

"Under the bed."

He finished his work, but said, "I can't pull any prints. Whoever did this must have worn gloves."

"Rubber or winter?"

"Can't tell. All I'm getting are smudges."

He turned on his side and looked under the bed. "Good housekeeping," he said. "No dust bunnies there."

He stood up, we looked around the rest of the room, and then left.

"Sorry to drag you out here a second time on a Sunday," I said, as Rochester and I walked him to the door of the building.

"All part of the job. The autopsy is tomorrow morning. He paused. "I've been thinking about another angle on this case. I still think there's a chance Dr. Ubeda is behind everything. But everyone's focused on protecting Yesenia - from Juan, from controversy, from herself. But what if someone's trying to destroy her instead? Make it look like she orchestrated everything, from the threats to the murder?"

He walked back to his car, and as I watched his taillights disappear down the hill, I considered his point. If someone wanted to frame Yesenia, they couldn't have planned it better - her knife as the murder weapon, her ex-boyfriend as the victim, her course as the backdrop.

The question was: who stood to gain from Yesenia's downfall?"

Chapter 27
The Light You Have

I texted Lili that Tony was finished, and that I'd meet her at our room. As I was walking down the hall, Maria and Raquel walked in, talking animatedly in Spanish. As soon as they saw me, though, they stopped.

"Did you hear?" Raquel asked me. "Someone stole those documents Yesenia found."

"Actually, Rochester found them between the walls," I said. "I really should have kept them until we could put them somewhere secure."

"I worry about her," Maria said, her hands moving restlessly, tugging at the buttons of her wool coat. "When my son married that Anglo woman from Oklahoma..." She adjusted the silk scarf at her neck. "He moved there and now he's embarrassed by me."

The simple gold band on her left hand caught the fluorescent hallway light as she twisted it round and round her finger. "Because I never went to college, because I speak with an accent." Her voice carried a brittle edge beneath its maternal warmth, like china about to crack. Her chin lifted defiantly even as her eyes grew over-bright with unshed tears.

"But Yesenia understands what it means to be caught between

two worlds." She fumbled with the clasp of her purse, opening and closing it repeatedly, the metal catch making tiny clicking sounds that punctuated her words. "She has become like a daughter to me."

When she spoke of Yesenia, her entire bearing changed. Her restless movements stilled and her gaze became fierce. "She's so brilliant, so accomplished. The way she explains our culture, our food—she makes people understand us." Her shoulders squared beneath her heavy winter coat, her voice taking on an almost possessive note of pride. "No one can deny what she's achieved."

For just a moment, her gloved hands clenched into tight fists before deliberately relaxing—a brief glimpse of the roiling tensions beneath her motherly exterior.

Raquel patted her on the shoulder. "You were a good mother to your son. I'm sure he will realize that someday."

Raquel looked at me. "I was thinking who could have taken those documents," she said, changing the subject. "I don't trust that boy, Bobby Cruz. We've been so nice to him, especially Maria, but learning that Juan Alfarero was his uncle makes me change my mind. That kind of behavior runs in families."

"Remember, Juan registered for this course under an alias," I said. "And Bobby says he didn't realize Juan was his uncle until he was already dead."

"And there's that strange man, Ken," Maria said. "We've been talking about him. He doesn't know anything about food. Maybe he was sent here to spy on Yesenia."

I shrugged. "He admitted to me that he doesn't know much about food, but he wanted a quiet place to get away from the office for a while, and he spotted this course."

Raquel frowned. "He still sounds shady to me."

I didn't tell them about the extra library card I'd found in another name, or his lack of a digital footprint. I shared Raquel's opinion of him.

Rochester and I went into our room, and he immediately went to his water bowl and slurped. Then he came over and tried to dry his face on my leg, but I pushed him away. "Not your napkin," I said. Then I rubbed the top of his head so he wouldn't think I was angry at him.

Lili came in a few minutes later. "Yesenia's going to pack up and head to campus," she said. "She and Deepti will drive over there in Yesenia's car and we're going to pick them up at Fields Hall at six-thirty for dinner in Leighville."

"Tony just suggested something interesting," I said, and shared his theory about someone trying to frame Yesenia rather than protect her.

Lili frowned. "That would explain a lot. And if that's true, we should see what kind of ammunition she's giving them." She grabbed her laptop and sat on the bed. "Let's see what she posted on Facebook this time."

We looked at what the volatile professor had uploaded. "*Dios mío*, someone needs to revoke Yesenia's posting privileges," Lili said, as we saw blurred copies of the documents and photos of the box and the cigars. A long rant about her family history in Cuba, and how her lineage went back beyond the 1959 fall of Batista.

"It's like she's challenging someone to steal those documents," Lili said. "Showing off what she has. And her followers already know that she's here."

"I keep coming back to the idea that this is all Yesenia's doing, to generate a buzz on social media that she can use to leverage herself into a TV show," I said. "Look at how many likes and comments she has already."

We scanned back through her recent posts. Some of them were about the food she was cooking and the lectures she was giving, and those got a lot of shares. She was spreading her reach, which was good for her future.

Even the posts about the threats against her got a lot of attention. "She still hasn't mentioned anything about Juan online," I said. "You'd think she'd love to get attention for his death, maybe even their past relationship."

"She's a complicated woman," Lili said. "I've got some research to do before tomorrow's lecture. You all right on your own for a while?"

I could take a hint. Though I loved being married, I appreciated that Lili and I needed our own space, too. I stood up. "Want to go to the office with me, puppy?" I asked Rochester, and he jumped up immediately.

I was glad that we'd be heading back to River Bend the next day. I loved Friar Lake and felt responsible for everything that happened there, but I wanted to be back in my own house, where I could spread out on the dining room table, where Lili could be up in the bedroom and Rochester sprawled on the floor in the kitchen.

As we walked to the gatehouse, I saw a group of the college kids heading toward the parking lot. Bobby Cruz was with them, but he disengaged and came over to me. "I spoke to my mom," he said, as Rochester sniffed his feet. "The police told her she's responsible for my uncle's body. Do you know when the police are going to let us bury him?"

"I understand the autopsy is going to be tomorrow," I said. "So probably after that."

He nodded.

"This must be tough for you," I said. "Finding out that your uncle was so close and just missing him."

"It's weird, you know? My mom and my aunts were upset that he wouldn't help us out when we all got here. They never really talked about him after that. He was sort of like this ghost. I knew that he lived in New York, and I thought maybe I'd get in touch with him when I came up here to go to school. But, like you know, it's hard to get into New York from here unless you have a car, and the chance never came up." He frowned. "Now it never will."

Rochester settled on the ground next to me. "Is the rest of your family as anti-Castro as he was?" I asked Bobby.

He shook his head. "Honestly, for my generation, Castro is like so in the rear-view mirror. Our lives in Florida are so much better than they were in Cuba. My mom's only regret is that we didn't leave sooner."

His friends called to him, and he hurried toward them, and Rochester and I continued to the office. I spent the next hour reviewing my budget and checking invoices, and then answered a few emails that had come in while I was busy with the course.

At four o'clock, I finished and locked the gatehouse. Rochester and I started a survey of the buildings, making sure the ones we weren't using were locked up. I was surprised to find Ken Gould in the library.

"Working late?" I asked.

Ken startled at my voice, his shoulders jerking as his fingers flew to minimize the window on his screen. A faint sheen of sweat appeared on his upper lip despite the library's chill. Though he tried to maintain his bland, middle-manager affect, his eyes darted away from mine and his right hand drummed a nervous pattern on the desk before he caught himself and forced it still.

"Oh, Steve. Just catching up on some office work. Nothing to do with the course."

His eyes darted away. "Just some... personal research."

I nodded, filing away this odd behavior for later consideration as he packed up his computer so I could lock the library.

Rochester took care of his business on our way back to the dormitory, and Lili and I left him with a bowl of food. We drove down the hill, still free of ice, and into Leighville to pick up Yesenia and Deepti. Both were bundled up against the cold, Yesenia in a down trenchcoat and Deepti in a parka and multicolored leggings. We drove to an Italian restaurant in the center of town, and with so many students still away from campus it was easy to park right in front.

After we ordered, I turned to Deepti. "I understand you're carrying on a freelance video business while you're here. That must be tough."

"A lot of what I do is editing," she said. "People upload their videos to me through Dropbox, and I either cut them down or add sound and video effects, like introductions, subtitles and so on. I also do a lot of converting documents and PowerPoint presentations to video. It's the kind of thing I can do in my spare time when I'm not working for Yesenia."

"How long have you two been working together?" Lili asked.

"Only a few months," Yesenia said. "I looked online for a videographer, and Deepti came highly recommended."

"Plus I had the flexibility to come out here to Pennsylvania for a month," she said.

The server brought us glasses of wine and a tray of garlic rolls. Lili lifted her glass. "To a smoother run for the rest of the class," she said.

We all clinked our glasses together. "I'm curious, Deepti," Lili said. "If I had a series of photographs I wanted to make into a video, how would I do that?"

She smiled, and light glinted off the multiple piercings in her ear. "Well, you could hire me, of course."

"And?" Lili asked.

"Well, you'd have to decide which of your photographs to include, and what your overall message would be. Yesenia showed me some of your work as we were getting ready to come out here, and you have a terrific eye. But the way your website is laid out, you're kind of all over the place. Landscape photos, pictures from your war correspondent work, lots of pictures of your dog. What would you want a video to do for you?"

"I was thinking I could put together a demo reel of images to apply for exhibitions," she said.

I looked at her. That wasn't something we'd discussed, and I was curious to hear more.

"Galleries?" Deepti asked.

Lili nodded.

"You should focus on those international photos," Deepti said. "They're super powerful. Especially the ones of women and children. Some of those shots legit made me cry."

She leaned forward, her nose ring catching the light. "Like, being South Asian myself, I hardly ever see us portrayed with dignity online. Your photos from Bangladesh? The way you showed those women rebuilding after the floods? That's the real stuff - not just clickbait disaster shots, but actual human stories."

"Thank you, I'll take that a compliment," Lili said. Our entrées arrived, and we began to eat.

"Another way to go, if you want, would be to focus on your more personal work," Deepti said, as we ate. "Landscapes, dogs, and so on. Or versatility—using the video format to show how your work has grown and changed."

"Very interesting," Lili said. "It's something I've been thinking about. I was going to have a small exhibition in Stewart's Crossing, where we live, but the gallery owner died and I'm still negotiating with the people who took it over."

I knew Lili had been offered a show at that gallery, but hadn't heard anything more about it after the owner's death. I was very curious to ask her more, but I wanted to wait until we were alone. We finally finished dinner, accompanied by cups of decaf cappuccino, and then we dropped Deepti and Yesenia off at Fields Hall.

"I'm not sure they'll really be safer there than at Friar Lake," I said, as we watched the two of them walk through the big wooden door. "As we learned, there's no real security in that building until they lock the doors at eleven. Do you think we ought to convince Yesenia to come back to Friar Lake and commute to campus for meals and classes?"

"I'm certainly worried," Lili said. "But right now I think we should stay the course. Suggesting a move would only make Yesenia more nervous."

The country road leading from Leighville to Friar Lake was dark and narrow, and I had to focus on driving. "I never realized how little light there is out here," I said, as I flipped my high beams on. "I guess we rarely come to Friar Lake at night."

"There's always darkness," Lili said. "It's all about finding your way with the light you have."

Chapter 28
Warning Signs

I didn't ask Lili about her conversation with Deepti until we were in bed together. "Have you been thinking about exhibitions for a while?" I asked.

"Since I started talking to Jonathan Wiesner," she said. He had moved to Stewart's Crossing to open a gallery devoted to photography the previous year. After his death, the gallery had been taken over by the man's sister and a business school classmate of my friend Tor.

"Have you been talking to Arie and Patty?"

"Just casually," she said. "They're still working out their business model. Arie's trying to drum up camera repair business while Patty goes through all the photos that her brother owned. They're thinking that in the spring they might be ready to sponsor a show."

"And making a video? Where did that come from?"

"From watching Deepti work," Lili said. "And hearing her talk about videography. It's just an idea right now. I might want to curate a video of student work for the Eastern website, or maybe, like I said, put together something to promote myself. I've been focused on teaching for the last few years, and it might be time to spread my wings again."

"You've always supported me," I said. "Even when I was getting myself in trouble. So you know I'll be there for you, whatever you need."

"I love you, Mr. Levitan," she said, and leaned over and kissed me.

"Back at you, Mrs. Levitan," I said. "Or Dr. Weinstock, whichever you prefer."

"I like them both."

We drifted to sleep then, and I woke up Monday morning ready to start my regular work week. After a brisk walk with Rochester, Lili and I packed up all our stuff and stowed it in my car, so the cleaning staff could get in and prepare the room for Joey and Mark.

I drove Lili to campus and we joined the students for breakfast at the dining commons. I was pleased that the special students had been able to find their way easily.

I left them to their lectures and drove back to Friar Lake, where I'd left Rochester slumbering in my office. I brought him a piece of muffin, which made him happy, and then settled down at my desk.

I dove into my college work but before I could answer more than a couple of emails, Joey came in. Rochester romped over to him for ear scratches. "How was the weekend?"

"Eventful." I explained about Tony's visits, though I didn't get into the details of who he suspected and why. "And Yesenia says someone stole those papers from the cigar box."

"We really need to get a better security camera system here if this kind of stuff is going to keep happening."

"Let's make sure we all survive the intersession before we start making big investments." We went over the rest of the week. "Mark's coming out this evening?"

"With Brody. He's bringing dinner."

"If anything more happens, call me right away," I said.

He stood up. "I'll get back to work. See you later."

I started boiling water for a cup of hot chocolate, and as I was finishing, Rochester started barking again and Tony Rinaldi arrived.

As he walked in the gatehouse, I held up my mug. "Hot chocolate?" I asked.

"That would be great," he said, as he peeled off his gloves. "I could use something warm."

As I prepared the cocoa for both of us, I asked, "Did you get hold of anyone who knew Claudia at her theater program last summer?"

"I did. Two different young women, about her age, there for college credit. And both of them called Ms. Monson an ice princess. Very talented on stage, but hard to connect with outside of the theater. One of them knew Ms. Monson was having an affair with a stagehand. But a lot of the students were dating or fooling around with each other or with theater personnel, so no one made a big deal about it."

I handed him a big mug, and he sipped it gratefully. "My mom used to make us hot chocolate in the winter. She'd shave chocolate bars into hot milk. But my sister and I wanted the kind that came in packets with tiny marshmallows."

He shook his head. "The kind of things we remember."

He sat down across from me. "Got the results of the autopsy," he said. "Death was quick, the result of what the pathologist called cardiac tamponade. Blood accumulated in the membrane surrounding the heart. That compressed the heart and reduced its ability to pump blood effectively."

"Any information about the stabber?"

"From the angle of entry of the knife wound, he says it was someone shorter than Mr. Alfarero. He couldn't tell me much more than that."

I did a quick run through in my head of our suspects. "All the people who were out of the room are shorter than he was, aren't they?"

"Ms. Jaceldo is tall, but I'm not ruling her out yet. Or any of the other suspects." He looked at me. "At least they're all staying put for a while, aren't they?"

"We can't hold them against their will, but yes, they're starting class on campus today. Fingers crossed nothing more happens."

"As a police officer, I've found crossing my fingers less than effective."

Chapter 29
Rubik's Cube

After Tony left, I kept hearing his phrase "as a police officer" in my head. That made me think of the other person in this situation who had a police background. Dan Lazerow. Was I too quick to assume he had nothing to do with Juan Alfarero's murder, because he had been a cop and was now in charge of Eastern's security?

I had invited him to the dinner at the last minute, and he didn't have access to the student roster before that. But could he have recognized Juan Alfarero from a case in New York? Perhaps one that had turned out badly for Dan?

Maybe I was being paranoid, but I opened my hacker laptop and set up a few more searches on him, trying to see if he had a New York connection to Juan Alfarero. Juan had been arrested a few times, possibly while Dan was on the force. But it was going to be tricky to find that information, and I certainly wasn't going to reveal to the head of college security that I was in possession of hacker tools, and sometimes commandeered the college network to use them.

I sat back. Was there anyone else I wasn't paying enough attention to? For some reason, the phrase I'd seen on the back of Juan's car came to mind. "You will be found." I hoped that meant that Juan's killer would be found.

In turn, that brought Max Abraham to mind. Where had he been when Juan was killed? I thought he had been in the refectory with everyone else, but I had been distracted. What if he and Juan had clashed when they worked together? Max was a strong guy, with arm muscles built up from kneading dough.

Though I was grasping at straws, I set up a search for connections between Juan and Max. While I was on the computer I saw that one of my online subscriptions – the legal kind—was expiring, and I had to renew it. I pulled out my wallet and extracted a credit card.

Somehow, while I was typing, my wallet must have fallen to the floor, because as I was getting ready to leave to meet Lili for lunch at the Cafette, I noticed Rochester had my wallet in his paws. He hadn't chewed it, but my credit cards had spilled out.

"I'll take care of any online ordering," I said to him. I gathered my cards and refilled my wallet, then put on my coat and hat and walked out. I left Rochester in my office with a pile of toys.

I turned the heat on full-blast in my SUV and navigated the barren country roads into Leighville. Weathered stone walls, built by farmers generations ago, lined the shoulders, their gray faces mottled with pale green lichen. Skeletal trees reached their bare branches toward a pewter sky, while here and there a cluster of evergreens offered the only spots of true color in the January landscape.

Eastern was lucky to have received acres of pastoral landscape along with the Fields endowment that set up the school. But all the leafless trees, and the few students on the street huddled in coats, hats and gloves, made the town look grim.

Lili was already at the Cafette when I arrived, with a roast beef sandwich and a bottle of black cherry wishniak soda for me. I shucked my coat and gloves, happy for the warmth provided by the fireplace.

"Tony came by my office this morning," I said. "He got the autopsy results on Juan Alfarero, but didn't learn anything new except that the assailant was probably shorter than Juan."

"Do you think whoever stole the documents from Yesenia also killed Juan?"

"I don't know. It's possible that Yesenia might be taking advantage of finding those documents to enhance her social media presence. Did you actually read them before they were stolen?"

She shook her head. "I've been focused on Brother Gervase's book, and looking that over with Yesenia."

"So we don't know that those papers really give her ownership of anything in Cuba. They could just be abbey records."

I chewed my sandwich. "Rick always asks cui bono, who benefits, when a crime takes place. So who benefits from those documents – let's call it 'disappearing,' rather than being stolen."

Lili picked up her cup of hot cocoa and sipped it. "Let's assume for the moment that the papers represent what Yesenia says they do. She loses the chance to stake a claim on that land if she doesn't have the proof of ownership. The converse is that the Cuban government benefits if the land grant paperwork disappears."

"That would mean there's an agent of the Cuban government at Friar Lake," I said. "I think that's a big stretch."

"I hate to throw countrymen under the bus, but besides me and Yesenia, there are three people of Cuban descent with us. Maria Cabrera, Raquel Jaceldo, and Bobby Cruz."

"You think one of them could be a mole, or a secret agent?"

She put her cup down on the saucer with a clatter. "I don't know. I'm a photographer and a professor. Not a specialist in espionage."

"You know, Rochester reminded me of something this morning," I said. I explained how he'd emptied my wallet of credit cards. "Anyone in the dorm with a credit card could have broken into Yesenia's room."

"And the whole class knew about the documents and what they could mean."

"What do we know about Deepti?" I asked. "She was staying in the room with Yesenia, so she had a key, and she must have seen the box. I'm sure Yesenia either told her what was inside, or she read about the papers on Facebook."

I wrapped up a couple of pieces of roast beef to bring back for Rochester. "She was a last-minute addition so I didn't do any research on her," I said. "I'll get to that this afternoon. She had the means and the opportunity to carry out the theft. We're just missing a motive."

"Yesenia said that she hoped the land grant could give her leverage with the Cuban government so that she could amp up her research and get a tenure-track academic position," Lili said. "What if she promised Deepti that if she got a Food Network gig she'd bring Deepti along? Stealing the documents might be a way to steer Yesenia toward TV, where Deepti could benefit by her coattails."

"I suppose," I said. "Not the strongest motive in the world, but we're talking about theft, not murder."

I sighed. "Which brings us back to Juan Alfarero. His death is the most important crime, and maybe his killer hopes we'll lose sight of that while we get distracted with the theft."

"I found Claudia Monson during the break this morning," Lili said. "I wanted to see if she needed anyone to talk to about Juan. You said his death didn't affect her, and I didn't believe it."

"What did you find out?"

"She's like a lot of pretty girls I knew in college. Totally concerned with themselves, and without much empathy for others. You're right, she was very blasé about the photos Juan took. But I don't think she was in love with him or anything, and she'd already moved on from him by the time she got back to campus."

"That's the impression Tony got from talking to two girls who were on the same program she was. Did you get any sense she might be lying?"

Lili shook her head. "Not at all. Maybe she's a great actress, but I don't believe his death affected her that much. And I doubt she had enough venom toward him to jump up, grab a knife, and chase him."

"And stab him in the stomach," I added.

"This is all very frustrating. I don't see how you and Rick keep doing this kind of thing."

"Did you ever have a Rubik's cube?" I asked.

"I've seen them, but I never tried to solve one."

"They were big when Rick and I were in high school. I could sit for an hour trying different combinations until I could solve it. It's kind of the same thing. You collect all these clues and keep turning them around until the solution falls into place."

"Only in this case you don't get a bunch of colors lined up. You get someone going to prison."

I shook my head. "That's not up to me. All I do is solve the puzzle. Rick and Tony and the criminal justice system do the rest."

I went back to Friar Lake and gave Rochester the scraps of roast beef. While he ate, I caught up on the latest email messages and signature requests. Then Tony called.

"You're right, that Toyota sedan in your parking lot is registered to Juan Alfarero. And the EZ Pass records show that he drove over the New Hope bridge on Tuesday afternoon. That gives him plenty of time to get to Leighville and slide that threat under Dr. Ubeda's door."

I looked at Rochester. Once again he'd provided an interesting clue.

"I reviewed security camera footage from the parking lot close to Fields Hall, and spotted him leaving the lot in the early evening, and then returning to his car about fifteen minutes later. Of course that doesn't guarantee he's the one who placed the threat, but it puts him on campus at the right time. He stayed over two nights at the Red Roof Inn off I-95 before he drove over to Friar Lake."

"Bobby Cruz was asking about his body," I said. "When you speak to Juan's sister, you can ask her what to do about his car. We don't want it to stay in our parking lot forever."

"I'm working on that. In the meantime I can have a truck tow it to the impound lot so it'll get out of your hair."

"I appreciate that." After I hung up, I sat at the hacker laptop and plugged Deepti's name into the various programs I had. While they worked, I reviewed what they'd pulled up on Max Abraham. The only connection my programs could bring up was when Max and Juan had worked together on the *Fiddler on the Roof* revival, which Max had mentioned.

Then I turned to Dan Lazerow. It was uncomfortable snooping into his life, because he was a colleague and someone I respected, and it was highly unlikely he'd killed Juan Alfarero. But I owed it to Tony, and to the dead man's memory, to explore every avenue.

Fortunately, I found an interview he'd given to a high school class in Manhattan a few years before, where he went through his background. He had graduated from high school in Forest Hills, Queens, and had a BA in criminal justice from Long Island University. He had completed the Police Academy in Manhattan and joined the NYPD as a patrol officer.

He served three years on patrol until he was offered a spot in an undercover narcotics unit, where he worked for two years. Then he was assigned to an investigative detail, where he spent 18 months learning investigative techniques while remaining a white shield, or police officer.

It took another year for a position as a detective to open up, and he received his gold shield. At the time of the interview, he was on the overdose squad in Manhattan, which was why he was reaching out to young people.

After that it was impossible to track his progress, until he was hired at Eastern a year before as director of campus security. The press release about him highlighted his experience working with young people as well as an MS in Criminal Justice from the University of Southern California.

I couldn't find any record of who he'd arrested or under what circumstances, but if he was focused on working with young people it was unlikely he'd have encountered Juan Alfarero, who'd been arrested by the precinct detective squads in the neighborhoods where he had been protesting.

Then I turned to the results on Deepti Patil. She was a graduate of the Parsons School of Design with a BFA in design and technology. Her senior project was a movie about her cousin's traditional Hindu wedding in Queens. She had posted clips of it on YouTube and it was fun to watch the various rituals, including her cousin's hands and arms being painted with henna.

She had credentials in web design and videography and was available to be hired for project work through Upwork and Fiverr. As my program dug through her connections, I recognized she was a hard-working young woman in need of a break. She had done good work, but it was all small potatoes, and in a blog post I found she had complained about applying for jobs at every television-related company in New York without success.

Including the Food Network, where she'd tried to become a camera operator for a show based on Indian food. She'd had five interviews, but eventually someone else was given the job.

How desperate was she, though? Would she steal those papers to push Yesenia toward a TV job? It seemed far-fetched, because there were so many other steps that had to take place before Yesenia would be before the cameras at the Food Network studios. And even though she'd promised to take Deepti with her, a new talent like Yesenia didn't walk in the door with much clout. She'd be more concerned with the details of her own contract than dragging Deepti along.

I sat back as Rochester shook himself, and fine golden hairs came flying off him. I grabbed the Furminator brush I kept in the office and sat on the floor with him, combing him out.

At home we called his fur angel wings, because he was our angel, and the tufts of hair floated in the air like the wings of angels. But that afternoon I was more concerned with combing out knots and removing as much loose hair as I could.

As I worked, I thought. We had three different crimes going on; how were they related?

First were the threats against Yesenia. Those stopped after Juan's death. Then there was Juan's outburst, followed by his murder. Finally, the theft of the documents from Yesenia's room.

The connecting thread was Yesenia, of course, but there had to be more. I started talking to the dog. "Yesenia. Cuba. Money. A TV program or a university appointment. The opportunity for Yesenia to go back to the island and use the grant paperwork to create power for herself."

I looked at Rochester. "Any ideas?"

He didn't even design to look at me. Instead I had to push him to roll him on his other side. He accumulated the most excess hair on his rear flanks, but the most tangles came around his head, probably because he dripped water there when he drank.

I kept brushing and thinking but didn't come up with anything new. When I was almost finished, Rochester squirmed away from me and jumped up, barking at the front window. I stood and looked out and saw Zenobia's car pull up. She, Enid, Maria and Raquel got out, all of them laughing and talking about something.

I was glad they were having a good time, despite everything happening around them. Their good reviews at the end of the course would be important to its success.

My phone rang with the ring tone I'd selected for Lili, a snippet of "Chan Chan" by the Buena Vista Social Club. It was lively and fun and reminded me of her. "Hey, I'm getting ready to come over and pick you up," I said.

"Good, because we've got trouble. After class finished this afternoon, Deepti was shutting down her equipment in the classroom on the ground floor of Granger Hall. Someone came in behind her and knocked her out, and walked off with the jump drive she's been storing her video files on."

"Oh, no. Is she all right?"

"Security found her and called 911, and then called me. The EMTs think she might have a concussion so they're taking her to the hospital in Doylestown for observation. Yesenia's going with her."

"I'll be right there. Have you called the police yet?"

"I did. Tony Rinaldi is on his way."

I grabbed my coat and the rest of the stuff I wanted to take home, including the hacker laptop. I was glad Lili and I had packed the car that morning. Rochester had a quick pee in the parking lot and then we were off.

Rochester stuck his head between the seats of the car. The air was still so cold that his breath was visible, making it look like he was a dragon about to breathe fire. He gave me his most pitiful "I haven't been fed in hours" look.

"Puppy, that sad face might work on Lili, but I know better," I said. He responded by breathing more dragon smoke in my direction.

Why had someone attacked Deepti? Did that mean she wasn't a suspect any longer? Things were getting more confusing all the time.

Chapter 30
Evidence Trail

Technically, dogs weren't allowed on the Eastern campus unless they were verified support animals, but I got special permission to bring Rochester with me when I worked at Fields Hall, and all the security guards knew him. As long as he didn't cause trouble, I had no problem bringing him with me, and I didn't want to leave him in the cold car while I found out what was going on with Deepti.

When we got to Granger Hall, Lili, Tony, and Dan Lazerow were in the hallway outside the classroom where Deepti had been attacked. I kept Rochester on a short leash as I went up to Lili and kissed her cheek, glad that she hadn't been the victim.

Then I turned to Dan and Tony. "What happened?"

Dan's face was flushed and he spoke rapidly. "The door to the classroom was open when one of my guards passed by, and he noticed Ms. Patil on the floor. He immediately called 911 and radioed the office. I was second on the scene, and Ms. Patil was still on the floor, awake but groggy. By the time the EMTs got here, she was able to stand up, and we ushered her out into the hall so they could do an assessment without damaging much of the crime scene."

Rochester smelled his agitation and wanted to go up and comfort him, but I held him back. I bet this was more excitement than Dan usually got at Eastern, a throwback to his time as a cop.

"Tony arrived and took over the classroom," Dan said. "A couple of the chairs around Ms. Patil were knocked over, and that indicates there was some kind of struggle between Ms. Patil and her assailant. She had no physical wounds, so the supposition is that someone might have used chloroform on Ms. Patil, and that's what knocked her out."

Dan continued, "The EMT said the worst case was that she'd have a bad headache for a while, but that she ought to be checked out anyway, to rule out a concussion when her head hit the ground. They took her to Doylestown Medical Center for observation, and Dr. Ubeda followed in her car."

Rochester slumped to the floor as Dan turned to Tony, who picked up the narrative. "Techs are inside dusting for fingerprints. I have two of my officers tracking down the students to find out who were the last ones to leave the class. I called the hospital ER and asked them to test Ms. Patil for chloroform. It doesn't stay in the body for long, so I asked them to expedite the test."

"Four of the special students are at Friar Lake," I said. "Zenobia, Enid, Raquel and María. I saw them arriving there as I was leaving."

"What are they doing there?" Tony asked.

"We don't have enough dorm rooms here for them, so five of them are staying out there. Well, we started with six, with Jose Alfarero. The other one is Ken Gould, but I haven't seen him today."

Tony pulled out his notebook and wrote that down.

"Could Deepti tell you anything before they took her away?" I asked.

"She was sitting at her computer processing the video she took today, and someone came up behind her and put something over her mouth. The next thing she knew she was waking up on the floor."

"Sounds like chloroform," I said. "Where can you get hold of that?"

"Online," Dan said. "Or in the chemistry lab here."

Tony said, "I have cell numbers for the five special students. I'm going to call them and see if they saw anything." He walked out the door, with his cell phone in his hand.

Dan's usual color had returned to his face and he was calmer, but Rochester kept an eye on him. "I didn't like having something happen out at Friar Lake, but at least that was isolated," he said. "Now this chaos is coming to campus, and I like that even less."

"The chaos started here," I said. "With the threat slipped under Yesenia's door the day she arrived."

"If someone other than Dr. Ubeda put it there," Dan said.

I crossed my arms over my chest as Rochester sat up on his haunches. "You've been talking to Tony."

"We share information. And the more I hear the more suspicious I become of our guest speaker. She had a reason to kill Mr. Alfarero based on their past relationship and their political opposition. Her knife was used, and she doesn't have an alibi for the time. It's possible she has created all this chaos around her to shield her from suspicion."

"Tony suspects her, that's for sure," I said. "But why would she sabotage the recording of her class? She's paying Deepti to record her lectures to use as a calling card to get herself a food TV program."

"I haven't worked that out yet," Dan said. "But I'll be thinking about it."

"It could be that someone wants us to think that," I said. "Tony suggested earlier that everything pointing to Yesenia might be too neat. Her knife as the murder weapon, her ex-boyfriend as the victim, threats that make her look unstable. If you wanted to destroy someone's academic career and TV prospects, you couldn't plan it better."

Dan shook his head. "Occam's Razor - the simplest explanation is usually correct."

"Maybe. But in my experience with investigations, the obvious solution isn't always the right one." I looked at Rochester, who had remained unusually alert throughout our conversation. "And something about this case feels off."

He walked away, leaving Lili, me, and the dog in the hallway. "I just don't believe Yesenia is behind all this," Lili said. Rochester stood up and nuzzled her hand, and she petted him. "I won't pretend to know her completely, but I understand her and what she wants from life. She wouldn't be sabotaging her ambitions this way."

"I trust your instincts," I said. "It means we need to double down on figuring out what's going on."

We walked outside, where we caught up with Tony Rinaldi again. "I spoke to the five special students," he said. "And they all agree they were the last ones to leave the classroom. Unfortunately they split up then."

"But four of them drove to Friar Lake together," I said.

He nodded and pulled out his notebook. "The four women. Mr. Gould hurried to his car and drove back to Friar Lake because he had a conference call. According to what the four women told me, they agreed to meet at Zenobia Willis's car. She wanted to get a cup of coffee from the Cafette to wake her up before driving. Raquel Jaceldo went for a brisk walk around the campus for a similar purpose. Maria Cabrera went to the ladies' room in Granger Hall, and Enid Garelick walked upstairs to look at the artwork on the walls from a higher level."

He looked back at us. "In each case they were on their own long enough to have gone back to the classroom, knocked out Ms. Patil, and then made it to the car on time."

"What about the regular college students?" I asked. "Any of them could have doubled back after the last students left the room."

He sighed. "I'll have to get in touch with each one of them and secure an alibi."

Rochester started pulling at his leash, and I relaxed it enough so that he could walk up to a tree and pee. "Lili said a jump drive was stolen?" I asked.

"According to Ms. Patil, she had the current day's film stored on her laptop and she was in the process of uploading it to a Dropbox account. The files on the jump drive that's missing were related to her other work."

Rochester kept nosing around. "It could have been put into a pocket easily," I said. "And whoever stole the drive might have thought it contained video of Yesenia's lectures."

I thought for a moment. "You could search the two rooms where the women are staying," I said. "See if you can find the jump drive, or any evidence of chloroform. I'm the person in control of the property, so I can give you permission to search."

Tony shook his head. "Your situation is like that of a hotel. If a person registers for a room and pays the fee, that room has similar Constitutional properties to a private house. I can't walk in without permission from each woman or a search warrant."

Rochester whimpered, and tugged on the leash, and I let him walk around the tree. On the far side, he stopped and plopped his butt on the ground.

"What is it, puppy?" I asked. I walked around the tree to where he sat. A torn piece of paper towel was on the ground.

"Do you have an evidence bag, Tony?" I asked.

He and Lili came over to where we stood, and he pointed at the ground. "What's that?"

"I don't know, but Rochester wanted to point it out to us."

"There's probably food on it."

I shook my head. "You've had some experience of Rochester," I said. "I think it's worth picking up and testing."

"For what?"

"Chloroform? Fingerprints?"

"Steve. This is a public area. Anyone could have dropped that."

A cold breeze swept through and I shivered. "I know. But it's on the way from Granger Hall to the parking lot and it looks relatively fresh. One of the women could have dropped it."

I waved my arm. "Look around. Do you see anyone out in this cold?"

His shoulders sagged. "I'll humor you. You're right, there's no one else around, and this could have been dropped by the person who knocked out Ms. Patil." He pulled an evidence bag out of his pocket and carefully slid the scrap of paper towel inside it.

As he sealed the bag, I thought about his theory that someone might be framing Yesenia. If that was true, they'd need to create a trail of evidence that pointed to her supporters - making it look like people were acting to protect her, when really they were being manipulated into creating a pattern of suspicious behavior around her. The paper towel could be part of that plan - leaving just enough evidence to connect the dots back to someone in Yesenia's circle.

"What's going on in that head of yours?" Tony asked.

"Just thinking about how neat all the evidence is," I said. "Every piece points to someone trying to protect Yesenia. Almost too neat. There could be a fine line between trying to protect her and trying to implicate her."

He nodded slowly. "Keep thinking like that. Sometimes the obvious answer isn't the right one."

Then he stood up. "I'm going to the hospital to talk to Ms. Patil again. I'll see if they can test this paper while I'm there."

Rochester stood up and pressed his head against my leg. "I know, puppy," I said. "You're cold. So are we." We said goodbye to Tony and walked back to my car.

"Things are heating up," I said. "I'm not sure we can guarantee the safety of anyone on the course at this point. Dan will have to report this occurrence to President Babson. And then we'll have to decide whether to continue."

Chapter 31
Theories and Threats

"Why would anyone want to steal that jump drive?" I asked Lili, as we drove through the deserted college town. The student-focused businesses along Main Street—the sandwich shops, the college bookstore, the coffee houses that usually buzzed with laptop-toting undergrads—had their lights dimmed or were shuttered entirely for the break. Salt-stained sidewalks stretched empty past brick storefronts with handwritten "Reduced Winter Hours" signs taped to their windows.

Even the popular sports bar where students usually crowded to watch games had only a few cars in its lot. Anyone who was at Eastern for the remainder of the winter break, or for the intersession, was inside sheltering against the cold.

"It had to be someone who wants to stop Yesenia from going on TV," Lili said. "And someone who didn't realize the files were being stored on the cloud."

"Cui bono," I said. "Once again, who benefits?"

"I don't know. Yesenia told me that Enid is very excited about the course and thinks she's a great instructor. She wants to recommend Yesenia to her school as an instructor."

"Yesenia could teach and go on TV," I said.

Rochester stuck his head between the seats. The air was still so cold that his breath was visible, like smoke in the air. The moment I recognized that, I said, "Smoke."

Lili turned to me. "Yes?"

"Could there be something to do with the cigars?" I asked. "Or the stolen paperwork? Suppose you wanted Yesenia to stop going to Cuba. How would you do that?"

"Why would I want to?"

"Work with me, here, Dr. Weinstock. How would you stop her?"

"Threats," she said. "Which she received, though those threats were aimed at the course, not at her research work."

"Research. What exactly is she researching, anyway?"

Lili thought for a moment. "Her specialty is food anthropology. How cuisine affects culture, and how immigrants have brought their recipes and their ingredients to the islands, and how that has changed what people eat."

I saw her thinking. "And having the documents in her possession could strengthen her relationship with the Cuban government," she continued. "She could force them to let her stay longer, talk to more people. Right now she has to go through a lot of paperwork. Permits to travel, restrictions on currency, having a chaperone when she talks to people. She's identified a lot of gaps in her knowledge, which would necessitate going out into the countryside to talk to people who might not trust her if there's an officer or a chaperone with her."

"That's a motive to steal the documents," I said. "To keep her from doing her research. And if she can't get a TV program, then she doesn't have a platform to spread her work. She makes a big point of Cubans on the island being like everyone else, concerned about living day to day, doesn't she?"

"She does."

"So showing Americans that Cubans are just like them could lead to a thaw in relations. Juan Alfarero was certainly against that. He didn't want this country to change its attitudes."

"Cubans are a very complex people," Lili said. "Take it from me.

I'm one of them. We have to juggle a lot of contradictions at once. One day I might agree with Yesenia, that we need to appease the Castros to help people on the island. Then the next day I might hear about a political prisoner or an information ban, and I'd be ready to kick them out."

As we drove along the barren riverfront, I saw the water burbling along in its relentless journey to Delaware Bay, and then the Atlantic. "Zenobia Willis wants her own show on the Food Network," I said. "Could she be sabotaging Yesenia? Trying to frame her for a murder, stealing the documents that would give her an advantage for a show, destroying the tapes she wants to use as her introduction?"

"I suppose it's possible, but that's not the vibe I get from her. She uses this term "people of color" to represent African-Americans and Latinos and South Asians and anyone who's not white. She wants to elevate programming by those under-represented minorities. So I don't think she'd sabotage one of her own."

"But isn't Yesenia like you? Latina but not Hispanic?"

She groaned. "Let's not get into that debate. People like Yesenia would say that distinction is one that is imposed by the white majority and it's all about the way the Spaniards conquered the indigenous people, and about racial purity. People whose families came from Spain are generally white, and therefore Hispanic."

She turned to face me. "But indigenous people, Black descendants of slaves, and mixed-race people are Latino because they live in Cuba and Central and South America and usually speak Spanish. That includes immigrants from other countries and their descendants. My niece and nephew in Miami identify as Jewish and American even though Fedi was born in Cuba. If either of them have kids, they'll only look at Cuba as a place where some family members were born while they stopped on their way to the US." She shook her head. "Race-based politics are so confusing."

We stopped at Ferry Street in Stewart's Crossing and waited for traffic to ease so we could make a left turn. Festive lights left over from Christmas still hung from the windows of the Drunken Hessian, the bar where I often went with Rick. The parking lot was busy despite the cold weather.

"Going back to Juan's murder, there were eight people with flimsy or no alibi," I said. "I don't think that ordinary college students like Bobby, Claudia, and Bradley could pull all this off, and none of them have a real motive, if you eliminate the connection between Bobby and Juan."

"Okay. So that's three out of eight eliminated, at least temporarily."

"Yesenia was out of the room, but despite what Tony thinks, I don't believe she wrote those threatening notes or that she would knock out Deepti," I said.

"Agreed. Who does that leave us with?"

I liked the way Lili used the word "us." I needed a solid human partner, and without Rick I was flailing. And Rochester was great to work with, but his inability to speak left me unable to brainstorm with him. I was glad to have Lili by my side.

"There's no reason for Dan Lazerow to cause chaos. It could only hurt his job. Maria and Raquel were both out of the room when Juan was murdered. They're both Cuban, but they're both fans of Yesenia. I don't see why either of them would want to hurt her. Ken Gould is a wild card, because we don't know much about him."

Rochester leaned forward and licked my neck. "I know you want to help, puppy," I said, as I was finally able to make the turn that would take us back to River Bend.

"Oh," I said, as I drove. "Maybe the person behind this doesn't want to hurt Yesenia, but to help her."

"Help her. How would that work?"

"Juan was her opponent. Killing him helps Yesenia, by removing a dissenting voice and someone who could keep interrupting the course."

"I get that."

"And suppose either Raquel or Maria thinks it's dangerous for Yesenia to poke the Castros, so one of them stole the documents."

Dog Grant Me

"Okay," Lili said. "But what about the threats?"

"There are two ways to think about those. One, that Tony and Dan are right. Yesenia manufactured them to generate controversy."

"Or?"

I tapped on the steering wheel. "Or Juan was the one who slipped Yesenia the threats. They stopped after he died."

"That fits his character."

I slowed down for the gate into River Bend to open.

"How does the attack on Deepti fit in?" Lili asked.

"Getting a program on the Food Network makes Yesenia a bigger personality, and potentially opens her up to threats. Maybe one of those women wants to keep Yesenia in her lane. Doing her research, collecting recipes, traveling to Cuba now and then on a tourist visa."

Lili frowned. "Where does that leave us?"

We pulled up in our driveway. As we got out of the car, a chill wind swept through the neighborhood, carrying the distant howl of a siren.

"The attack on Deepti, the theft of the documents - those all seem directly connected to either protecting or undermining Yesenia. Until we figure out which one of those, we won't know how to proceed."

Chapter 32
We Survived

We had too much to do when we got home to spend more time brainstorming. We had to unload the car, and I had to take Rochester for his walk. While I was out, Lili threw a load of wash in and called for a pizza delivery.

By the time we were sitting at the table, with Rochester by my side waiting for crust, we'd both had some time to think things through. The rich aroma of cheese, tomato sauce and sausage rose around us, making me salivate. As much as I loved Lili's cooking, and Cuban food in general, it was nice to have a good pizza.

"It's like the Rubik's Cube you were mentioning," she said, between bites. "When you get the pieces lined up."

"So we're agreed that the person who killed Juan, stole the documents, and assaulted Deepti did all those things to help Yesenia?"

"As strange as it sounds, yes. Don't you and Rick have those four L's you talk about?"

"Lust, love, loathing and lucre," I said. "Whoever killed Juan did so either out of love for Yesenia or loathing for Juan and what he stood for. Which in the end is the same thing."

"And knocking out Deepti?"

"I think we come back to love for that. Protection is a kind of love. I've read about men who kill their wives because they're protecting them from leaving the marriage. Or cult leaders who feel they're protecting their congregations from Satan by having them kill themselves."

Lili shivered. "It's like living a class in abnormal psychology. When are you going to share this theory with Tony?"

"I want to sleep on it first. Let my subconscious work out any details. Do you think anyone else is in immediate danger?"

"That depends on what Yesenia does," Lili said, as she fed Rochester a piece of crust. "If she goes on Facebook and starts ranting about the attack on Deepti, then the attacker might feel like Yesenia resents them and doesn't value them. That could lead them to do something else."

"Then you need to talk to your friend. Convince her to shut up for a day or two."

"Easier said than done."

After we cleared the dinner table and tossed the pizza box in the recycling bin, Lili took her phone upstairs to call Yesenia, and I opened the hacker laptop. I wanted to go back to what I'd learned about Maria Cabrera and Raquel Jaceldo and see if there was any indication which one could be responsible.

I looked through everything I'd been able to turn up on Raquel, and she was as she appeared to be. A retired cook whose specialty was Cuban cuisine. Everything she posted online was either about her family or cooking. Yes, occasionally she veered into educational politics, lobbying for higher wages for all workers in the education system except administrators.

She had been born in Union City, New Jersey, a town full of Cuban émigrés, to parents who had left the island while Batista was still in power. Her Cuban heritage was only a part of who she was. Yes, she'd attended some Hispanic Heritage Month events, but for the food, not the politics.

Then I turned to Maria Cabrera. Her name was so common that

the programs had trouble parsing her out. Thousands of matches on LinkedIn, Facebook, Spokeo, and other big sites. I remembered she had said that she used her middle name to differentiate herself from her cousins on Facebook, and I set up a new search for Maria de los Angeles Cabrera.

I kicked off all the programs and let them do their work. I sat back and considered. Could I do something to poke either of them? I might say something negative about Cuba, or Yesenia, in casual conversation, and see how they responded.

I certainly had reasons to complain about our speaker. She had brought a great deal of danger to our placid rural campus, and her actions could lead to the course being cancelled, a big hole in my budget, and perhaps even to a bad situation for Friar Lake or the whole intersession program.

I'd have to be careful to put all the blame on Yesenia, not my wife. I didn't want to sic either Maria or Raquel on Lili to protect Yesenia from blame.

Lili came back downstairs. "Limited success," she said. "Yesenia has agreed not to post anything about the attack on Deepti until Deepti is better, and they can see if any harm was done."

"How is Deepti?"

"She has a mild headache, and the hospital gave her a couple of Tylenol and discharged her. Yesenia drove her back to Fields Hall, and she's going back and forth between her room and Deepti's to check on her."

"Any results of the chloroform test?"

"Yes. She spoke to Tony at the hospital. There was chloroform residue around Deepti's lips and in her blood. And the paper towel Rochester found had traces of chloroform on it too."

I reached down and ruffled Rochester's fur. "Good boy," I said, and he rolled over on his back and wagged his legs in the air.

I got down beside him and rubbed his belly. "Any fingerprints on the paper towel" I asked.

"Tony wouldn't say. But you could ask him yourself tomorrow. When you pass on our theory."

"I'll do that."

"Did you dig up anything more in your research?"

"Nothing on Raquel. She just wants to cook and she's interested in all different cuisines and ingredients. She was married to a man from Spain and her identity is equal parts Spanish and Cuban, with an emphasis on the Spanish."

"The way mine is Jewish and Cuban, with an emphasis on the Jewish," Lili said. "My niece and nephew identify more with being Jewish than being Cuban, especially because their mother doesn't speak much Spanish or cook Cuban food. And I think there's an economic thing going on, too, though no one will say so. The Hispanic kids in their classes are generally poorer and don't speak English as well."

"There's a socioeconomic study for you," I said. "The assimilation of the Jubans into American society and the end of the Juban identity."

"I agree. But if they have to lose a part of their heritage I'd rather they lost the Cuban part than the Jewish part."

"It's like they say at the Passover seder, 'they tried to kill us, we survived, let's eat.'"

Lili laughed. "Maybe they say that at your family seder."

She joined me to take Rochester for a quick walk, and as we returned and approached the front door, something stopped my dog, and he sniffed at a folded piece of paper tucked into the handle of Lili's car.

"What's that?" I asked, pulling it free.

Lili unfolded it and scanned the contents, her brow furrowing. "It's a note. Handwritten in Spanish. The translation says, 'The truth lies in the past. Trust no one.'"

I felt a trickle of unease. "Yesenia's handwriting?"

Lili nodded. "And it was left here, on my car, while we were away at Friar Lake. Which means…"

She trailed off, but I could hear the implication in her words. If Yesenia had come here, to our home, without our knowledge, what else might she have done? The threats, the stolen documents - were they really as simple as they seemed?

I gripped the note tightly, a chill running down my spine. This case was far from over.

Chapter 33
Café Cubano

We went inside, and I sat across from her. "Yesenia was here on Tuesday night for dinner," I said. "You haven't used your car since then, have you?"

"No. It's been in the driveway all this time."

"If Yesenia tried to show up here while we were at Friar Lake, the security guard would have called us," I said. "So that makes it reasonable that she put that note on the car when she was here. Before Juan was murdered."

Lili pushed the paper away from her. "It's creepy. What do you think she meant?"

"It's a warning. But why? Do you think she knew that Juan was coming to the class, even though he registered under a false name? That in case he caused trouble, she wanted us to know that the reason was the history between them?"

"Possibly. Maybe she was frightened that someone would come after her because of things she's said or done in the past."

"Will you talk to her tomorrow? If there's something else brewing we need to know about it."

Lili promised she would.

As I took Rochester out for his last walk, I thought about the question again. He seemed happy to be back on familiar ground, but I couldn't share his happiness. I was still trying to puzzle out the series of events that had begun with the threats against Yesenia and ended, at least so far, with the attack on Deepti.

The more I went over the facts, the more I agreed with the idea that one of the two older Cuban women had orchestrated things to protect Yesenia. It was the only theory that fit with all the actions. Someone wanted to help or protect Yesenia, and they'd killed Juan, stolen the documents, and stolen the jump drive too. Maybe their ideas were misplaced, and certainly murder had to be punished, but they'd started from a good place.

It was going to be tough to convince Tony Rinaldi of that. I hoped that the piece of paper towel Rochester had found would prove to have a fingerprint on it, which could lead him to the right conclusion.

Tuesday morning, when I returned from walking Rochester, Lili was in the kitchen making tiny cups of café Cubano for us. It was a sweet espresso drink made with strong, dark roast espresso sweetened with a thick sugar foam, and she had brought her special machine back with us from Friar Lake. She had a matching one at her office, along with a store of dark roasted beans and a bean grinder.

After I divested myself of my parka and gloves, she handed me a china cup and I lifted it to my lips and inhaled. "The nectar of the gods," I said, before I took a sip.

Rochester was very interested in the machine, which was unusual for him, because he usually found the smell too strong. But he sat on the floor beside it and barked a couple of times.

"You don't want coffee," I said.

He barked again.

"Fine." I dipped my finger in my cup and offered it to him to lick. He did, but it was clear he didn't like it. He spat once and then sat on the floor beside me, licking his jowls.

"See, I told you so," I said.

I turned to Lili. "What's on your agenda today?"

"Yesenia is doing the morning lecture, so I have time to catch up on email and paperwork. I'll go downstairs for their ten-thirty break and that's when I'll ask her about the note you found on the car."

"Well, technically Rochester found it," I said.

She grimaced. "Of course. After the break, we'll talk to the class about food traditions for an hour, then send them off to lunch. They meet again for an hour and a half in the afternoon, but then have the rest of the day off."

"Are you happy with the way things are going? I mean, aside from murder and assault."

She laughed, then sobered. "I know, murder is nothing to laugh at. But the way you phrased it. Yes, I'm happy. The students are interested in the material, and they ask lots of questions and they're all willing to share their own food experiences. If we don't have any more drama, I'll consider this a success."

We left soon after, in our separate cars. I was in my office when Rochester began barking. I looked out the window and saw Tony Rinaldi getting out of his car. He came into my office, bringing a gust of cold air with him.

Tony began pulling off his gloves and his wool hat. "Man, it's cold out there. Tanya has been putting up photographs of Puerto Rico all over the kitchen, trying to remind herself that she comes from a warm place. Not so subtle hints I need to take her on vacation soon."

"We were in Miami the Christmas before last, for Lili's mother's funeral," I said. "It was really nice to be away from the cold and snow."

He shucked his jacket and sat down across from me. "I'm not going anywhere until I find out who killed Juan Alfarero. The techs in Doylestown were able to lift a fingerprint from the paper towel," he said. "But it doesn't match anyone in the system. Which means I'm going to need to take fingerprints from some of your students."

"They're all in class on the Eastern campus," I said. "The room in Granger Hall where Deepti was attacked. They have a break at eleven o'clock. You could take prints then."

"I'm afraid I'll spook the killer into doing something else," Tony said. "But I don't see any way around it other than taking prints from everyone in the class. It's not like the murder, when we had a limited number of suspects based on who was out of the room at the time. I'd rather not make the connection between the two crimes right away, in case they aren't related."

"Let me run a theory past you." I told him the ideas Lili and I had. "That narrows the suspect pool down to two." I looked down at Rochester and remembered the way he'd barked at the coffee maker that morning, and I had a burst of inspiration. "I might be able to get you their prints."

"How would you do that?"

Without referring to the dog, I said, "Lili has a special coffeemaker in her office for Cuban coffee. The students have a break at ten-thirty and she's going down there to hang out with them. Why don't I have her make coffee for the Cuban-American students, call it a little taste of home. She serves it in china cups. I'll collect the cups for washing up, and you can take the prints from them."

"I like it. How will I get the cups?"

"You can come over to Lili's office and wait there."

He nodded. "Sounds good to me."

Rochester, apparently tired of all this crime talk, grabbed his favorite squeaky toy and dropped it directly on top of Tony's case notes. When neither of us immediately responded to this obvious invitation to play, he picked it up and squeaked it three times in quick succession, his tail wagging hopefully. "Your dog has interesting ideas about proper police procedure," Tony said.

He left, agreeing to meet us at Lili's office after the break, and I called Lili and told her the plan.

"I don't like singling the Cuban-Americans out, but they're the most likely suspects. And I don't have enough cups for everyone. All I have is a half-dozen china mugs and then a stack of tiny plastic cups for cortaditos."

"How about if you make cafecitos for everyone, but give a bigger cup to the Cubans. You can call it a taste of home."

"I can do that. I'll have to get Matilda to help me carry everything downstairs."

"I'll help you. Is there a classroom nearby where we can set up? I'll stop on my way to campus and get extra milk."

"Yes, there's an empty room across the hall. We can invite everyone over there. You know that bakery on Main Street? They sometimes have guava pastry. See if you can get some of that, too. We'll make it a Cuban break."

"I can do that. Do you have paper plates to serve the cake on?"

"I do. Left over from a student party we had in December."

"There's still a possibility that we're looking at this all wrong,' I said. "Remember, Tony suggested that someone might be trying to frame Yesenia rather than protect her."

"Think about it - whoever's behind this would need to know her habits, her relationships. They'd have to know which knife was her favorite, that she dated Juan Alfarero, even how she'd react to threats. That suggests someone who's been watching her closely."

Lili frowned. "Like a devoted follower on social media? Or someone who's been tracking her movements?"

I remembered the shady figure I'd seen walking in the dark, when Rochester had growled. "Exactly. And they'd need to understand Cuban exile politics well enough to manipulate people's reactions." I glanced at my watch. "We'd better get moving if we're going to set up this coffee break.'

We firmed up the arrangements, and I went back to work until I had to leave for Leighville. Rochester peed on the way to the car, and then waited in the back seat while I dashed into the grocery and the bakery. He was very interested in what I had on the front seat and I had to keep pushing his nose back.

He was delighted to trot alongside me as we walked toward Granger Hall, and equally happy to have the attention of all the dog-loving students.

Our little coffee party went smoothly. Lili poured the espresso shots and I handed them out to the students, and then she mixed up the bigger mugs of café Cubano for Maria, Raquel, and Bobby. We couldn't eliminate him without causing suspicion.

Some of the regular students found the cafecito too strong, but Bobby promised them that if they ever came to Miami, he'd get them accustomed to it. The rest of the class, including the special students, were happy to have a little Cuban coffee break.

I saw Lili pull Yesenia aside for a few minutes. I wanted to know what they were talking about, but I held back. Lili would let me know what she discovered.

When they went back to their regular classroom, I called Tony's cell and asked him to come downstairs. He arrived with evidence bags, and I'd been careful to keep aside the mugs that Raquel and Maria had used.

"I'm going to test all three," he said. "Just to be fair in case this ends up being evidence in court."

He took all three mugs away, and I cleaned up the trash and carried the coffee maker and the foam machine upstairs to Lili's office, where Matilda gave Rochester a lot of love.

I was back in my office late that afternoon when Tony called. "I had one of my colleagues who's particularly skilled at fingerprints lift them from the mugs," he said.

"Did you get any match to what was on the paper towel?"

"I did," he said. "But I'm sorry to tell you that your hypothesis was wrong. The print on the towel doesn't match either of the older women. The person I believe attacked Ms. Patil is your student, Bobby Cruz."

Chapter 34
Breaking Point

"Bobby Cruz!" I said. "But why would he attack Deepti?"

"That's what I'm going to figure out. I've called Dan Lazerow, and he's going to have one of his security guards escort Mr. Cruz over to his office, where he has an interview room I can use. I don't want to make a big deal out of this until I have to."

He ended the call, and I immediately called Lili and told her what Tony had discovered. "That shoots a big hole in our theory," she said.

"Unless the attack on Deepti isn't related to anything else. Maybe Bobby asked Deepti out and she rebuffed him."

"What does knocking her out with chloroform accomplish?"

"I don't know. But male brains aren't fully formed until they're in their twenties. Maybe he didn't think it through. He asked her out, and she said no."

"And then he went back with chloroform? Or maybe he walked in on her with it? Steve, you're not making sense."

"None of this does. I'm going to head over to the security office and see if Dan and Tony will let me observe the interview."

"I'll meet you there. This is my course."

It took some convincing, but Dan finally agreed that Lili and I could join him in a room next door to the interview room, which had an observation window. "You wouldn't be able to get away with this in a police station," Dan said. "But campus politics are different, and I understand how much the success of this program matters to both of you. And in a larger sense to Eastern College as well."

We followed him into the room and took chairs facing the window. Bobby was already in the room, perched on the edge of his chair like he might bolt at any moment. His hands twisted the strings of his Eastern hoodie into knots, then methodically smoothed them out, only to start the process again.

The confident college athlete was gone - this was a scared kid who'd never been in trouble before. When he glanced up at the window, his eyes were red-rimmed and he kept swallowing hard and licking his lips, as if his mouth had gone dry. Every few seconds, he'd start to run his fingers through his thick black hair, then catch himself and drop his hand back to the hoodie strings, a nervous cycle that revealed just how thoroughly his usual self-assurance had crumbled.

Tony entered with the same measured calm he'd shown throughout the investigation. "Bobby, I'm Detective Rinaldi," he said.

"I know who you are," Bobby said. His voice had lost its usual swagger, replaced by the higher pitch of anxiety.

"Good. I'm going to turn on this recording equipment, and we'll have a conversation."

"I didn't kill that guy," he said. "Yeah, I know now that he was my uncle but I didn't know then."

"That's okay," Tony said. "Let me get everything set up before you start talking."

He positioned his chair at an angle - close enough to establish connection but not so near as to seem threatening - and kept his movements deliberate and unhurried as he turned on the recorder. "My name is Detective Tony Rinaldi and I'm in an interview room in the Eastern College campus security office with Robert Cruz, a student at the college," he said.

He added he date and time, and asked Bobby if he agreed to be interviewed, and Bobby nodded.

"You have to speak for the tape," he said.

"Yes, I agree."

"Can you state your age, please?"

"I turned twenty-one in December."

"Thank you. Let's talk about yesterday afternoon. What time did your class end?"

Bobby tilted his head for a moment, and then his shoulders sagged. "Professor Ubeda finished around three-thirty," he said.

Tony's body language mirrored Bobby's anxiety with strategic patience: when Bobby leaned forward, Tony would lean back slightly, giving him space; when Bobby's voice rose with tension, Tony's grew quieter, forcing the young man to focus and slow down.

"And what did you do afterwards?"

"I hung around for a few minutes with some of the other students."

"Which ones?"

"Maria and Raquel. They've been kind of like aunties to me. I miss my family in Miami and I hate the cold."

"What did you talk about?"

He shrugged. "Just stuff. And then Raquel left."

"Leaving you with Ms. Cabrera?"

"Yes."

"Where were you?"

"In the hall outside the classroom."

I looked at Lili but neither of us spoke. If she was thinking what I was, then we were both very curious to see what was going to happen next.

"And then what?" Tony asked.

"She pulled this plastic bottle out of her purse, and a bunch of paper towels. She said something like, 'just put this over her mouth and she'll pass out. Don't worry, she won't remember anything, and she won't be hurt.'"

"When Ms. Cabrera said 'she' who was she referring to?"

"Deepti."

"So you and Ms. Cabrera had a previous conversation about Deepti?"

"We did. Or well, it wasn't about Deepti. It was about the recordings."

Tony made a couple of notes in his notebook. "What about the recordings?"

"Maria thought it was a bad idea for Dr. Ubeda to have a TV program. That she would cause a lot of controversy for Cuban exiles. That she should stick to being a professor."

"Interesting," Tony said. "What did you do after Ms. Cabrera pulled out the items from her purse?"

"She poured some liquid on the paper towels and then handed it to me. She told me not to smell it but that I had to move quickly."

"And what did you do then?"

"I opened the door to the classroom and walked in. Deepti had her headphones on so she didn't hear me. I went up behind her and put the paper towels over her mouth like Maria told me to."

"What happened then?"

He looked angry. "Maria said she would pass out right away, but she didn't. She started trying to push the paper off her face, and I had to press down harder. Then she pushed at me and we knocked over a couple of chairs. Finally she collapsed on the floor."

I looked over at Lili. Her mouth was open slightly and her eyes wide. I knew that look; I'd felt it myself when I'd heard examples of what people did to each other.

"What did you do after Ms. Patil passed out?"

"Maria was watching through the window in the classroom door. She came in then and grabbed the jump drive from Deepti's computer. She told me I had done a very good thing and the Cuban people would be proud of me. She told me to find a garbage can away from the building to toss the paper towels. Then she left."

"What did you do?"

"I was in kind of a daze. I put my coat on and walked out, back toward my dorm. I guess I was nervous because I was kind of tearing at the paper. I finally found a trash can outside the dorm and tossed it. Then I went upstairs and took a shower before dinner."

Tony asked him a few more questions, clarifying things, but I knew the interview was over. Bobby had admitted to the assault, but fingered Maria Cabrera as the thief and the mastermind.

Now it was up to Tony to make the next move.

Chapter 35
Protecting Yesenia

While Tony wrapped up his interview with Bobby Cruz, I stood up. "Where are you going?" Lili asked.

"Over to Friar Lake. I want to make sure Maria doesn't leave before Tony can arrest her."

"He can send cops over there," she said.

"I know, and I'm sure he will. But I know where to find her, and I'll have Rochester." I slipped my sleeves into my parka, and Rochester stood up.

"You're not going to confront her, are you?"

"Not at all. Just stall her until Tony or his guys can get there."

Lili crossed her arms over her chest. "I don't know, Steve. I don't think that's a wise idea. I asked Yesenia about that note she left in the door of my car, and she apologized for being so cryptic. She said when she arrived at Eastern, she was already on edge from all the online threats she had been receiving. Then she spotted someone watching her - she thinks it was Ken Gould, though she couldn't place where she knew him from. She was afraid her phone and email were being monitored, so leaving me a hidden warning seemed like the safest option."

"If I get both Maria and Raquel together, Maria won't do

anything," I said. "And I'm sure it won't take long for Tony to get there." I grabbed Rochester's leash. "Come on, boy, let's go."

He understood the urgency in my voice, and nearly dragged me toward the parking lot, not bothering to stop and sniff or pee. We jumped into the SUV and I backed out of the spot, and drove out to Main Street.

My adrenaline levels were pumping. I had no idea if Maria knew she was under suspicion, or how she could escape. I looked over at Rochester, sitting up on the seat beside me, and his presence calmed me enough to start thinking.

Maria and Raquel had taken a bus from New York to New Hope, and then an Uber from there to Friar Lake. She could call a car service again, but I didn't know how often the buses ran.

I came to a stop light on River Road and used my phone to find the number for the bus station in New Hope. "When's the next bus from New Hope to New York?" I asked, when the operator came on.

"Six-fifty this evening," she said.

I thanked her and hung up. It was four-thirty by then. Plenty of time for Maria to get to New Hope by car. New Hope was full of stores and restaurants where she could hide out until the bus was about to leave.

If I missed her at Friar Lake, there was also enough time for Tony to get cops out to the bus station to stop her.

But what if she had another plan in mind? I thought about how she'd been getting back and forth between Friar Lake and Leighville. Zenobia had driven her.

What if she stole Zenobia's car keys and took off? It would be a big effort to track her. If she was smart, and I was sure she was, she wouldn't head directly home to the city. She might drive around until she found a country inn or motel, and lie low for a few days. There were plenty of those in the countryside, and around New Hope.

If I were her, I'd do that, and lurk around the bus terminal until the police had given up. Or she might head to her apartment in the city, using back roads, which would make it more difficult to track her and requiring Tony to involve New York city cops to arrest her.

Rochester and I finally pulled into the Friar Lake parking lot. The only cars there were Joey's truck, an SUV with Jersey plates that I believed belonged to Ken Gould, and a sedan with New York plates that looked like the one Zenobia drove.

If Maria was planning to escape in Zenobia's car, she hadn't gone yet. And there weren't any Leighville police cars there yet, either.

I jumped out of the car and instead of waiting as he usually did for me to open the other door, Rochester hopped over my seat and out my door.

I didn't bother to put on his leash. He was right by my side as I hurried toward the dormitory. I knocked on the door to the room Maria and Raquel were sharing, and Raquel opened it. "Hey, Steve, what's up?" she asked.

Rochester nosed past Raquel into the room, and she said, "Wait a minute. Where's your dog going?"

I looked over her shoulder and saw Maria at her bed, packing a bag. "Going somewhere, Maria?" I asked. "The class has barely started."

"I have an emergency at home. I need to get back."

Raquel stepped back so I could enter the room. It looked a lot like the ones in the Eastern dormitories, with a bed and nightstand on either side with a shaded lamp. A shared desk, and the room to the bathroom, which was open. Each room had at least one of Lili's landscape photos on the wall. This one showed Bowman's Tower in fall, at the height of the leaf color.

"What kind of emergency?" I asked.

Maria's movements grew increasingly erratic as she tossed clothes into her bag, her earlier methodical packing dissolving into chaos. Her hands shook so badly she dropped a sweater twice before managing to stuff it in. The same protective intensity I'd seen her display toward Yesenia now had a wild, unhinged quality.

"It's personal."

"You're not hurrying out because you know the police are talking to Bobby Cruz, are you?"

"Why are the police talking to him?" Raquel asked.

I turned to her. "Maria didn't tell you about the chloroform?"

Raquel cocked her head. "Chloroform?"

I smiled, trying not to appear threatening despite what I had to say. "She gave Bobby chloroform to use to knock out Deepti so he could steal the jump drive with all of Dr. Ubeda's videos on them."

"No," Raquel said. "She wouldn't do that." She turned to Maria. "Would you? Did you? He's such a nice boy. He told us we reminded him of his aunties back in Cuba."

Maria stopped packing. Her voice shifted rapidly between defensive anger and something close to pleading. "I had to," she insisted, her accent growing thicker with emotion. "It wouldn't be safe for Yesenia to go on TV." Her eyes darted between me and the door, never settling, while sweat beaded along her hairline despite the room's winter chill.

"Why not?" I asked.

Her speech took on an almost fevered quality, the words tumbling out faster and faster. "I knew he dated Yesenia… he said he was coming to confront her… I had to protect her…" Her chest heaved with rapid, shallow breaths.

"You don't know," she continued. "These anti-Castro people are everywhere. Juan could have hurt Yesenia if someone hadn't taken care of him first."

"Someone like you?" I asked.

Rochester's steady presence beside her leg seemed to unnerve her further - each time he shifted or sniffed, she flinched. The woman who had played the role of protective mother figure was crumbling before my eyes, revealing someone whose fierce devotion had curdled into dangerous obsession.

Rochester started barking as she reached into her suitcase, and when she withdrew her hand there was a pistol in it. "You should leave now," she said. "Zenobia is going to be here any minute to drive me to the bus station."

"The police will be here before then, to arrest you," I said. "Bobby told Detective Rinaldi what you did. How you gave him the chloroform and the paper towels, and then when poor Deepti was knocked out, you stole the jump drive."

Raquel backed away from Maria. "Put the gun down, *mija*," she said. "Nobody needs to get hurt."

"You go," she said, waving the gun at Raquel. "Go on, get out."

Raquel didn't need another prompt. She ducked past me out into the hall and I heard her running away.

My hands started to shake slightly - they always did when adrenaline kicked in - and I shoved them into the pockets of my khakis, trying to project calm authority despite my racing heart. At six-foot-one I usually had height advantage in confrontations, but that meant little against someone with a weapon.

"You know the police are going to catch you, Maria," I said. "Why don't you tell me why you did what you did. Detective Rinaldi is a friend of mine. I can try to convince him to ask the judge for a lighter sentence if I know your motivation."

Of course I couldn't do that. Tony had no influence on what a prosecuting attorney or a judge would do, but I hoped she'd watched enough police TV shows to think it possible.

"I knew Juan in New York," she said. "We used to run into each other at rallies. He believed in a free Cuba. There's so much propaganda out there, from all sides, that you have to be careful who you listen to. Juan started hanging around with the wrong people and he started to go crazy."

Rochester sat at attention beside her. She'd stopped packing, but she still held the pistol in front of her. Her grip was white-knuckled and unsteady, the weapon wavering between pointing at me and dropping toward the floor.

"I knew he dated Yesenia a while ago, and they broke up. I saw him a few weeks ago and he said he was coming to this class to confront her. I'm a passionate fan of hers, you know that, so I registered for the class too, to look out for her."

"You're a good person," I said.

"I am. I just wanted to protect her."

I nodded. "I can understand you got upset when he jumped up and started yelling."

"Anyone who cared about her would," Maria said. "I grabbed the knife from the counter and went after him. I was going to convince him to leave. But he wouldn't listen, and he lunged at me, and the knife was in my hand."

Her whole body seemed to coil inward, shoulders hunching as if physically reliving the moment. The gun trembled more violently in her grip.

"An accident," I said. "Self-defense. You just have to tell the police that."

"I wasn't really thinking," she said, her voice cracking. "Just acting on instinct." The desperate pride in her expression suggested she still believed she'd done the right thing, even as the reality of her situation visibly crashed over her.

"Yesenia doesn't understand how much danger she's in. I knew that if she started posting those videos on YouTube, and lobbying to get a TV show, she'd put herself in more danger. So I had to stop that girl from filming her. I figured she'd be so scared she would leave."

"And then Yesenia could go on teaching," I said. "Did you mind that she went to Cuba?"

Rochester started nosing around Maria's feet, and she stepped away, still holding the gun out.

"It's important to her work to visit the island and talk to the people," she said. "If she tried to challenge the Castros for ownership of that property, they'd stop her. She didn't understand that. So I had to get those documents away from her, too." She shook her head. "She can be so naïve sometimes."

"Other people can be, too."

I heard Tony's voice behind me. "Like guys and their dogs who think they can do police work. Steve, you need to step aside, and Ms. Cabrera, you have to put the gun down."

Chapter 36
Stupid

I did as I was told and stepped back. "Rochester, come to me," I said. I didn't want Maria to think she could hold my dog hostage.

He scrambled across the floor to me, and I grabbed his collar and pulled him out into the hallway with me.

The gentle, probing investigator I'd come to know had disappeared, replaced by a coiled spring of focused tactical alertness. Tony's voice carried the crisp authority of his training, each word precise and commanding.

"You heard me, Ms. Cabrera," Tony said. "Please put the gun down."

His movements became economical and purposeful as he positioned himself in the doorway, and though his gun was drawn, his stance remained controlled rather than aggressive - the practiced balance of someone who knew how to de-escalate while staying ready for anything. Even his breathing had changed, becoming measured and steady, a calm center in the charged atmosphere of the room.

"I overheard some of what you were telling Steve. That maybe you had an argument with Mr. Alfarero and there was an accident. We can talk about that at the station."

I saw Raquel hovering nearby. "I didn't know any of this," she said to me in a low voice. "And I certainly didn't know that Maria had a gun with her! I never would have agreed to share a room with her if I'd known."

"I'm sure Detective Rinaldi will want to talk to you again," I said. I looked toward the room, where Tony remained in the doorway, his gun drawn in a stalemate with Maria.

Raquel came up to stand by me. Despite years commanding busy kitchens, Raquel's professional composure cracked as she watched her roommate's standoff with Tony. Her usual patient, nurturing demeanor dissolved into something raw and vulnerable.

Where she typically moved with confident authority among the students, offering gentle corrections and warm encouragement, now her hands trembled as she looked over Tony's shoulder and saw Maria, and she began to cry.

Her voice, which had guided so many young cooks through complex recipes, shook as she called out, "*Mija*, please, put the gun down. No cause is worth losing your life."

"Sometimes it is necessary," Maria said. "Juan gave his life."

"Not voluntarily," Raquel said. "Don't be foolish, *mija*. Put the gun down."

Maria moved her gun hand, and for a moment I thought she was going to put the barrel up to her head. But she dropped it on the floor, and then kicked it toward Tony.

He bent down and picked it up. "You made the right choice, Ms. Cabrera," he said. He hit a button on the radio attached to his coat. "I need two uniforms in here to take custody of the suspect."

A moment later, the two officers came inside, and Raquel and Rochester and I stepped back. Tony escorted Maria into the hallway, and one of the officers handcuffed her and led her to the exit.

"¡Ay, Dios mio!" Raquel said, and she sagged against me. "I was so frightened. For myself, but also for Maria."

I put my arm around her shoulders, and Rochester nudged her hand. "It'll be okay," I said.

"What about the boy?"

We both looked to Tony. "Only the district attorney can decide what charges to press against him," he said. "What he did was wrong, but he may be able to claim that Ms. Cabrera forced him into it."

"He's a good boy," Raquel said. "I need to lie down. May I go inside?"

"There's one thing," I said. "Rochester was very interested in something Maria had under the bed. Tony, can you look under there?"

"Why not? The dog probably has more sense than you do."

He walked into the room and got down on his knees. He pulled a flashlight from his belt and shone it under the bed. Then he used its edge to tug something out. "Looks like the missing documents," he said. "Though my Spanish is usually confined to endearments to my wife, I can make out a few words."

He put the pages in an evidence bag and then allowed Raquel back into the room. He and I walked outside together, with Rochester by my side.

"Confronting her was pretty stupid," he said to me.

"I wanted to make sure she didn't leave. I didn't realize she had a gun." I looked at him. "Will you be able to use anything you overheard?"

"She confessed freely, before she was under arrest. I hope she'll talk more at the station."

"Do you think it might have been an accident? That she didn't mean to kill Juan Alfarero?"

"She grabbed a knife and went after him. I'd say she was planning on more than just talking to him. But she'll have an opportunity to present her side of the argument, and we may have to bring in a psychologist to examine her state of mind."

As we walked outside, I saw Lili pull up in the parking lot, and Rochester rushed off to greet her. Tony tipped his hat to her and walked off to his own car.

"What happened?" she asked. "Where's Maria?"

"Taken away in handcuffs," I said. "She confessed to everything.

As we thought, she was trying to protect Yesenia. But there has to be more than that. She's not stable."

"I'm going to call Yesenia and tell her what happened. I'm sure the police will want to talk to her again."

"Yes, there's still a lot to mop up. But I hope the rest of the course will be less exciting."

While Lili spoke to Yesenia, I called Dan Lazerow, and then at his suggestion I called President Babson's cell phone and explained the situation.

"Is everyone safe now?" he asked.

"I believe so," I said. "Maria Cabrera and Bobby Cruz are in custody. Deepti Patil hasn't suffered any ill effects from her attack, and I'm sure Detective Rinaldi will find the missing jump drive."

"Do you think we should continue the course, given all that's happened?" he asked. "Or cancel it, refund the money, and take our lumps."

"I'd like the chance to show that we can bounce back." I looked over at the chapel, standing tall against the graying sky. The old stone building had weathered centuries of storms and changes, just as we would weather this crisis. Even now, sunlight pierced through the stained-glass windows, casting jewel-toned patterns across the dry grass—a reminder that beauty could emerge from darkness.

"Let us keep the class going, unless the students want to drop out. I think we can finish it successfully."

"I'll give you that chance, because I want to blunt any bad feelings faculty and others have about the intersession. Fortunately, the other classes are all going well, and the students and faculty who are participating are excited by the opportunities."

"We'll make sure this course continues on a positive note," I said. "And ends in a way that brings credit to the college."

As I hung up the phone, I couldn't help but think of Professor Salazar's ominous warning at the start of the intersession. She had made it clear she disapproved of Yesenia's involvement, calling her a "known supporter of the Castro regime." And her feud with Lili went back years.

What if Salazar was still plotting to undermine the program, even now that the worst of the drama had passed? She had the ear of many senior faculty, and if she decided to renew her campaign against Yesenia, it could jeopardize not just the rest of this course, but the entire future of the intersession.

I felt a growing sense of unease churning in my gut. With Salazar and her allies still out there, I had a feeling our troubles were far from over.

Chapter 37
Mysteries of the Universe

Ken Gould approached me about a week into the course. "I wanted to let you know I'm leaving," he said. "I won't ask for a refund or anything."

"Is it something about the course?" I asked.

He pursed his lips, and then his shoulders sagged. "My wife was killed in a car crash about six months ago," he said. Rochester moved over to lean against his leg.

"It really knocked me out, especially because she did all the cooking. I was living on coffee and fast food and my boss suggested I take some time off, get out into the country and rest. He told me about this class and said I might be able to pick up some cooking tips."

"I'm so sorry," I said.

He nodded. "I'm getting better. My boss was right, coming somewhere different was good for me. But I'm never going to learn to cook, and honestly, I don't feel like doing the academic work. So I'm heading to my sister's place for a week, and then I'll go back to work."

I put my hand on his shoulder, and shook his hand. "I'm glad we could help in a small way," I said. "Though you probably didn't expect to end up in the middle of a murder."

"It woke me up, you know? Like seeing how much passion

everyone else put into what they care about, whether it's food or Cuba or acting or whatever. And that we only have a finite time on earth, so we should make the most of it."

He smiled. "I know I sound like a Hallmark card, but I didn't want you to think I was bailing because the course was crap. Because it's not."

That evening at home, I thought about investigating Ken's story, seeing if I could find anything online about his wife's accident. But that was prying into his privacy, and it didn't matter to me or Friar Lake. I wanted to thank him for participating, so I sent an email to the address he'd registered from.

It was returned as undeliverable. I couldn't help myself—I looked for the company he said he worked for. The website for that company had gone off-line as well. It was as if except for the time he'd spent at Eastern, he didn't exist.

A lot of people disdain sites like Facebook and Twitter, and many professionals like doctors and lawyers kept off them to preserve their privacy. But it was strange how I'd never been able to find anything specific about him online.

As I sat at the dining room table and reviewed the emails about the course continuation, Rochester kept pushing his nose under my elbow, gradually lifting my arm off the table until I couldn't type. "You have a bed right there," I said, pointing to his cushion by the wall. He gave me the same look he used when I suggested he didn't need another cookie. "Fine," I said. "Ten minutes of belly rubs, then back to work." His tail thumped against the floor in victory.

Lili came in as I was on the floor with Rochester, and she sat on one of the cane-backed chairs across from us.

"Do you think Ken was a spy?" I asked. "Sent to watch Yesenia and see what she was up to?"

"That sounds silly," she said.

I started counting on my fingers. "First, the company email address he gave me is no longer in service. Second, he has no digital footprint anywhere. Third, Rochester found that library card with his picture and another name, which suggests he has experience in assuming other identities. And fourth, it's strange that he left the class after a week. I'm not going to investigate the story he gave us, but I don't believe any of it."

"There must be another reason why his identity has fallen apart."

"Remember that note Yesenia put in your car door, before the course started? Could he be the person she was worried about, who was there to listen to what she said and twist it around? She said she thought she saw him when she arrived at Eastern that first day, and that he looked familiar. She was afraid he was planted by some law enforcement agency to spy on her."

Lili shook her head. "You don't believe he was involved in Juan's death, do you?"

"Not at all."

"Then let it go," she said. "You can't solve all the mysteries of the universe."

That was true. And I had enough to do in the spring term, with events scheduled at Friar Lake weekly, and the need to start planning for the summer and fall, as well as our trip to El Salvador for the family wedding. Still, Ken Gould's disappearance nagged at me like an itch I couldn't scratch. The fact that his identity seemed to dissolve the moment he left campus suggested there was more to the intersession drama than just Maria's obsession with Yesenia.

But as January drew to a close, even that mystery had to take a backseat to the successful completion of our first intersession course. Through her contacts on the campus grapevine Matilda reported that the other experimental courses had gone well too. Faculty were pleased with student engagement, and the extra tuition revenue had more than covered operating expenses. Despite the drama that had unfolded at Friar Lake, we'd managed to salvage both our course and the intersession concept.

That sense of accomplishment filled the refectory on our final evening, as Yesenia stood at the front of the room wearing a dress in the red, white, and blue of the Cuban flag (well, the American flag, too, but something about the way she wore it seemed Cuban) while we served the last meal of the program.

The students had worked in groups to research dishes, source the ingredients, and then prepare them. Lili beamed proudly from her place beside Yesenia, and the room was filled with delicious aromas.

Both Maria and Bobby had been forced to drop out of the class. He had gone home to Miami until the spring semester started, and he was waiting to see if the district attorney would file assault charges against him. He'd also have to face the committee that handled student behavior in the spring.

Maria was in pre-trial custody in Doylestown, and Yesenia had gone to see her several times. Yesenia was distraught that Maria had acted on her behalf and she and Lili had several deep conversations about how Yesenia could have behaved differently, and what she could do in the future.

Tony had returned the original documents to Yesenia, though he'd kept a copy for his records and if necessary to use in prosecuting Maria. He'd also returned the jump drive to Deepti. For a few days it had been touch and go if Deepti would stay, but once she got back to her rhythm, she had been able to continue filming and uploading files throughout the course, as well as continuing to do remote work for her other clients.

The remaining students had rallied, and they all expressed their satisfaction with the class and what they'd learned.

Raquel had been very upset, worrying that her friendship with Maria had blinded her to what the other woman was doing, but Yesenia had reassured her, and their bond had strengthened. Raquel had led a team presenting the first course, a white bean soup of Spanish origin called caldo Gallego.

I had spent a few minutes watching her team prepare. In the kitchen, Raquel had found her way back to herself, her calm professionalism restored as she directed her team with the precise, practiced gestures of an experienced chef. Though a shadow crossed her face whenever Maria's name came up in conversation, she threw herself into teaching the younger students.

Raquel's team also gave a brief presentation on the ingredients and how the soup had come to be popular in Cuba. It was delicious and the team did a great job presenting the information. It was clear that Raquel had found healing in sharing her expertise and watching the students' enthusiasm for Cuban cuisine grow.

Enid and Zenobia's team had taken on the main course, and they prepared bacalao, a dish of salted codfish with a history that stretched back not only to Spain but to Scandinavia as well. A team led by Claudia Monson prepared a side dish of pigeon peas and rice to accompany it.

Max and his group had baked a fabulous rum cake with chocolate icing for dessert. I could have eaten several slices if Lili had let me.

Sadly, there was nothing on the menu Rochester could eat, so we left him at home with a bowl of kibble with peanut butter cookies crumbled into it.

Yesenia appeared to have learned a few lessons as she was teaching. She had promised Lili and me to scale back her social media presence while she was still with us, and she had, focusing only on what she was cooking and what the students were learning.

As the rum cake was being devoured, she stood up and moved back to the prep island. "I have an important announcement to make," she said. "Thanks to you all, and your encouragement and participation, Deepti was able to put together a great demo roll of what I could do in a program for the Food Network."

The room buzzed. "Are you going to have a show?" Claudia asked. "Can I be a part of it?"

Students laughed. "Nothing is definite yet," Yesenia said. "But we presented the demo roll to executives, and they like it. They're especially interested in a classroom-type program based on food anthropology, because they don't have one like that on their network. There's still a lot to work out."

"Will you be able to go back to Cuba for research?" Raquel asked.

"I am planning a trip *este verano*," Yesenia said. "And no, I'm not going to divulge anything more about those documents I found. I'm keeping them to myself for now."

That night, Lili and I drove home. Rochester barked his approval that we had come back to him, as if he worried we never might.

Lili accompanied me as we walked him through the darkened streets of River Bend. I had one hand in hers and one on his leash, and that was the way I wanted to keep going through life.

Author's Note

This book was inspired by the mystery fiction of Raquel Reyes, who writes about a food historian in her Miami-based novels, beginning with *Mango, Mambo and Murder*.

I am blessed to live a rich Jewish life, because of all the sacrifices of my ancestors, and that heritage finds its way into everything I write. In particular, if my grandparents hadn't been able to emigrate to the United States, I might have grown up like Lili and Yesenia in another country.

I would also like to pay tribute to the passengers aboard the St. Louis. According to the United States Holocaust Memorial Museum, in May 1939, the German liner *St. Louis* sailed from Hamburg, Germany, to Havana, Cuba. The 937 passengers were almost all Jewish refugees. Cuba's government refused to allow the ship to land. The United States and Canada were also unwilling to admit the passengers.

The *St. Louis* passengers were finally permitted to land in western European countries rather than return to Nazi Germany. Ultimately, 254 St. Louis passengers were killed in the Holocaust. Lili's and Yesenia's ancestors were truly lucky to have been allowed to enter, and thrive in, the Pearl of the Antilles, even if they eventually were forced to continue their journeys onward. A movie was made in 1976 about the journey of the St. Louis, called *Voyage of the Damned*, and starring Faye Dunaway.

Acknowledgments

Once again, Randall Klein provided outstanding editorial services, and Kelly Nichols created an adorable cover that reflects the book. My friends and colleagues Lourdes Rodriguez-Florido and Elisa Albo have inspired me with their stories of their Cuban backgrounds. I would also like to pay tribute to all the Jubans I have encountered in my thirty-eight years in Miami, and the great cooks in my family, including my grandmother Rose Kobrin Globus, my great-aunt Sarah Kobrin Deitch, and my aunt, Rebecca Fais Globus. I was thinking of their mouth-watering meals as I wrote this.

Broward College provided me the academic background for Eastern College during my twenty-year tenure there as a professor of English. The college also funded my travel to various mystery conferences during my time there, for which I am grateful.

I appreciate the help of my beta readers in scouring this manuscript for errors and helping me make it the best it can be for readers. Thanks to Alex Spijkerman, Andy Jackson, Bob Kman, Bob Ronai, Faith Lapidus Weiner, Judith Levitsky, and Tim Brehme. And thanks to you, dear readers, for your support of Steve and Rochester. If you're so inclined, I'd love a review of this book at Amazon or wherever you get your books. It helps new readers discover the series.

And if you haven't already, please sign up for my newsletter, where I sent out regular missives about what I'm writing.

New from La Tazza

We proudly introduces our new Cuban pastry collection

Experience the sweet flavors of Havana, expertly crafted by Master Baker Max Abraham with the help of food anthropologist Yesenia Ubeda Goldstein.

Daily Specials

- • Pastelitos de Guayaba (Guava Pastries)
- • Quesitos (Cream Cheese Rolls)
- • Refugiados (Guava & Cheese)
- • Señoritas (Puff Pastry Cookies)
- • Tocino del Cielo (Heavenly Bacon)

New from La Tazza

Weekend Specials

- Coquitos (Coconut Macaroons)
- Capuchinos (Cone Pastries)
- Tortica de Morón (Butter Cookies)
- Masa Real (Royal Marzipan)

Perfect with our signature Café Cubano!

New from La Tazza

La Tazza Café
237 Main Street •
Potter's Harbor, PA

Open Daily 7am - 6pm
"Where Every Bite Tells a Story"

Friar Lake Conference Center

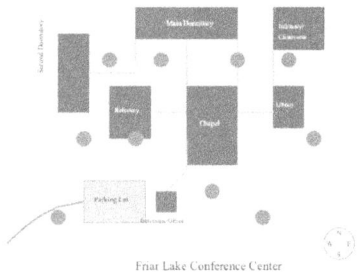

Friar Lake Conference Center

Friar Lake continues to evolve as I write more books in the series. There wasn't a need for a library in earlier books, for example. The drive to the left leads down the hill. Picture the rest of the property surrounded by woods that Rochester can investigate!

www.ingramcontent.com/pod-product-compliance
Lightning Source LLC
LaVergne TN
LVHW011947060526
838201LV00061B/4241